Strange Alliances

Braided Dimensions Series

~ Book 3 ~

A Novel

Marie Judson

STRANGE ALLIANCES

Copyright © 2020 by Marie Judson

Contact the author for information: **www.mariejudson.com**

Paperback ISBN: 978-1-64456-731-9
Library of Congress Control Number: 2024908196

Listing category for shelving: Fantasy Science Fiction, Fantasy & Futuristic Romance, Time Travel Fantasy, Epic Fantasy

Front Cover Art by Tatiana Villa
Formatted by The Book Khaleesi

Rights to the Heron bird Celtic ornament on title page was purchased from VectorStock

INDIES UNITED PUBLISHING HOUSE, LLC
P.O. BOX 3071
QUINCY, IL 62305-3071

Books by Marie Judson

Braided Dimensions Series

Braided Dimensions: Book 1
Stretched Across Time: Book 2
Strange Alliances: Book 3
Pasts Undone: Book 4

Lost Xentu Series

Elf Stone of the Neyna: Book 1
A Far Cry: Book 2

Braided Dimensions Reviews

"Fascinating, with well-written characters in a unique, complex world. I absolutely loved this book and look forward to reading more of this series. Fantastic, a must-read!"

—Laure Eccleston

"I thoroughly enjoyed being caught up in this imaginative tale. The characters are compelling. I will be looking forward to the next installment!"

—Bernadette Wulf

"Judson's story rips you away from the mundane world. We need Book 2!"

—Richard Devall

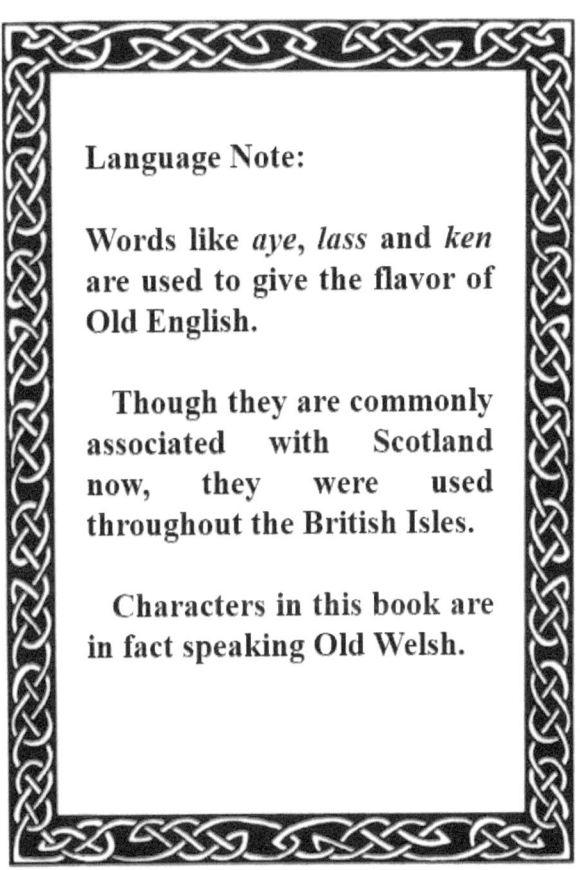

Language Note:

Words like *aye*, *lass* and *ken* are used to give the flavor of Old English.

   Though they are commonly associated with Scotland now, they were used throughout the British Isles.

   Characters in this book are in fact speaking Old Welsh.

For Piper and Soren

Chapter 1

Ew cloth formed on my loom, wholly different from any I'd woven before, unique in feeling as well as design. The Brand of the Thirteen—a sygil made of runes burned into my shoulder by Aelfwyn so I could stand in the power circle of ancient Wales—burned as I worked. It was not painful, more a warmth strong enough to make me wiggle my arm.

Baird got up from the chair behind me, where he'd been trying to decipher a modern book with its lines of regular typeset, and knelt at my side. "Ye alright, Dove?" he asked, keeping his face averted from the cloth I wove.

"You can see it now. It's barely started but feeling very…interesting," I said.

I'd never imagined a domestic evening with Baird, in *my* home. It had to be only a respite. Certainly, he could never be happy here, long term.

He leaned in to study the pattern.

I slipped off my low chair and knelt to examine it with him, pressing against his side.

"Might be a place I know." Baird's voice was soft, as though not to wake something, or someone. "I can no' be sure. Mun see more o' it."

As I touched the short length, the diamond shapes on

my Ing ring shimmered. I heard voices. My stomach clenched as I recognized Thorgisl, smooth and sinister.

I pulled away from the loom, feeling panic as I turned to Baird and whispered, "I just heard Thorgisl." I hesitated, "*His* voice. Do you think the design drew him?"

"We can no' be certain, love."

"My ring reacted. Maybe it's a warning, though I've never known that purpose for it." I'd worn the silver ring with a circlet of Ing runes etched around it since Aelfwyn, master healer of Baird and Kyna's time, handed it to me, months before. I always wore it, along with the silver pendant, also crafted by Kyna's brother, Duff.

Kyna, my twin of medieval time, Baird's partner, could have advised me. Having lived in her spirit for a week, I'd gained much of her knowledge: how to speak old Welsh, how to weave, some ancient lore. But since she was in hiding in the twelfth century, I seldom had contact with her now. Nor did Baird.

He appeared to be considering, then took my hands in his. "We need to stay calm and think clearly."

I took in a long, deep breath, blew out. After a silent moment, I said, "Do you think the weaving might somehow allow him to see us? Ever since he came into this house, I've been worried he might have left something that allowed him to spy on me."

"You have to weave more so we can see the place."

"What if he's controlling it?" I asked.

"The sylphs created protection 'round yer house, did they not? Did not Boldo send one here?"

I nodded, thinking about Boldo, the ancient Traveler who'd been woven so intimately into my life. Sometimes it seemed like a betrayal to Baird. Did I need to explain to him how often Boldo and I were connected by my boots?

"I believe they know if some ought has crossed the boundary, or any danger is within. Shall I call her now? I believe it's *Bedw* who crosses time easily."

"Would you?" I wondered if I'd be able to call her myself someday. "That's the name of the sylph who came before? *Bedw?*"

"Aye. She's named fer the birch, the tree she favors."

"Lovely. The tree that grows first in new soil, after a fire or anything catastrophic."

"Indeed." He kissed my forehead. "It be good t' know our trees." He strode out the back door, pulling me along.

Oz found us and rubbed against my leg, purring, happy to have us outside with him after dark.

"It'll be stronger if ye join me."

It was a beautiful night, with almost no moon, or coastal overcast. The Milky Way stretched, a dusty cloud-road over us. As I gazed up, a strange shifting in the air above signaled the presence of a sylph, only apparent where she blocked the stars. Her sweet-as-honey voice — not quite a sound, more a feeling that held music — filled me. Fear of Thorgisl diminished into a bare whisper at the back of my mind, and I felt I might have over-imagined the threat.

After a few moments, Baird whistled a sort of birdcall.

I no longer made out the air elemental's shape against the sky. The sweet song had left me. "Is she gone?"

"Aye, she returned to her home."

"But we learned nothing."

"Not true. She told me the Jutland mage — tick, more like, ye ask me — has not been here. Or there be no taint o' 'im."

"But … she knew instantly?"

"She'd already been investigatin'. She and Ylva've taken a liking t' each other and are makin' it their mission t' protect ye."

"Seriously?" I felt warmth rise to my cheeks. "She told you all that?" Could I be so fortunate as to have these two powerful guardians? Ylva, shamaness of ancient Norway I'd first met when flung to her mountaintop by Aelfwyn, had saved my more than once.

"Ye've done well t' draw a pair such as that t' yer side, Dove. At least I believe so. I still donna entirely know about the Norwigi witch."

"She calls me witch, too." I laughed, not knowing how I felt about it. Had I even earned the label?

"No offense intended. Not yet. I'm grateful fer her help wi' Duff. Mightily." He put an arm around me. "Not t' mention yer fine *crychydd*." He used the Welsh name for heron. I looked around for my spirit bird. She rarely appeared—only in dire circumstances, it seemed. But she'd been there at the rescue from Thorgisl's fort. I wondered if I'd ever grow to know her, to be able to call her to me. I determined to ask Ylva. Though Baird took animal forms, he seemed to dwell within the actual animal, not call upon spirit ones. Ylva, on the other hand, seemed familiar with both. She'd given us gopher spirit-form long enough to enter enemy territory in the Harz mountains of Old Germania. I'd seen her take wolf form. I had a feeling she knew quite a lot about calling animal spirits.

We walked toward the back steps. "I guess I can go on weaving without any worry," I said as we climbed to the back porch. Still, the worry did not entirely dissipate, that I'd heard his voice, felt his presence in my home as I wove. Even if the taint of him was not there, I would not be at ease.

"Mayhap t'will empower ye to gain insight int' his plans, rather than that he be spyin' on ye," he suggested, holding the door for me.

"That's very positive thinking," I said as we crossed the enclosed porch and entered the warm, cozy living room. I stopped near the archway to the kitchen. "Are you hungry?"

"Dove—"

I knew that tone. He must be leaving. "What draws you home?" I asked.

Since he'd said he might start staying longer, there'd been more sense of relationship between us. With his son trying to be in the twenty-first century with my daughter, he seemed to be contemplating anchoring himself in this time as well. I didn't know how to feel about it. I wanted as much time with him 's I could have, yet parting was inevitable, and always wrenching.

"I want t' see about th' amber—the safety o' its storage, and plans for it."

"You'll go to Norway, then?" I asked.

We had received no news of Duff and Ylva's travels to her homeland, removing Thorgisl's amber power stone from the Wanderers' midst. That object had drawn Thorgisl and his men to the *Silwy* clan of Travelers—attacking and harming men, women and children—and abducting the clan leader, Mora, who often joined the Council of Thirteen in Kyna's tower for their magical workings, was still missing.

"First, I'll check on my son, see if Hamelyn wants t' travel with me. Perchance, we can accompany Duff back."

"That might be a fine journey," I said.

"Aye, that it might. Those are fair mountains."

Had I been angling for an invitation? If so, it did not come. I felt my heart drop as he kissed me good-bye.

I sat in the living room and pondered. I had heard Thorgisl's voice as I touched my weaving, not anywhere else. Despite the assurance by *Bedw* that there was no sign of the Jutlander's invasion, by spirit or otherwise, I would not feel safe until I resolved what the connection was, and what it meant.

I lifted Ylva's wolf carving and stroked it. My own animal guide, *crychydd*—came to mind. She was so elusive. I wondered if I would ever find out how I was tied to her.

Deep within, I harbored a faint hope that the cloth I was weaving would show if Otho—abducting Traveler pirate, Boldo's cousin, mysteriously estranged from the Silwy clan—had Mora, and if so, where and why. But what if Throgisl read my thoughts as I wove?

With my fingertips, I explored the wolf—Ylva's totem—and heard her voice in my mind. "Greetings, Kay."

"Hello, Ylva, my friend. I hope I'm not interrupting anything."

"Duff and I are near my home. One more night we camp. We were making the fire."

"That's great. You haven't encountered any trouble on the way?" I asked. "All's well with the amber?"

"No problems. The amber is safe, as are we. I am enjoying the trip and regret its ending. Duff says hello."

"Give him a hug for me," I said.

"I can give him numerous embraces for you. Duff and I have become lovers," she said.

Her candor made me grin. Unsure if there might be a formal way to receive such news, I merely communicated, "I'm happy for you, and for Duff. Ylva, I'd like to speak with you soon about spirit animals. How to get to know mine."

"Ah. That is a subject I like. It will make me joyous to impart what I know. It should probably be done in facing one another on one plane. But for now, it is best to honor your totem animal. I will carve a talisman you can wear, or keep in a pocket. I have started one at home, of your heron. Spirit animals choose places. Go to where you have seen her. Call out your craving to become more one with her. Those are my thoughts now."

"Thank you, Ylva. Enjoy your meal."

"Soon I will come, or call you, *Fremtidens heks.*" *Witch of the future.* I received the words and meaning at the same time. It gave me a jolt. To her, witch meant one who could wield magic, I assumed, something akin to her role as shaman for her people. To control powers would mean safety. She had to hope for that.

Our connection faded away.

Go to where I'd seen my heron spirit. The Welsh word *crychydd* sounded a bit like cricket. How amazing to receive a fond name from one's spirit animal, or that's how I thought of her. Could I give her a nickname, too, or would it be disrespectful? I'd seen her first at the Franklin Street Café, which was now a sports bar. Maybe not auspicious for a deep spiritual connection. Then I'd sighted her at the edge of the woods on the hillside in ancient Wales. I could travel back in time, but if she'd come to me once in my era, I might be able to build power with her here, in regard to my weaving, first of all.

My passion for this idea mounted by the minute. I pulled on a light, hooded jacket from cloth I'd woven, and left the house, aiming for Franklin Street. I didn't walk in that direction often, toward the south end of downtown.

The restaurant, I discovered, had changed hands again. It was now Luna Tratorria. Better than a sports bar, but I felt sad to never return to where I'd first seen my heron, and fellow gardeners Jarl and Joaquin. Things kept changing.

A robust garlic and crust aroma assailed me. Clinking

and conversation from diners and the kitchen filled the air. A waiter hurried, eager to seat me. His balding head came only to my chin.

I quickly thought up an excuse. "Can I check the back room to see if my friend is here?"

"Certainly." He gestured magnanimously.

I thanked him and crossed to the curtain separating the first and second rooms, where I'd seen my heron stalk for the very first time. In the middle room, I slowed, imagining how I might call out my longing to my heron amidst the hubbub.

Carefully I brought to mind the first sight of the gangling bird—taller than most men—taking slow, graceful steps. I squeezed past tables, holding the image. The patrons glanced my way. A waiter bustled past me with a full tray and I scooted aside with an apology.

The image of the *crychydd*, which had for a moment come back to me clearly, diminished as I stepped into the last room. On that first encounter, she'd seemed to lead me to meet Jarl and Joaquin, or so I'd interpreted things. I gazed toward the corner where they'd sat, dressed for Halloween, as Mayan shaman and Grim Reaper, before I'd known a friendship would develop between us.

I stood still, remembering, and noticed faces turned toward me. Self-conscious, I left. Back on the street, I walked, at first aimlessly, then with purpose, turning onto Partridge Street and the old oak in the overgrown yard. The two-story house appeared as abandoned as ever. I walked to the gnarled tree and leaned against its trunk.

"Why do we end up here?" I asked no one in particular. "Is this a magical place, that I would find Baird here, that I would return from ancient time within you?" Now I was speaking to the tree.

I turned to the tree and breathed in its scent, felt the rough bark with probing fingers. "Was it my magic or yours, that I could survive inside you?" The yard remained shadowed, as if in permanent twilight. I hoped to see my heron, drawn to my great longing, as Ylva had suggested. When I was in trouble, imprisoned in the Jutland fort, she'd brought Ylva to me, saved me. It seemed she came when my need was true, not when I felt I needed her.

I'd never approached the deserted-looking house. Something about it shouted, "Go away!" But I felt curious to walk around the back. Retracing my steps to the end of the block, I turned right instead of left at the corner. Behind the house at this juncture, I discovered a park I'd never seen before. A path skirted the rear yards.

At the back of the house with the oak, bushes lined all along a solid fence. There was no gate. I glanced up at the roof, curious. This side of the house seemed far less decrepit. I was tempted to climb over. As I stood still, scanning the premises, my thumb found my Ing ring. The Brand of the Thirteen tingled. Instantly I saw inside the house.

A voice, slightly familiar, said, "Well, if you're goin' t' spy, ye may as well come in."

Chapter 2

I stood in a comfortable kitchen, golden from lamp light. A wood-burning stove crackled, exuding soft warmth through the room.

The woman I'd spoken with in line at the library, whose sylvan green outfit had drawn my attention, sat now at a rustic farm table, sorting herbs. Her dark eyes took me in. "Tea?"

"If you have herbal," I said.

"Do I have herbal?" She opened the pantry door where jars from floor to ceiling exhibited a vast variety of herbs, roots, and seeds. Drying plants hung from twine crisscrossing overhead. "What do you wish it to do for ye?" she asked.

"Give me sight, if possible." I took her question literally, only partially playful.

A sly smile creased one corner of her mouth. She hefted a full water pot onto the stove, then opened the double door of the wood-burner to shove in a gnarly log. After this, she perused shelves packed with jars. "What kind o' sight ye be after?" She turned to me. "Sit." She gestured to the table.

I settled into a sturdy wood chair. "I have a spirit bird, a heron, that comes to me randomly. She's saved my life. I don't know what else. I've rarely seen her but they seem like important moments."

She brought several jars to the table. "Intriguing."

I said, "Your accent reminds me of...someone, some people I know."

"From the past?"

I took in a surprised breath. "Yes."

Crumbling handfuls of herbs into a tea sieve, she explained, "I came here to escape...troubles."

"You came ... to this property? The oak?"

Instead of responding, she selected a cup for me. "I saw you at Samhain."

"Yes," I said, "our festival in the community gardens. You seemed sad." I hesitated. "I saw some ephemerals, ancestors, there. Were they some of your people?"

"T'weren't lookin' at the phantoms," she said. "T'wer lookin' at the band." Her eyes filled.

"Harper in the Glen?"

"That's right." She lifted the pot as a low whistle emanated, and poured through the sieve.

"Someone in particular?" I asked.

"Ian be my son."

I sat in stunned silence as she pushed a full cup to me and filled her own.

"You know Galfride," she said.

My mind raced to follow this leap. Galfride, who'd captured me, attacked my mind, held Kyna's daughter, Gwynedd captive. But he had also helped us lately. Whatever did this woman know of him? "I do know a Galfride, someone who lived far in the past." What could he have to do with this?

She took some time with her tea. "Honey?"

I accepted, and she brought a cunning little container

from the shelf, with a dipper, from a past era.

Then she related her story. "I took him in, as a young boy.

"*Galfride*?" I couldn't fathom this. Her story, by some miraculous coincidence, crossed mine in so many ways. I tested sending her a mental image to see if she spoke of the same Galfride.

"I know it's the same one," she said, "though he was maybe twelve when I took him into my home in Cornwall. He was skin and bones, doin' tricks fer change, sleepin' rough. Sometimes he had bruises or cuts. I couldn't bear it. I brought him home, fed him, bathed and clothed him." She stopped to sip her tea. "My son, Ian, was younger by a couple o' years. My name be Marget, by the by."

I stared at her, reconciling this new image of Galfride's past. "Nice to meet you, Marget. I'm Kay."

We nodded at each other, acknowledging the introduction.

"This is astounding. You've filled in several blanks in the story for me." I told her of Galfride's family's involvement in the burning of Kyna's village, of his hitching a ride with the Travelers who'd saved her and her brother. "Did he explain how he came to leave his home in *Germania*?"

Marget shook her head. "Not that I recall. He had a strange accent. But he wouldn't talk much about himself."

I sipped my tea. It had an earthy flavor. I wondered if it did indeed give sight and what sort I should expect.

"I got him healthy, put him in school for a time. He learned fast, loved learning." A fragile crumpling occurred in her face.

"What happened?" My throat was tight seeing her distress, and the question came out a hoarse whisper.

"He grew too confident. He started explorin' my workroom when I went out t' tend to neighbors' needs or l' shop." She drew in a long shuddering breath. "He got my son int' some mischief. And soon t'wer worse than mischief. T'was what drew th' town's attention. They were comin' fer us, a friend told me. We went int' hidin', left the house I loved. But my son's mind was linked with Galfride's. I couldn't break his hold.

"I'm shortenin' the story. There was more. But I found this portal in my scryin', and made the decision. I tied our entry into the portal with a break in Ian's memory so that he'd ferget Galfride, and Galfride would not find him. We'd leave no trace, no trail. When we arrived here, I realized I'd broken Ian's tie to the past altogether. I dinna dare go back. Ian walked away. I was a stranger."

I listened, wide-eyed, imagining that happening with my son, Rousseau.

"Th' house were empty, some spell upon it. Seemed t' be waitin' fer me. Now I bide my time, tryin' t' find a way t' bring Ian's memories back while no' drawin' Galfride to him."

"Ian's been intensely interested in my time travel," I said. "I had a gold crystal that he could hardly keep away from. He seemed to resent my having it. I think there's something deep inside him that senses the past."

"What happened to the crystal?" she asked, eyes wide and bright.

"It made its way back to its original owner." I wondered, all of a sudden, how candid I should be with her. Pushing away my half-finished tea, I got up. "I need to go. But we should talk again."

Suddenly torn, I knew I wanted Marget as an ally, but the uncanny intertwining of her history with my life unnerved me. I needed time to sort this out. How had she ended up in my town, in the very house with the oak that had changed my life? How could we both know Galfride, someone who lived a thousand years ago?

Marget got to her feet as well. "Of course, my dear." She came to me and lifted her hands so that I had to take them.

I liked this woman. There was kindness, warmth, and intelligence in her eyes. I'd been drawn to her from the start, at the library. "Your clothes inspired my costume last year," I said.

"Did they? But ye were a faery, were ye not?"

She remembered.

"Have you known whenever I came here, to the tree?" I asked.

"Oh yes. Look." She took my hand and we walked up a hallway. The front sitting room was dark. There was a veil accross the middle of the room; beyond it, the front yard was like a stage seen through smoke.

I gazed beyond the gauzy barrier at the old oak, its wide trunk dominating the front end of the yard. "That's where I first met Baird." I pointed at the tree. "He took me to the past." I turned to her. "To your time. And ever after that, I searched to return. I've been caught in a web, traveling back and forth, ever since."

She came to stand by me, nodding.

"You knew about all this?"

"Oh, no. Not all the details."

"Have you ever caught a glimpse of me, coming to the yard, standing by the tree?"

"Of course. You understand, no one else even perceives the property. It be glamoured. But you have the sight."

"Oh." I pondered that, stomach roiling with potent emotions. Self-consciousness, curiosity, doubt. "You sit in here often?" I asked. Then realized, of course she did. She hoped her son would come back.

"I do. I'm a woman with time." She took my hand. "T'is always wise t' be cautious." There was wisdom in her hazel eyes.

"Do you know how it has come to pass? That our paths have crossed, in so many ways?"

"Come. T'is brighter at the back." She led me upstairs to a sitting room facing the park, bordered by willows along a stream.

We sat in plump chairs covered in gingham. There were sewing machine and fabrics, books, a writing desk with a Mac laptop.

"You have a nice situation here," I said. "What do you do for an income, if you don't mind me asking? Or can you get what you need by magic?"

Her eyes twinkled. "Not everythin'. I'm handy with craftin'. The sewin' machine o' today be miraculous. I make herbal sachets, sell 'em in the little what-not shops, and at wee fairs. I make other items as they come t' mind. Fer the seasons and all."

"Now that I think of it, I believe you had a booth at our Samhain fest."

She nodded agreement. "My favorite holiday, o' course. I made miniature scenes o' scarecrows in fields and the like."

"I saw those. Fabulous!" I reached to finger a stitched pillow embroidered with unfamiliar markings. "I like it here. May I visit you sometimes?" I again made ready to leave.

"Please do. I'd love t' have a true friend in this time. I've made a few but there's so little they can know about my life."

"I just feel a little uneasy that we have these uncanny

connections. You've been aware of some of them but never approached me. You almost seem to ..." I hesitated, not wishing to be offensive, "have watched me."

She looked down at her hands folded in her lap. "A bit, I confess."

"Because?"

"I had to know that I could trust you. And wanted to understand these connections as well."

"Maybe on a long rainy evening, we can explore what all you know and go from there." I'd made a decision. "I have friends in your time who might be able to help you with Ian. I'm not sure. They have troubles, as well. Galfride has been one of their worst."

"I think I might know." She laid her hand on mine. "What can I do t' assure you that I have nothin' but good-will toward you and your loved ones?"

Tears sprang into my eyes, unbidden. She had been nothing but kind, and she was here in my time, in my town, ostracized from the past and all she'd known, even from her own son. How could I not embrace her wholeheart-edly? Where was suspicion going to get me? I sat back. "I want to open up to you, Marget. Some things I've experi-enced have made me wary. There's someone after me in your time who imprisoned me, stole my memories. There's something he wants and he'll go to any lengths to find it. I heard him in my mind recently when I was weaving. I'm so frightened for my kids if he finds them through my mind." It all spilled out and, for a moment, I felt purged, sharing my worries.

Chapter 3

Her somber eyes took in all that I said with intensity. "I might be able to help with that, if I could come to your weaving place."

Still as a stone, I weighed what I had shared, the merit in exposing all and allying with this mysterious woman. To have an ally seemed more and more deeply appealing.

I stood, smiled, nodded. Just like that, we were walking out the back door together.

I hadn't seen Marget's backyard—she'd drawn me directly into her kitchen when I arrived on the outside of her fence. The garden was lush, organized yet wild, with herbs everywhere in a tamed tangle. Some vegetables allowed to "go to seed" were in their full flowering. I stopped by a low-growing shrub and touched a serrated leaf. "Is this one chamomile? I feel like I recognize it."

"I risked goin' back t' Herne Croft fer that one."

"Is that the name of your home town?"

"My homestead, coast o' Cornwall. Closest hamlet be Saveock Water." She pointed at the plant. "Pinch the leaf and sniff it."

I did. "Smells like apple!" I said, holding it to my nose.

She nodded with a little smile. *"Treneague.* 'Tis Cornish chamomile."

We walked out of the park, she in her rust-colored lay-ers—long skirt, crocheted sweater belted at the waist, shawl and boots.

Several blocks later, as were passing the community gardens, my cell phone rang. With an apologetic glance, I checked. It was Sophie. I answered. "Hi, sweetie."

I heard her sobbing.

"What is it?" I asked her.

Marget watched my face.

"I … I can't do it, Mom. I tried."

"Can't do what, darling?" I slowed my own breathing as if to communicate to my daughter to do the same.

"I tried to go to the past and I couldn't. I got super sick. I've been spewing my guts out."

"You tried by yourself?"

"No. With Hamelyn and Baird."

My insides roiled. Trying to take my daughter to me-dieval time without me? Without my even knowing? "Sometimes it takes a bit of practice, honey." I wouldn't get angry and take a chance on alienating her.

"We've tried and tried. All different ways. I can never do it. I've been blacking out. Horrible voices come to me, like nightmares."

What could it be? I wondered. Oh, I'd be making a visit to the past and very soon. *Many times?* "You know night-mares aren't usually dangerous in the outside world. They just mean we're processing—"

"—something in the psyche. I know, Mom. Now's not the time for Jungian theory." My daughter's voice shook on the verge of more tears.

Marget's eloquent dark brows twisted in a question mark.

I mouthed, "Sorry," pointing at the phone.

"Are you with someone?" Sophie asked.

"A neighbor. Sweetheart, please don't try again, even if Baird and Hamelyn encourage you. Not until we talk more."

"I just finished my last exam. Can I come visit you?" Her voice was thick with emotion.

"Of course. Come now. Do you have enough money?"

"Yeah, I saved when I was working full time in Paris." She sniffed.

"Good for you. So smart."

"Can't just jump, like you and Baird." Her voice had a bitter tinge. "Can't jump anywhere. I'm pathetic." She hiccupped.

"We'll talk about it when you get here, my love. Just let me know the flight time and I'll be there to pick you up."

"Okay," she said, quiet voice sounding young and vulnerable.

"I love you."

"Love you, too, Mom. Talk to you soon." She rang off.

"Is that Sophie?" Marget asked.

"Yes. She can't time travel. Or not so far."

"Some can't. It's a form of evolution," she said, as though stating a fact.

"Have you made a study of it?" I laughed as we moved on down the block. My mind was split now, going over and over what I would say to Baird.

"Some of us have, yes. We have a group on the internet. Carefully encrypted of course. Dark web and all that."

"Oh my god. You're a hacker." The incongruity of it nearly sent me into giggles—this medieval witch comes to my time and becomes a total techie. I added, more soberly, "I thought I was alone."

"No, honey. Though there are not many of us."

STRANGE ALLIANCES

We rounded the corner of my block. Approaching my home, Marget slowed, then knelt at the edge of my yard — a spiral of carefully cultivated native plants in tiny paths, with some patches of indigenous ground cover as "lawn". I watched as she whispered.

Bedw appeared in the shadows beneath a coastal fern sheltering an interweaving of succulents and fairy grass.

Soon Marget nodded and stepped carefully into my yard, looking spellbound, eyes twinkling.

"I guess she approved of you," I said.

"I know her in my time," she explained. "She was surprised to find me here. I'll be glad to have her bless my garden."

Oz joined us on the porch. Entering the house, we walked straight to the loom.

Marget's visit ended up lasting far into the night. She spent time exploring my weaving space. We made dinner and ate companionably in the kitchen. She shared more about her past over lentil soup and artisan bread.

I hadn't counted on a lesson in scrying. She'd brought an obsidian bowl, wide and shallow. In the wee hours, we sat by candle light on the back porch, seeing visions on the surface of the water in the shallow vessel.

Two days later, Sophie arrived at the San Francisco airport. I picked her up and we made our way through the city, stopping for Chinese food along Nineteenth Avenue.

"So," I said over dim sum, "you tried to go back in time. And it didn't work out? How did that come about? Baird and Hamelyn popped in one day and offered to take you to their time?" I picked up a rice crepe, dipped it in sauce, and took a bite.

"Hamelyn came. He's been visiting briefly since I last saw you." Tears welled in her eyes. "He can't ever stay long," she whispered around a tight throat, pushing her chopsticks at a sesame ball. "I asked him to take me back with him. 'Maybe we can be together in your time,' I said. He told me he had no idea how to bring me with him, that he'd get his dad's help." She carefully picked up a rice noodle and nibbled the end, then set it back down. "Baird came with him the next time."

I tried to picture how this fit in between the time I was with him and Sophie's call.

"He said he'd better ask you but I begged him to just try. I wanted to know." She stared down at her lap. "Pride, too. I wanted to share it all with you when we were next together, that I'd been there. Not complicate things with, you know, your worries." She looked up, apology in her eyes.

"I have no special ability to help. Aelfwyn might be able to," I said, regret in my heart.

"They told me she *was* helping. Aelfwyn says I'm not one who can do it." Now her tears were ready to spill and I saw a storm of weeping on its way. "It basically means Hamelyn and I can't be together, since he gets sick staying in my time and I can't go to his."

"Darling." I wrapped my arms around her, ignoring the restaurant clientele. After a deep breath, I whispered, "We'll explore this more. Come home with me. Walk on the beach, see my garden, meet my new friends."

Her tears subsided. She sucked in air, pressed her eyes,

and sat up straight. "Let's eat this marvelous lunch, Mom." She popped a shrimp dumpling into her mouth, followed swiftly by a bite of steamed lotus paste bun. "Mmm…" She pulled a tissue from her bag, delicately dabbed her eyes, breathed deep and tucked into her lunch with gusto.

"That's my girl," I said, chewing thoughtfully. "How'd your exams go? Do you know yet?"

Half-finishing a bite, she nodded. "Good. I squeezed in a Welsh history class. Well, it covered the South West of the UK, including Cornwall."

"Interesting. I've been doing a bit of research on that area myself," I said.

"Have you?"

"I have a new friend from Cornwall."

"The neighbor?"

"Almost sort of a neighbor. She lives on the far side of the gardens. I met her first at the library and we've run into each other here and there. I'll explain more on the drive." We were coming to the end of our food.

Soon we were back in traffic. Sophie's gift of gab kicked in and she chatted about Aberystwyth, her friends, her classes. Then she waxed nostalgic about San Francisco. "I've always loved this city. It's been a dream of mine to live here someday."

"I remember that." Was this a hint that Aberystwyth was losing its claim on her? "When I did my Master's here, I brought you to the City quite a bit."

"I remember going to class with you. I loved it—the campus, the buildings. And we played here. Cable cars, North Beach, Coit Tower, Ghirardelli Square. The hike from the Marina. People flying kites. We'd park by the boats and climb those long stairs. Sometimes in the mist."

I nodded, enjoying her reminiscence, joining in with

other details. "Remember the time we thought we'd walk to the Square from the ferry and it started raining. We had no gear…"

"With Gramma and Grampa! And your brother and the cousins…"

"That's right."

"I thought Grampa might keel over it ended up such a long walk."

"It wouldn't have been so bad if we weren't hurrying to make it for the tree-lighting."

"And you were carrying your niece, Niamh, all the way on your shoulders," Sophie reminded us.

We drifted into silence, thinking of my parents, now dead, and my estranged brother, Keith. He'd become religious, up in Oregon. When I wouldn't come to Jesus the way he wanted, he'd dropped me.

On the long drive through the countryside—fields with old oaks, vineyards, redwoods—Sophie fell asleep and I drifted into troubled thoughts: my daughter's distress over her time-travel malfunction, and my automatic reversion to deception, in regard to Marget. It hadn't been outright lying, yet. But it would, if I didn't share soon. I'd started on a new road of transparency when I visited Sophie in Wales, and I'd aimed to continue that way.

I determined to set it straight when she woke—who Marget was, where she was from, *when* she was from.

I thought back to two nights before. Marget had knelt by my loom, run her hands over the frame and the emerging cloth, crawled around it. Then she'd beckoned me to join her on the floor.

"Open yer mind to me," she'd said.

I'd done so, as with Baird, closing my eyes, sensing her tapping gently at the edges.

"You've built a wall around some thoughts."

"To protect them. My children's childhood, that sort of thing."

"We can deal with that later. It's good. You've done well. It seems very strong." After a time, she said, "I've entered the areas with Thorgisl. There are memories you've shoved into your unconscious, though. It will be uncomfortable if I go deeper. Your protective instincts will rise up to keep me out. But I must go there if I'm to find all I can about this *Thorg* and his doings."

I cringed at the thought of recovering memories of the Jutland mage and my time imprisoned with him, but settled myself more comfortably with my back to the footstool, readying. She scooted against the other chair.

"T'would be better if we had somethin' o' his, somethin' he touches. But I don't think we need to collect that immediately."

"Boldo and Baird have both explored his laboratory. I suspect Ylva has as well. I could ask one of them to collect an object."

"Yes, let's do that. Soon. For now, I want to see all that's in you. Then we'll use a scrying bowl to find out what he's thinkin'." She took my hands. Our knees touched. As I gazed into her eyes, I prepared mentally for this enigmatic woman to know much more of me.

Chapter 4

When she broke away at last, I felt exhausted. I sagged back against the ottoman. "What did you find out?" I asked, with trepidation.

"He does not see you in this time. I believe Baird may have been right that your hearing him is a sign that a residue of him remains in you, from his deep probing into your mind."

"Ick," I said.

"We must make ye safe from that bit o' him growin' and influencin' you."

"It's like a parasite in me?" I asked with horror.

"Mm. A tad like that. We need to enclose it, and use it for our own purpose."

"Do you know how?" I asked.

"I did something like it with my son, against Galfride, but I had to do much more with him," she said. "I must conceive of a container for this Thorg energy. For that, we need to scry."

As promised, we'd gone to her house for the instrument of sight. We climbed a different set of stairs, this one narrow and wallpapered, giving directly off the kitchen near the back door. At the top of a third set of stairs was a long, narrow room with a slanted peak to the shape of the roof, and dormer windows. Along one wall, an altar stretched, filled with mysterious objects. A black, veined bowl held center place.

She smiled. "Plymouth marble. I bartered with tin and copper from my home region."

"But this is very special. I can't—"

"It's important to us all," she said, cutting me off.

We lugged it through the dark from her place to mine. She also brought a filled, corked urn on her back. "Sacred well water. Special algae in it cleans so it never stagnates. It's important to let the liquid we've scryed upon stay pure. In the same way, we could look into Thorg's sight-waters and determine what he's seen. Do ye have an attic or basement?"

"Attic," I said.

"We need to let the place cocoon over time in overlapping spells. The magic grows in the air." We hauled the heavy bowl up the ladder.

"So, it's important to keep this bowl hidden away," I suggested.

"Another reason t' keep it in the attic, out o' sight," she agreed.

If we were to spend much time there, I thought I might have Joaquin raise parts of the ceiling, maybe even put an outside stair. I wouldn't want to draw attention, though. Maybe he'd have to build a stairway with railing at his place and bring it in his truck. Was that possible?

Sophie stirred and opened her eyes. Taking a deep breath, I shared the bare bones of Marget's story with Sophie: where she was from and bits of our acquaintance. But not about the scrying bowl in the attic. And not about Marget's son.

Next morning, my daughter stood at the door of my guest room—the place that should have been my office, with its back window looking out on the yard. When I'd moved there, I'd intended to line the walls with books and continue scholarly endeavors at the desk. Instead, for the past two years, I'd kept the room mostly closed, books boxed. Much of my research remained in the attic.

Sophie rubbed her eyes. Behind her, the futon couch was rumpled with covers.

"What would you like to do today?" I handed her a cup of hot java with cream.

She sipped. "Mm. Beaujolais blend?"

"Yep. You know it." That was our favorite Mendocino roast.

"Let's see. I want you to show me the gardens, introduce me to Jarl and Joaquin. Maybe eat lunch at Headlands Café. Do you think Shelley could meet us?"

"You don't want to spend all day with my old friends, do you?"

"Yes. And Marget. I want to meet her. And maybe see her house that you've said so much about!"

We settled in the breakfast booth with almond-flour scones I'd picked up from the bakery the day before.

"Okay, let's make our way to the garden. I need to check in there anyway. And I'll text people."

As it happened, all four met us at the firepit with bag lunches. They made a fuss over Sophie.

"You're beautiful!" Marget had to look up to my daughter's five-foot-nine height. "I love the way your curls pick up glints of sun."

"Thanks," said my elegant daughter, dressed today in

crocheted and batiked layers.

Jarl, Joaquin, and Shelley hugged her and commented on how long it had taken to meet her.

"Harper in the Glen tonight at Duck 'n Hen," Jarl announced.

Marget blanched, hearing the band name. I knew the anguish she felt, having made her son forget his own mother. She asked, "Are you still chef there?"

"Part-time," Jarl said. "Also at Ravens."

"Yummy," Marget answered.

"I'm also doing website work, mostly coding," he added.

"That's good, modernizing your engineering capabilities," I remarked.

Marget's eyes lit with the mention of web and coding. Future hacking chums?

"What's Ravens?" Sophie asked.

"Expensive," Joaquin put in. We all agreed.

"Ravens is vegetarian haute-cuisine near Mendocino," I explained. "I'll take you, but you can't order the whole menu."

"I don't do that anymore," Sophie protested. "Are we going to Harper in the Glen tonight?"

I glanced at Marget. She gave a quick chin-lift—acquiescence.

"We must," I said. "You'll love the pizza. They have a non-cheese."

"I'll splurge with dairy," said my lactose-intolerant daughter.

"Eggplant and bell." I waggled my brows, knowing she'd adore the combo, as I bit into a filled Mid-East pita bread.

That evening, I pulled on a skirt outfit of my own making.

"So cute. Will you make me something?" Sophie asked.

She touched my sleeve and got the dreamy look I expected.

"You're not getting a taste for my tree bark styles, are you? I'll make you an outfit. We can pick out the fabric together."

"Okay."

I felt relief that she wasn't asking me to weave cloth from my ancient fibers for her. The way the touch of it affected her worried me.

"Maybe tomorrow we can go over to Yakota. There's a fabric store there, with more up-to-date patterns and styles than we have here in town."

"Great!" She twirled, showing me a linen blouse, embroidered at the edges, belted and draped over a batik skirt. "How do I look?"

"Like you stepped out of a fashion magazine," I said, "as always."

"I can't believe I'm going to meet the band. Isn't it the same one that played on that first Samhain when you met Baird?"

"Yes, indeed," I agreed. It would be intense with Marget there.

I'd never told Sophie about Ian's weirdness toward my crystal. Hopefully all would go well. Surely, he wouldn't do any of his strange stuff around my daughter.

"I'm going to check in your mirror," Sophie said and scurried into my room.

As I passed the loom, I felt a prickle. I stopped and tried to interpret the feeling. The cloth called to me to finish it. Could I weave with my daughter here? I seemed to be waiting until the end of her visit, but surely that was silly. As I stood reflecting, darkness came into my heart. I shivered and wrenched away. Hurrying to the kitchen, I gulped down a glass of reverse-osmosis water from a jug on the counter.

Sophie called from the front hall, "Is it time to go?"

I grabbed my bag from my room and joined her. She'd pulled on misty aqua-marine boots to go with her skirt of deep jewel tones that swirled around her calves. I drew on my own boots.

Boldo popped into my mind. "Greetin's, *dewis crëyr glas!*" Heron-chosen, he'd called me, referring to my spirit animal.

I thought to him, "Hello, friend. I haven't heard from you in a long time. You're well?"

"I am. Thank you for inquiring. This must be your famed daughter."

"You saw her in Wales. When I was there, in modern time?"

"I think not."

He was right. Sophie had not been with us when he called for help on that terrible day, when his clan was attacked by Thorgisl. Only Baird and I had been in our hotel room.

"You're doing a weird thing, Mom," Sophie said. "Your eyelids are, like, fluttering. It's creepy."

"I'm sorry, sweetheart. Let's get going." To Boldo, I thought, again, "Where are you?"

"Far and away, Ceirwen. I'll need t' keep my location obscured from ye fer a while as I search. I only pray, with me gone from them, my clan be safe."

"But why hide? Isn't that worse for your people, if Thorgisl can't find you?"

"I'm workin' with Ylva. She gives him visions. By th' time he gets t' where I've been, I'm gone," Boldo explained.

"You're doing it again, Mom."

"I'd better work on that." As I hurried up the front walk, I thought to Boldo, "Please contact me again soon. I want to know you're safe."

Duck 'n Hen was packed for the popular Celtic band. To Sophie's combined amusement and glee, some of the English dancing participants did cotillions and quadrilles along one side of the dance floor, right out of Jane Austen. The rest did freestyle interpretations.

Shelley and Joaquin grabbed a table near the band. We made greetings over the general hubbub.

Sophie's eyes opened wide as she took in the band members she'd been hearing about, trying to put names to them, I imagined. Ian and Shane were easy, since Ian was always lead singer. "Candace?" she mouthed, tilting her head toward the flautist.

"That's right. I'll introduce you at the break." We draped coats and bags on chairs, then returned to the front to order.

Once settled at our table with a pitcher of dark Death and Taxes lager shared around, Sophie sat back and listened dreamily, foot tapping to a reel. As Ian picked up a fiddle and jammed on it for a solo moment, she leaned forward. "Mom, that's old," she said. "You know the fiddle emerged in the UK in the 10th century. Isn't that the time—" She stopped and glanced at Shelley and Joaquin who were trying to hear her.

Just then, Marget entered from the street. She searched, then aimed for our table. Joaquin pulled a chair up for her. She thanked him and sat.

She wore her usual mid-calf skirt, incongruously topped by a plum-colored hoody with *Pomo Bluffs* stitched on one side. Her eyes traveled to the stage where her son played. As he set the archaic instrument carefully in its case, his eyes darted to Marget, or at least to our table. I looked back and forth from mother to son. Withdrawing his attention, Ian grabbed the mic and sang, grinning his charming crooked smile. Sophie watched, as did Marget. I pondered. How might he have gotten such an old instrument? It looked like it belonged in a museum. Perhaps he'd found it at a sale.

Marget hadn't dared to gift it to him, had she? She'd returned to her time for herbs. Why not for a fiddle? But would she risk his regaining his memories?

At the first break, Harper members joined us. Sophie leaned toward Ian and asked him about the fiddle.

Electricity zinged the air. Clearly, Marget felt it as well. Her eyes met mine.

"Soph, this is Ian," I said, unnecessarily. A feeling of dread crept in as his gaze remained pinned on my daughter. The feeling seemed to attach to the shadow already growing in my heart.

Chapter 5

Shelley, Joaquin and I joined the dancers on the floor to practice Appalachian steps. When Jarl was able to leave the kitchen, we had four for paired-off configurations.

Out of the corner of my eye, I noticed Ian on stage showing Sophie the ancient fiddle. Then they were gone for a while. I half-watched the door while we danced to Wayfaring Stranger played over the sound system.

The band returned to their instruments and Sophie found us. Shelley showed her steps which she learned easily.

Not long before midnight, the band finished playing.

"So nice to meet your daughter," Sarah said as we gathered to say good night. "How long will she be here?"

I turned to Sophie. She shrugged. "I'm out for summer. Not sure of my plans."

As we walked home, I asked about her flat in Aberystwyth. "Did you sublet your room?"

"We cleared it before I came here. A friend is storing my boxes."

"You didn't say," I said, thrown off. "You have to find a new place then, before fall?"

"That won't be hard," she said, but wasn't looking at me. *What was going on?*

At nine next morning, Sophie and I again sat in the breakfast alcove with coffee.

"Ian asked me to meet him at ten at Highland Café," she said.

My heart jumped. "Oh?" Dread crept in as I recalled the Ian I'd known. Finding out his early relationship with Galfride had, if anything, made me fear him more. I did feel empathy, and thought I had greater understanding. But I wanted to say, "Galfride is lurking somewhere in that boy's unconscious. Stay away from him." Could he be lurking *in* Ian's mind, watching us? How would we know?

Galfride had seemed different when he helped us on the Brocken. The last I'd seen him he was near the Jutland fort. All the time I was held captive, until I lost my memories, I wondered if he might break me out. Where was he? What was he up to? Was he in league with Thorgisl?

"What are you thinking about?" Sophie asked.

Pulled from reverie, I brought my eyes to hers. I could not be the one to say who Ian was. He did not even know about his mother. That problem had to be solved first. "Sorry. My mind drifted, thinking about my weaving."

"The one you've started?"

"Yes. It's felt different from others I've made. They always sort of weave themselves. But this one almost seems to be answering a question, one I don't know I'm asking." I laughed, a short huff. "I must sound strange."

"It seems cool. Like any artwork or creative thing we do, maybe. Right? Like we're reaching. 'What's my deep question?' 'What's my yearning?'"

"You're so clever."

"Aren't I though?" She laughed and got up. "I'm going to go hog your bathroom for a long time getting ready, okay?"

"Sure, babe." I got up, too, and kissed her cheek. "Take as long as you want."

When she'd disappeared into my room with an armload of clothing and toiletry bags, I stood for a while by the back door. Guiltily, I realized that I wanted a little break in order to summon connection with my fae world. I wanted to reach out to Ylva, perhaps *Bedw*. My heron? I would enjoy the silence and privacy in my home for just a little while. For now, I took a second cup of java to the back steps and sat.

Oz leaned into my shoulder, pressing the Brand of the Thirteen. I gasped and shuddered. Oz bonked his head into my chin, kneaded my lap.

"You rascal, activating my powers. Did you get a rush?"

For a second, he turned his green-gold eyes to me. Then he clipped my chin once more with his hard head before flopping in a patch of sun that threatened to be brief as clouds scuttled across the morning sky.

Stroking him, I tried to identify messages coming from the Brand scorched into my flesh. Often, when the brand was activated, one of the runes flashed. This time the whole archaic heron motif appeared, hovering. As I watched, the yard dimmed and I saw only a chamber, or stark room, like a chapel. I stared, trying to make out noises, shapes, movement, breathing slowly so as not to disturb the image.

"What do you think?"

Startled, I turned.

Sophie stood behind me in perfect fitting pale green jeans, vest and boots, jacket in hand.

"Adorable," I said. "You'll want that jacket. Or a heavier one. I think the clouds are gathering."

How long had I grappled with the mysterious image, trying to bring it into focus and failing? Was it even important, or active imagining?

"I think you're right. I'll get a warmer one." From the front hall, she called, "You have some great capes hanging here. Maybe I'll grab one."

For an instant, I panicked. Should she wear one from the past? I wasn't used to having anyone there and had left the ancient ones hanging with mine. I scurried in after her. "Do you want this one?" I handed her the forest green one I'd woven.

"Are you sure? It seems so special. You know what? I'm going to take one of mine."

She returned to her room and came back holding a hooded coat, quilted plaid.

"Smashing," I said. "Is it rain resistant?"

"Oh, aye. It's Scottish," she answered.

"I'll bet it'll be adequate then," I responded, giving her a kiss as she headed for the door.

After my daughter left, I walked slowly to the loom.

Marget and I hadn't finished the work we'd started — we hadn't accessed Thorgisl's scrying stone yet, though she assured me we could — but she did say it was safe to weave. Still, when I approached the loom, something stopped me. Here was my chance to get some work done, yet I froze.

Instead, I gathered gardening tools from the back shed. Carrying the kneeling cushion and a trowel to the front yard, I knelt by the fern where I'd last seen *Bedw* and began meticulously weeding around nasturtiums, following crab grass imposters to their roots and decamping them, digging my fingers in among ice plants to pick out nascent intruders, and trimming brown stems, until Sophie returned.

She dropped down next to me. "This is looking great. You've completely replaced the lawn Gramma and Grampa had."

"Took too much water to keep it nice," I said, tugging at one of my least favorite weeds.

"Do you know Ian can't remember his childhood?" she asked.

My head jerked up and my heart pounded. I felt on the spot. How should I answer?

"He has that strong Cornish accent—I know it well from living in Wales," she added as if she thought I might doubt her. "Yet he can only remember ever being in Northern California."

I took a deep breath, plotting out what to say.

"He does get flashes, though, he said."

"Flashes?" I felt a little faint. At what point would it be utter negligence not to impart to my daughter what I knew about him? But how much was mine to share?

"Yeah. Dreams. And … just other times." Her fingers fiddled with clover-type grass.

"I—" I started a sentence, having no idea where I might go with it.

"He invited me to come to Berkeley," she hurried on. "They have some gigs down there. Freight & Salvage. Ashkenaz. That'd be so fun, wouldn't it? They share an apartment."

"So … you're going to go? For how long?" *Should I tell her? How much?*

"Maybe a week?"

"But … you hardly know him," I squeaked. *She's an adult*, I reminded myself. *She's going to do what she wants.*

"Not just Ian. I really like Candice and Sara. Shane, too. Mom, I've been totally immersed in music theory, not really experiencing. Playing even! Ian's ancient fiddle brought all the ideas to life. Touching it, hearing it, knowing it's from a thousand years ago, maybe."

"Have you mentioned Hamelyn or time travel to him?" I asked suddenly.

She stared at me. "No."

"Maybe you shouldn't for now."

"Why not?"

"Ian acted strangely about the golden crystal. He even…got a little hostile." When her eyes widened, I hurried to say, "But I think he was drunk." I didn't need to ruin what they had.

What about at the English dancing, when we'd stood in line and I'd heard his thoughts about Galfride's portrait? Well, now I understood. It must have been one of his flashes, remembering his early influence, the older boy.

"I don't mean to scare you but…he is Marget's son. And he doesn't remember. Because Galfride took over his mind, just like he took over his niece, Branwyn's. And then held Gwynedd captive. Before he and Marget came to this time, they broke the connection by deeply suppressing his memories. Only it went too deep. He doesn't recall his past at all. Which might be the safest for now."

"Why didn't you say this before?"

"I only just learned it from Marget," I slightly prevaricated.

"But how will I be with him and not talk about it?"

"Practice your acting skills?" I suggested. "We are going to work on a plan to get his memories restored. While you're away, we're going to plan."

She gazed at me a moment longer. "They want to hear

me play flute." She grinned shyly. "I'm nervous to, but Mom, what if I could … like, play with them a little. Learn to play old Celtic music. And new. They play both." She was alight. Her eyes glowed.

Hamelyn seemed to be far from her thoughts. I could not deny that was a relief. But *Ian*? And would it be worse if we helped him to recover his past? "It does sound fun, honey."

"I want to see our old haunts around the East Bay, from the years we lived there. What better opportunity, staying in a flat in that area?"

I nodded. I'd have to explore this all with Marget. "When do you go?"

"Tomorrow." She hugged me, that tight grip that said she felt alive, soaring.

At least, I suspected, gratefully, that she might be done with living in Europe. And I had been honest.

Now for the next steps.

Chapter 6

Midmorning next day, a knock came at the door. I opened it to find Ian on my doorstep.

"We've come to fetch Sophie," he said, seeming a little unsure of his welcome.

Past him, I saw a true 60's-style VW van, with a Harper in the Glen scene painted on the side. From inside, the other three band members waved. "That's a classic vehicle," I said, waving back. "Sophie?" I called, then asked Ian, "Do you guys want to come in?"

"I'm ready," Sophie said, entering the hall with a travel bag over one shoulder. She wore patterned leggings and a soft skirt for the long drive.

As she approached, I looked from her to Ian, feeling panic. Should I be letting her go?

"Send me pics and all that," I said, kissing her.

"I will, Mom. I'll chat you, as always." She kissed me back, and they were out the door.

Oz came and sat by me, black tail-tip looped perfectly around his white front paws. I watched them load her bag and re-establish positions in the car. They put Sophie up front. Ian drove. I stepped out the door as they pulled away, and waved them all the way down the block, until they turned and disappeared.

I took a few deep breaths, stood there a moment longer, then returned to the house. Who to contact first, Marget or Aelwyn? Should I bring Marget with me and have the two women chat? I texted Marget, "Are you up for a visit today?"

"Certainly. Do come," she responded.

I put on a light jacket—summer on the Northern California coast is rarely shirtsleeve weather—and walked the several blocks to Marget's. I sent the old oak a greeting, feeling a glimmer of tree-answer as I skirted around to the park at the back of the house. Marget had tea water ready.

I went straight to the point. "Sophie went with Ian and the band to the East Bay for the week."

She listened intently, nodding.

"I told her," I said.

Her eyes grew wide.

"Ian told her, about not remembering his past. He said he gets flashes. I felt she had to be warned, on her guard. I don't know …" I watched her expression closely. "He's your son. You haven't told me that much about him, what he's really like. Just that Galfride influenced him."

"I understand. Of course, you want to be careful, for your daughter's sake."

"I suggested she not say what she knows, for now, about his past, or who you are. That we're working on bringing his memories back but we should do things carefully."

She stared down at her hands pressed together in her lap, then at last looked up. "I will give you my story now. Why I left…my time, Cornwall. I said 'witch hunt' but of course what we know as witch hunts now started in the fifteenth century. I was hunted by my own kind. Banished is more accurate. In the world of magic-workers—crafters—banishment can be quite harsh."

"Was it … due to Galfride?" I asked.

"Yes. Because I'd allowed him to learn from my materials. His abilities at that time leaned toward the dark."

"He was still that way quite recently," I said. "I have seen it." I recalled Gwynedd, seated frozen on the cave-wall bench, unable to call out. And my own moments of horror in his caverns deep in the Haute Alpes.

"They were coming for us," she went on, expression haunted. "Friends—the few I had left—warned us. The Guild would have stripped our powers which essentially leaves one a drooling imbecile. Galfride went into hiding, I knew not where. I gathered my most cherished items and traveled to Wales. I'd heard of the workings of the Thirteen. I planned to present my situation to them. But I feared they might be influenced by the Crafters of Cornwall Guild.

"For several years, Ian and I lived modestly and quietly, in Borth and Machynlleth. But I knew Ian was still influenced by Galfride from afar." She stared at me, eyes jewelling with unshed tears. "He had been such a brilliant, joyous young man, loved in our town. He learned to play fiddle with men who gathered 'round the taverns."

She sat silent, then went on, "But he was different after Galfride came. 'Where is he?' I'd ask him. 'I don't know,' he'd say. But I knew there was still a connection. Finally, I had to take a risk. I approached Kyna. Ian was perhaps thirteen. She worked with him t' sever th' tie t' Galfride. Aelfwyn sometimes helped, too. But Galfride would find him again, and he'd turn into a different person, mean, and sneaky.

"In the long hours we'd spent together, stitching, talking, gathering herbs, Kyna told me of your visit. I begged them to try to send me to where the crystal had sent you. They weren't sure if it was another time. Not yet."

I stared at her. So there really was no coincidence at all.

She went on, "I think she was as curious as I. At last she agreed. They worked one final time with Ian to make sure he would not be found by Galfride. Ian was by this time in his late teens.

"When we arrived by the oak, he had no memory of his past. He did not know who I was. He walked away from me. He found himself work, playing music he'd learned as a boy. That's a memory he didn't lose." She ended with, "I've wanted to get their help to restore his memories but feared Galfride."

"I see. Well, I think it's time we spoke with them and decided how best to do it. Do you think the Crafters of Cornwall are still after you?"

"Perhaps not. Especially not in Wales. Are you able to take yourself there?" she asked.

"I usually get help. Otherwise, I've been known to … go astray." I paused. "Marget, I made another friend recently, a woman in Norway, of your time. She has formidable powers. I would ask for her help as well, if you're amenable."

"Ylva?" she asked.

"Yes, you *have* been spying." I laughed. I did not mind, nor did I blame her. She was isolated, away from her time, from her kind.

"You have some wonderful allies," she said.

"I do. I think so." But it was not all sunshine. I thought of Thorgisl. "And some enemies as well."

"They're not your enemies though, are they?"

"They threaten my friends. I was captured by Thorgisl. I'm not certain if he or Ansgor might hurt me and my kids." I was relieved that Sophie was no longer in Aberystwyth and seemed less reachable, yet the tentacles spread in surprising ways, like Rousseau being driven to write stories too close to Otho and Thorgisl's doings. "Thank you for entrusting me with your history. It makes sense. You have connections to Kyna and Aelfwyn. I just wonder why I didn't see it sooner."

She reached across the table and took my hand, which was warming on the cup.

"I don't mean I'm hurt you didn't reveal this sooner," I said. "It just seems like I would have stumbled upon the information, here or in the past."

"Baird did not know. No one else knew. I asked them to keep my secret," she said.

"That makes sense. I'm going home and contact Ylva." I smiled, gave her hand a squeeze and released it.

"Yes. We'll make plans." She took a deep breath as we both stood. "I'm a little frightened about when he remembers."

"That … he might be angry? About the memories being closed off all those years?"

"I have no idea. He might go immediately back to where he left off. With the dark thoughts and … interests."

"We won't just let him go off half-cocked," I said. Would she know that expression?

"That's a good saying," she said.

"These are women who know a lot about the mind. As I know you do as well."

"Not like they do," she said, walking me to her back door.

I made my way through her vibrant garden and turned as I reached the fence. I waved, then paused. Since I didn't practice my arts every day—though I should—they were not automatic. Holding the silver piece with my Ing ring hand, I accessed a sense of the heron brand, and immediately saw beyond the fence. No one was in the park. I made myself move to the other side. It wasn't even exactly going *through* the fence, but just *being* on the far side. To Marget, I must have vanished. I could have hopped to the gardens the same way but that wouldn't get me any cardiovascular, so I walked briskly past a mix of houses, some charming old wood structures from the early 1900's, most more mundane, from recent decades.

I entered the community gardens and spent time checking all the rows, making sure plots were generally in order. Then I tended to my own weeding, watering, and harvesting. Sophie had only been with me a few days but I felt the freedom of time. What a loner I'd become! I loved seeing her, finally having a chance to catch up, yet at the moment, all was fraught with complexity, uncertainty, and even danger.

As I left the gardens, my cell phone rang. On it, I saw a photo of Sophie with the band in front of the van, the Berkeley marina behind them. She was tucked against Ian who was clearly taking the selfie. His eyes bore into mine. I wrote, "Thanks for the pic! Have fun!"

Then I texted Marget. "Are you able to scry a bit—see what's happening with our kids?" I felt like a rat.

"I can," she said, adding a pirate emoticon, unpatched eye winking. It amazed me that she was from a thousand years ago yet had settled into the 21st century—dark web and all—like a native. A clever, witchy-techy native.

"Ha ha," I responded.

"Should we continue our work with your scryin' skills?" she texted.

I thought a moment. What first? I longed to contact Ylva. I also needed to check on Rousseau. How long had it been since he last chatted me?

"I'm going to putter around and try to get my mind clear for a bit, if that's okay," I told Marget.

"Take your time," she answered.

I texted Rousseau, "How are you?" That message left, I tackled my most immediate concern: keeping my daughter safe. Normally I bowed to the wisdom of Baird, Kyna, and Aelfwyn for matters of the mind that were out of my range, such as hiding or retrieving memories. Ian's memories had been suppressed with magic. Could Sophie be safe with a man who was tormented by a past he did not remember? In my study of language, I had explored depth psychology. I had a feeling there might be a healthier, less invasive way of connecting Ian to his memories, through healing. Ylva had healed Duff—reconnected him with his soul, it seemed. Perhaps we needed to consider a modern approach, if he was to develop in a healthy direction.

Along with Shelley's midwifery, she'd studied depth psychology as well. She always said only so much could be dealt with through medicine, or even herbs. "Birth. Breastfeeding. These are things which call upon our inner resources, our relationship with self." Could we bring depth psychology to the table with Ian's memory retrieval? Marget had said he'd been a beautiful lad—bright, well-loved, quick learner. We needed to tie him to his soul as he remembered his past.

I texted Shelley, inviting her to join me for lunch soon.

In the study, I explored book boxes until I found my Jungian library. I pulled out the relevant collection. My symbol books had normally sat next to my thorough personal library of the world's writing systems. I chose a spot on the empty shelves my dad built. I hadn't yet made this room my office.

Shelley texted back, agreeing to lunch the next day.

I texted Marget. "Yes, I'd love further scrying lessons. Please come for dinner." So much for alone time.

Chapter 7

Next day, after a most enjoyable meal with Shelley at Headlands, at which we'd explored the concept of memory restoration from a Jungian standpoint, I returned home to find Ylva and Duff sitting in my living room. Both stood and their heads brushed the ceiling, Duff with his red hair tied back, bangs wildly chopped, Ylva in her signature floor-length crimson coat, hair a similar scarlet shade. I rushed to Duff, arms open, crying out with a sob.

I'd known he'd been healed, but to see him in my home, well and jolly, after his ordeal in the Harz Mountains, warmed my heart. He bent and wrapped me in his arms. Then I hugged Ylva.

"Is this your first time coming to my era?" I asked Duff, wishing I'd already replaced my parents' couch. I'd meant to shop for something bigger, but hadn't gotten around to it.

"We came to let you know of our efforts to find Otho, and of Boldo," Ylva explained.

"I want to hear everything! About the amber, how you're protecting it. If you've discovered more powers in it. How is Boldo's clan being kept safe? Any news of finding Mora?"

"So many questions," Duff said. "How about some tea?"

"Yes, tea!" I jumped up, reminded of courtesy. I rustled around in the cupboard for butter cookies Sophie'd picked out. It would have been fun for her to meet my friends.

Carefully, I brought a full tea pot, steeping, and cups and saucers to set by my guests. I rolled a chair from the den. "Boldo has only contacted me once. He said you were helping to obscure his trail from Thorgisl."

"Yes," Ylva said. "That's true." She stretched out her legs from the couch, boots like snow-shoes crossed.

"So, you're able to scry what Thorgisl sees?" I asked.

"To some extent," Ylva said.

I set out their cups and plates. Then, turning one of the comfy chairs so I faced them, I told them about my weaving and how I'd felt Thorgisl in my thoughts. "It's kept me from weaving further."

"We will have to find a solution for this. The cloth you weave must be of importance." Ylva crossed the room and knelt by the loom, nearly doubling over to see the short stretch of fabric. After a moment she returned to the couch.

Oz sauntered in and leapt onto my work table. Curled on his side, head upside down, he opened his eyes halfway.

Duff and Ylva watched with amusement.

"His dragon pose, Sophie calls it."

They laughed. Duff demolished two cookies in a wink.

"Duff, did you ever meet someone named Marget, at Kyna's home?" I asked.

"I donna think so," he said, pouring himself more tea. Two more cookies disappeared into his mouth, followed by a substantial gulp of tea. "Perfect."

"She's from Cornwall, and she's been to Kyna's. She

worked with Kyna and Ylva," I said.

"Mayhap I never came inside when she be there."

"Would you mind if I invite her over? She lives in this time."

"Of course. We should meet her. I think I've felt her observing when I was here before," Ylva said.

I stared, gulped my tea. I texted Marget, while Ylva and Duff watched.

"May I see it?" Ylva reached out.

I showed them pictures on the phone. They stared in amazement.

Marget made good time and was soon knocking on the door. Her eyes did not widen at the sight of the two giant redheads who greeted her; she'd probably scryed the scene. I made introductions.

Marget settled with tea, which rolled into dinner, as I satisfied myself that Mora's clan was safe and all possible was being done to find her. My work space became the dining table it was meant to be. For once, I set four places. It was only the second time I'd entertained a group there. The other was Harper in the Glade, that first Winter Solstice I'd know them.

"Do you think there's an enchantment on Mora, that she's actually at the Jutland fort?" I asked Ylva.

"That is my guess. I can reach much of Thorgisl's mind but … if you have an ice wall, he has a glacier."

"I'm sure," I said, knowing well the steely discipline inside that mind; I'd dwelt there far too many hours, finding out only what he wanted me to know.

Marget shared her full story. We broached the topic of Galfride's influence on her son's mind and his loss of memory in order to keep him and everyone else safe.

Duff moaned. "I hate to hear that, a young man turned

into Galfride's pawn. And he recalls none of it now?"

"He may remember glimmerings," I said. "My daughter is spending time with the band, and he told Sophie he gets snatches of memories he doesn't understand."

"You're lettin' her stay with him?" Duff asked. "Should we go and check on 'er?"

"There's been no sign of him doing anything sinister since he's lived here." I looked at Marget, who agreed. His strange fascination with my crystal and the drawing of Galfride could be explained, I told myself. "And Marget can look in on them with her scrying."

Sometime after midnight, Marget and I started yawning.

"I can make up beds, if you'd all like to stay," I offered. I thought about where I could accommodate Ylva and Duff if they accepted. I could give them my queen-sized bed and use the roll-out in the den.

"It's not far for me to walk home," Marget said.

Ylva said, "It takes only an instant to be at our home. We will return soon. I have brought you something." From a pocket inside her voluminous red coat, she drew out a carved heron, brightly polished, about eight inches tall.

As she placed it in my hands, I felt a quaking in my belly. It seized the brand on my shoulder. For a moment, I stood motionless, in the grip of a tremor that soon subsided. Ylva and I had a new connection.

After everyone left, I lay in bed holding my heron statue. "Can you help me call my spirit-animal?" I asked it, touching its sloping back with a tentative fingertip. I felt nothing.

Next morning, my phone vibrated against the bedside table as I was waking. "

Mom, you were right. A week is too long with people I hardly know," Sophie texted. "I'm going to bus to Marin and catch the shuttle to you."

"Looked like you had some fun, though. At the Marina?"

"Yeah, I'll catch you up when I get there."

"Sounds good. I'll be at the stop behind Harvest Market to meet your shuttle," I texted back.

What had happened? I had all day to conjecture.

Sophie stepped off the shuttle with other passengers wearing a fringed hippy vest and bell bottoms with mirrored spangles running down the lined pattern.

"Aren't you a blast from the past," I said, tossing her bag into the back of the car.

"Scored these at Buffalo Exchange." She climbed into the passenger seat. "I love that era. It's not fair that I was too late for it."

As we pulled away from the curb, she asked, "Hey, Mom, has Rousseau been in touch lately?"

As I turned onto Highway One, the main street through town, I glanced at her. "He and I are in contact about once a week, I think. I texted him yesterday. Haven't heard back yet."

"Does he usually take that long to reply?" Sophie asked.

"Sometimes. He goes on trips with his college mates, or gets wound up in a case."

"Or a basketball tournament. Should you call him?"

"Do you have some reason to be worried? Did he say something to you?"

"No. He and I barely communicate. I'm not great about it but he's worse. I just … wondered. You told me about him writing stories. That sounded weird. He feels like he's being controlled?"

"Yes. Well, sort of driven. But as you say, creative endeavors often grab and run with us. Should we pick up crab at Noyo?"

"Sounds great," she said. "I love to go down there. Let's walk on the sand, too."

We turned onto the narrow, curved road that descended to the harbour flats. At the top, the view opened out over fishing and pleasure boats, warehouse structures with stacks of crab traps. The blue Noyo River, sparkling in the lowering sun, curved past a row of restaurants connected by boardwalks, then past RV parks and picnic areas, to enter wooded hills.

We parked and climbed a short stairway alongside a loading door crowded with crab cages looking old and rusty. Fish and saltwater smells filled the air. Inside, a no-nonsense shop with worn linoleum flooring contained bread shelves and a single glass-fronted fridge offering seafood-related fare. A handwritten sign behind the scraped and dented counter offered the day's catch.

I ordered crab and picked out a loaf of French bread.

"Can we get shrimp cocktails?" Sophie asked. "We could bring 'em out by the water."

We did. Following the harbor road on past the last of the restaurants, then through the tall piers of Noyo Bridge to a parking lot that sided the curved beach.

As we settled on a tilted, broken-off concrete block facing the river mouth, with its comings and goings of fishing trawlers, I said, "I want to hear about your visit to the East Bay." Reaching into the bag, I pulled out a shrimp cocktail and fork for each of us.

Sophie opened hers and popped a bite of cocktail, chewing for a moment. "I had a lot of fun, especially at first."

"Then what happened?" I tasted mine with its tangy sauce. "Mm, pretty good!"

"Yeah, it is. Well, Ian started asking a lot about you, and if I'd seen a golden crystal in your house. Or a drawing of a guy. He described it. Sounds cool. You'll have to show it to me. But he acted all weird and intense. I know you warned me that he'd been strange with you." She took another bite.

"I understand it better now, knowing how his memory was wiped," I said. "But was he...scary? Forceful?"

"A little freaky. When I said I hadn't seen those things, he pressed on and then finally kind of laughed, made some of his jokes. Have you worked on getting his memories back?"

"I've been laying some groundwork."

"Do you think it'll be safe? Once he remembers?"

I searched her eyes, remembering all too well Ian reaching for my chest where the glowing crystal lay under my shirt, how he'd pinned me against the wall of Duck 'n Hen, before Jarl came along. "Honey, has he scared you?"

"Not really."

We stared out to sea as the waves lapped in and shushed back across the sand at our feet.

Around a bite of shrimp cocktail, Sophie said, "This is so good."

"It is particularly fresh," I agreed.

"Let's fly to Boston and check on Rouss," she said.

"Whoa. That's a bit extreme, though I'd love to visit him. I'll try calling him tonight." Why was she so anxious to reach her brother all of a sudden? Most of the time, she ignored him.

We stood and brushed off the sand.

That evening, I tried to call Rousseau. Not reaching him, I left a message.

We were sitting at the table, playing a card game. I'd lit a fire as the evening had turned cold and blustery. Oz lay on the rug by the fire.

"Let's do it. Let's go to Boston," Sophie said.

"Well. We can think about it."

We finished our game. I picked up a book—*The Dream and the Underworld*, by James Hillman.

Sophie opened her laptop. After a few minutes, she said, "There are some good prices, SF to Boston, right now."

Chapter 8

And, just like that, we planned a trip back East.
The next day, my son called. "I got your message. You're coming to visit me?"

"We're looking into it. Will that work this week for you?" I asked.

"For sure! I think it's great. Sophie's coming? How's she doing?"

"She seems unsure about returning to Wales."

When I got off the phone, Sophie said, "I haven't told you, I visited UC Berkeley. I might transfer to a Master's program there. Folklore is about the closest to what I've been studying, and I can choose a concentration in media studies. I talked to the department head."

"That sounds wonderful, sweetheart! You'd be closer to me, too. What do you think you'll do with it?"

"I don't know. Film. Writing. Get a Ph.D. and teach?"

"You'll do great, whatever you choose."

"Thanks, Mom."

A day and a half later, Sophie and I were in the air over the Midwest. She slept and I stared out at clouds. It was strange to get on with my life while a part of me was embroiled in worries of a thousand years ago.

Rousseau met us at Logan. He wore jeans, high tops,

and cardigan for East Coast summer weather. Each lugging a carry-on, we left the airport to catch an electric shuttle, a bendy bus that curved into a dimly lit tunnel.

Shouting over the noise as we climbed with other passengers to the Red Line to Somerville, we caught each other up on our news. After dumping our bags at his upstairs apartment, we ambled down the street to a Japanese restaurant.

"I can't believe I've never seen where you live," Sophie said, hugging her brother. Both tall, they leaned against the wall, waiting for our name to be called. I found a seat next to them and watched them, admiring. Sophie filled him in about her possible Master's program at UC Berkeley.

"You might be at Mom's old school," Rousseau said.

"I did my undergrad there, you know."

"Oh, yeah." He grinned at his sister. "I remember."

"Just because it's not Harvard."

They made faces at each other. Our name was called.

That night, Rousseau put fresh sheets on his bed for us and took the fold-out couch for himself.

"You know I'll have to work in the morning, right?"

"Of course, sweetie," I said, rummaging in his hall closet for a blanket. I stopped short. Under a quilt was a coat very much like Otho's, and a pair of old breeches. Very old. I picked them up and sniffed. Tenth century. I was sure of it.

"Rousseau?" I called. My heart beat an aching tap dance.

Rousseau came up behind me. I held out the jacket and pants to him.

He was somber, lids slightly lowered in that look when he both wanted to share and didn't. "You didn't see the shirt that goes with it, hanging in my bedroom."

"Boots, too?" I swallowed.

"'Course."

Sophie came up beside him, probably sensing a tone. She looked from him to me to the clothing but said nothing. "Have any chocolate, Rouss? I'll make Mexican spiced, and you can tell me about it."

"In the kitchen cupboard," he said. "I'll help."

I sat in the one big chair. When hot cocoa was ready, Rouss and Sophie scooted to the back of the roll-out bed.

Rousseau blew on his drink, then set it on a coaster. "I was writing one day. And…" he took a breath, glancing at Sophie, "I noticed I was moving. Everything was moving. I wasn't in my room anymore. I smelled salt air and heard sea gulls. Then I realized that all around me, from perches on the desk, animals and birds were staring at me."

I gripped my cup, despite its burning heat, in fact welcoming the distraction from my fears.

He chuckled nervously. "Of course, I thought, 'Now that's getting too involved in a story,' and wondered if I was going insane. A man burst in the door."

"Was it Otho? Were you on his ship, the *Kauli Pishom*?"

"That's the one. The ship I'd sent you stories about."

"You never told me about this, Mom," Sophie said.

"That ship disappears, Rouss. You could be on it when it… we don't even know where it goes. I saw it get snatched out of thin air. We have to figure out how to keep that world from grabbing you."

"I can't even time-travel," Sophie mumbled.

Rousseau wore a troubled, unreadable look. I set down my hot drink and scooted onto the bed, wrapping my arms around my son. He hugged me back.

After a moment and several long, slow breaths, I sat away and turned toward him. "Cough up the worst. How many times have you been to the past without me knowing? Summarize before my heart implodes."

He sighed. "You're one to talk. Reading my stories and not even saying you'd been there, that you knew the people I was writing about."

"I'm sorry. At first, I hoped it wasn't related. As my suspicions grew, I thought I could disentangle myself before you kids got pulled in… Every time I thought that, I seemed to just get more deeply involved."

"Now I know how that can happen."

"You're scaring me even more. Have you been drawn other times? Who've you met?"

"I know Galfride, Mom." He licked his lips. "And I know Thorgisl."

"What?" My voice dropped to a low register, feeling sick. I studied his face. He looked too peaceful. "Do you know what these men have done? Do you have any idea?"

"I know some. What danger have *you* been in without *me* knowing?"

"Score," said Sophie.

That night, we slept little as I relayed my adventures, the three of us lined up on his couch.

"Boldo is Otho's cousin?" Rousseau asked. "Sounds like you two are close."

I sighed. "Purely platonic. So Otho found you sitting on his ship, at his desk."

"Yeah. Remember in my story where they anchored and Otho went to shore? It's like I knew, from his mind, that he'd been to that tavern, that he'd gone to the alley with the huge guy and the little man, just like in my story. He got back, boarded the ship, threw open his cabin door, and there I was. He carried a bundle. When he saw me, he stopped, then snarled, "Who the hell are you?" I think I could read his mind. Basically, I could understand him. I knew he'd wanted to hide what he was holding and didn't want me there to see. He shouted, "Get out. If you're a new crewman, you got a hell of a nerve, sittin' at my desk."

"I ran out, then crept around the ship, searching for a hiding place. It was cold on the sea. I put on a warm cape thing with a hood, then hid under some sails and waited, hoping they didn't find me. At almost dawn, I saw them readying a boat to go ashore, so I crawled in; it was still pretty dark. No one saw me. I hid under a heap of ropes. They rowed to shore and pulled the boat onto the sand. When they'd left, I climbed out and followed. They went into a tavern. I waited a few seconds, then went in after them. It was warm in there and I didn't know where else to go. Seemed safer than just hanging out god knows where."

I curved my hands around my cup, seeking warmth, and sipped the last of my cocoa.

"I was sitting in the shadows, kind of close to the fire—as close as I could get while still staying out of the light—when a guy sat across from me. So much for hiding. He said, 'You're related t' her, aren't ya?' Good looking guy. Well-dressed. I could understand him. Mind-speak, I guess. 'To who?' I asked.

"Whom," I said, automatically.

"Yeah, well, I eschewed niceties. Anyway, he was reading my mind. Ceirwen, he called you. I had no idea they call you that, but he put a picture in my head. 'That's my mom,' I said. 'And you're from a town in Cimru, right?' he asked. I knew he was fishing for something you didn't want him to know, so I said, 'Yeah, it's too shrimpy to have a name.' 'I want to show you something,' he said. He took my arm and we left. I knew he was Galfride. I guess he told me. I knew that name from my story, that he was the one having Gwinydd brought to him.

"We walked a long time up a kind of frozen road, next to swampy flats, until we came to a low stone fort. 'Your mother was held captive here,' he told me. Then this guy comes walking up the road toward us. 'Thorgisl,' Galfride growled. Thorgisl invited us to his place. Galfride wouldn't go, but I was curious."

I groaned.

"Well, I was a little disbelieving. My mom? In medieval times? But I also kind of suspected. You'd acted strange about my stories. I had a feeling you knew the guy I saw on the subway, and that he was from another time. I wanted to see what you'd seen. I didn't know anything about Thorgisl. But Galfride said you'd been held captive in the fort."

"Didn't you fear he might imprison you?"

"I didn't get that sense from him."

Oh, so calm. I could throttle him.

"Anyway, we went up to his tower, leaving Galfride outside. Thorgisl told me, 'Anyone can read your mind. It's open like the workings of a clock. I like it but you're not safe.' He seemed to want to train me or something."

"You're in danger with him, Rouss. He sent his men to slaughter Mora's clan. He took Boldo prisoner, and now he has Mora. He's had her for months." I paused. "She's important. The leader of a clan that has great abilities. They're the main members of the Thirteen!"

He looked puzzled.

"Kyna's and Aelfwyn's powerful circle. They brought me back from outer space when I shot myself out there. They can do amazing things. With Galfride's help, we moved the clan's whole caravan out of danger."

Rousseau listened, a tiny quirk of a smile playing at his

lips, an echoing twitch at his brow.

"You don't believe me."

"I wouldn't have six months ago."

"Good god, Mom," Sophie said, hands clenched together.

I laid my hand on hers. I had a feeling Boldo was listening, even though I wasn't wearing my boots; my stocking feet were curled under me on the couch between my kids. "How did you get away?"

"Something startled me and suddenly I was back at my desk, here in the apartment."

"You haven't returned to that time, though, have you?" I asked.

"I can't exactly control it. Not yet, anyway."

"You've been to Otho's ship again. You have clothes like his."

"Can I share the rest tomorrow?" He yawned.

Sophie had fallen asleep, despite her efforts to hear it all.

"Come on, sweetie," I said, tucking fingers under her shoulder. Rousseau and I coaxed her to his bed.

"I'm gonna be a wreck for work," Rousseau said. "But that's okay. I'm glad to have you here." He ruffled my hair.

"I'm glad to be here." I gave him a quick hug. "I should have come sooner, should have asked more about the stories."

"How could you know? 'Night, Mom."

I glanced at the window where dawn light filtered in. "Such night as remains to us."

I'd barely slept when I heard Rousseau leave.

After a few hours with eye masks to keep out light, Soph and I walked around the neighborhood. We chose a café called Three Little Figs, ordered and found a spot to perch at a high table. Amid the noises of chattering patrons, espresso machines, glasses clinking, chairs scraping the floor, we pulled out our laptops. I gulped my mocha from its tall glass, then emailed Marget, "I'm in the Boston area, with my kids. I have lots of news."

Soon she replied, "How was Sophie's time in Berkeley? It hasn't been a week."

"She came home early," I answered. "And we just flew to the East Coast."

"We need to put dark web on your computer," she wrote.

"Okay," I said, baffled.

"When do you return?" she asked.

"Sunday."

"I'll have a little surprise for you."

My mind went wild trying to imagine what it might be. "You're mysterious."

She sent a laughing emoji and we closed off.

That evening, Rousseau took us to a Greek restaurant. We'd received full plates and begun eating when I asked one of my many burning questions. "Have you learned to take yourself to the past, or are you always drawn unexpectedly?"

Rousseau chewed thoughtfully. Then he said, "I have a stone."

Chapter 9

What kind of stone?" I asked, nibbling a lightly fried zucchini appetizer.

"It's amber color," he said, shrugging. "I don't know much about it yet but Thorgisl said it'll help me come back and forth."

"Does he know you come to another time?" I asked calmly, as if my heart weren't a bass drum hammering my chest.

"I don't know. He never said that."

"Never?" I squeaked.

Sophie chewed braised eggplant, glancing from me to her brother. "I can't believe what I'm hearing," she said, "even though I've met Baird and know Hamelyn." Her eyes filmed and she ducked her head, taking another bite.

"I want to hear about him," Rousseau said. "And about your plans. Do you think you'll move back to Berkeley?"

"I'm considering."

"I am, too. How about you, Mom?" Rousseau bit into his chicken *souvlaki*.

"Not quite yet." I allowed the change in conversation. What could be solved by grilling him? He probably didn't know the answer. One thing was sure. I had to get Ylva to his apartment to check the stone.

"I have to go into the office for a few hours this morning," Rousseau announced, then finished blending a protein concoction.

"Do you get enough fresh fruits and veggies, dear?" I asked. I'd noticed he'd barely touched his salad the night before.

"Yes, Mother." He quirked a half-smile.

I snickered and tickled his waist.

Sophie entered, rubbing her eyes, scuffing in her brother's size-eleven slippers. "Where's the coffee?"

"Out," Rousseau said. "I don't really stock it since I don't drink it."

"How is that possible?" she asked.

"Green tea?"

"Yeah, I'll take that."

"Water's still hot. I gotta run. I'll be back by noon. Promise. And we'll go see some traditional Boston sights."

"Oh, by the way, can you show me the stone you have?" I asked in a deliberately light tone.

"Um, okay." He appeared reluctant but disappeared into his room. He came out with a wood chest. Inside, folded into velvety cloth, was a wafer of amber. My insides shook at the similarity to the one that had been seared into Boldo's flesh.

"Can I keep it out here for a while?" I asked, not wanting him to hide it away again.

"Sure, Mom. Don't go anywhere with it, though, okay?" He kissed the top of my head. Wearing a dapper suit jacket with jeans, he pulled a workbag over his shoulder. In the doorway, he waved his smoothie bottle, then departed.

"Let's go back to that café," Sophie suggested.

"Can I come in a bit?"

"Are you doing something secret? You're not going back in time, are you?" she called from the bedroom. "That's okay. There was a cute guy working there. Maybe I'll flirt a little before you come."

This would be perfect, I thought. "Good. I want to write a bit."

"Okay, I'm showering," she yelled from the bathroom and closed the door.

After Sophie, I showered and dressed. She left and I sat down on the couch. Touching my Ing Ring hand to the silver pendant, I felt the strength that came from the Brand at those times of concentration. "Ylva," I spoke in my mind.

The woman appeared before me. "This is a different place, with homes below us," she said.

"Yes." I stood. "This is my son's place. We're near Boston, far from my town. Will you sit?"

She settled next to me on the couch. I scooted the coffee table out, seeing that it cramped her long legs.

"Can I get you tea? Coffee?"

"I have dined recently," she said.

"My son was given amber by Thorgisl. I wondered if you might check to see if he is tracking him. Any possible threats you might detect."

"Let me see," Ylva said.

I set the open box between us.

She unfolded the cloth to expose the amber, a little over an inch in width, almost half an inch thick at the center. Holding the stone in her immense palm, she closed her eyes. After a moment, she said, "I want to be certain." To my astonishment, she stood and took off all her clothes. Then she set the amber on the rug, diminished to a tiny size and leapt into the stone.

I lay on the rug and stared in. There she was, curled at the center, a perfect nude being, red braid coiled over her.

She returned to full size. "This must not remain here."

I grimaced. "My son won't like that."

"I will put with the other until we know."

I thought for a moment. "I'll promise to take him to visit you and see where his amber is."

"Thorgisl has not come here?"

"No, Rousseau was drawn to your time."

"I will explore more. Don't worry. I'll not let anything happen to your son."

"Thank you, Ylva." I didn't see how she could protect Rouss but I could hope. "Can I bring him to see you?"

"Yes, of course."

"How's Duff?" I asked.

"He is well."

"He still stays with you?"

"He does," she said, looking pleased.

I wondered, then, how much he might be missed at Kyna's home, which brought me to thoughts of Baird. I'd had no contact with him for weeks and felt the absence keenly.

Thinking of taking Rousseau to these places, meeting my friends of the Middle Ages made my heart soar. *But how jealous Sophie would be.*

Ylva stood. "I will take this now." She shoved the stone, still wrapped in cloth, into her immense pocket.

I got up and hugged her. "My profound thanks for your

help. You always come when I ask. It's a great comfort."

She smiled down at me. "We are spirit-pack." She laid a great hand on my head. Then she was gone.

I put on a light jacket and grabbed my backpack. All the while, my heart felt sore. What would I tell Rousseau about his stone, I wondered, as I descended the three flights of stairs to the ground floor.

Walking down the street, warm with sunshine, I wondered what was possible between me and my son. If he was learning to mind-speak, might I send him mental messages? I pondered how I'd bring him to Ylva. She would probably have to bring us. I seemed to reach her more easily than Baird. But I hadn't even made an effort to reach him recently. Why was that? Could it be that I was angry with him for trying to bring my daughter to the past without asking me?

I entered Three Little Figs Café and found Sophie settled near the counter. Gazing around the general milieu, I searched for the cute waiter. Not seeing him, I approached and set my laptop on the counter next to her. She looked up, noticing me for the first time. "Mom!"

"Hi, sweetie." I stepped to the counter to order, thinking of the challenges that lay ahead.

Rousseau returned at noon, as promised. I'd laid out lunch makings from a local deli. When we'd sat, I told him about the stone.

"This Norwegian shamaness was in the apartment?" Sophie asked, wide-eyed. "That's why you wanted me out of here?"

I nodded.

"Can't trust you for a minute," Rousseau said, mouth

full of sandwich. He swallowed. "Actually, I'm glad. The thing was making me nervous. I got a feeling when I touched it, and really didn't know how to use it."

I felt a wash of relief and leaned to hug him, kissing his temple.

That evening, after trekking the open markets near Boston's waterfront, sampling various chowders, and keeping Sophie from buying too much clothing, we rode the T back to Cambridge.

Late, Sophie crashed, exhausted. Rousseau and I stayed sitting on the couch, chatting quietly so Sophie wouldn't hear. "She can't travel to the past," I whispered, legs pulled up in a curl in my comfy yoga pants.

"I got that," he replied. "Weird, isn't it?"

"Yeah. Ylva invited you to visit."

"That would be awesome. To see ancient Norway? And meet this giantess?"

"But we're playing with fire. None of this time travel is really safe, you know." I didn't want him to think we were just waltzing around in the past without possible consequence. My gut wrenched as I thought of him getting stuck there, me here, somehow, and never seeing him again. I took his hand and looked earnestly into his eyes.

"I know, Mom. It's no game. That's why I want to learn what I'm doing." He'd always had a serious, philosophical side. And an abundance of curiosity.

"Me, too. I'm still a novice." For some reason, at that moment my brand burned. I winced.

"What's wrong?" he asked.

I showed him the mark on my shoulder, pulling my slouchy t-shirt out of the way.

He stared. "Did that hurt?"

"It did."

"What's it about?"

"It's part of the Thirteen, allowing me to be in the circle."

"The Thirteen is the powerful group that hangs out in Kyna's tower? Lots of Welsh Travelers?" He summarized what I'd told him.

"That's right."

"Would it help me to have something like that?" he asked.

"I'm not sure you need it," I said. "You know, Aelfwyn always wanted to involve you. It's ironic that you got pulled in." *Or is it?* I asked myself. "Sweetie, we go home tomorrow. I want to talk so much more about all of it. I want to know how many times you've gone to the past, what Thorgisl has said to you, what happened on the ship. This hasn't been enough time."

"We'll keep talking," he said, brow furrowed. "Should I come out west to visit you?"

I squeezed his hand. "Can you take the time off? I have a friend in town, Marget, I want you to meet. She's given me a scrying bowl and is teaching me to use it." I grinned.

"A what?"

"It helps you see, on the water. Maybe that can help connect us." I thought about my boots and how Boldo and I shared thoughts easily. "I'm just trying to say, there may be ways we can communicate thoughts when we're on opposite coasts."

"Or if I live in Berkeley," he said. "I'm considering moving back west."

"I'd love that so much, sweetheart," I said warmly. "Do

you have a timetable?"

"Not yet."

"Well, until then, since I know you could be pulled into the past anytime, I want our communication to be the best it can be."

"So that I could call you from the past?"

"Yes, and maybe reach others. Friends. Even Galfride. He's been an enemy but recently he's helped. If he's hanging out in Jutland and you're pulled there again..." I wondered again why he was there. To locate Mora, when no one else had been able to and win himself some points? Was he curious about the power-stone Thorgisl was after? Or just wanting to know more about Thorgisl?

I yawned mightily. Rousseau caught the bug and echoed with a cavernous yawn of his own.

"We'd better get some sleep. Has the couch been okay?"

"It's fine."

"Let's get it made up for you."

"I'm tempted to just roll up in a blanket."

"You'll regret it in a few hours."

"True."

Together, we made the fold-out bed.

"'Night, Mom."

"Night, honey." I tiptoed into the bedroom to check on my daughter. She was fast asleep with ear buds in. Gently, I removed them, turned out the light, and slipped in beside her.

Chapter 10

O z leapt onto the car as we came to a stop in our California driveway. Padding to the center of the roof, he rolled over as I got out. He pressed his chin to the metal surface and slid like an otter on snow. I reached up and stopped him before he fell off the side. "You nut," I said, rubbing his belly. He purred.

Sophie lugged her bag toward the front door. He trotted off the car and after her as I got out my luggage.

Inside, mail was scattered onto the hardwood hallway floor. Sophie bent down.

"U.C. Berkeley," she said, picking up an envelope.

"Already?" I called, setting my carry-on in the bedroom.

"Just a letter from one of the faculty I spoke with," she said, coming in with torn-open envelope. "She says they're very interested in the interdisciplinary approach, since I've studied in Wales." She tucked the letter back in. "I'm going to finish my application now." She hurried to the guest room.

I loved seeing her excited. It seemed like everything was coming together for her. I returned to the hall and gathered the rest of the mail. Flipping through, I came to a violet envelope, addressed to Kay Ceirwen Halefin, with delicate flowers lining the sealed closure. Smiling, I sniffed it. There was a sweet scent. I opened it. "You are cordially invited to tea on the morrow, 2 p.m.," it said, signed Marget Tregarthen.

So that was her full name. I savored being invited to tea by mail. It had no postmark; she'd clearly walked here and put it through the mail slot.

I stood the card, open, on my desk and checked on Sophie. She was already hard at work on her laptop.

"Want a snack?"

"Sure. What do you have in mind?"

"Toasted sprouted grain tortilla with rosemary, and guacamole."

"Sounds great," she answered, grinning.

"How's it going?"

"My essay?" she said. "Want to read it over when I'm done?"

"Of course."

"Ya know, Mom, you should put a sliding door from this room out into the yard, and a full-length window at the end looking out on a pretty garden. The windows are too high and cramped."

"Less room for books."

"Look. You hardly have any on the shelves." She swept an arm toward the long, empty spaces.

"I'll see if Joaquin wants to help. Are you going to design the garden?"

"Absolutely. You and Shelly should add herbs to it. Hey, let's check when Harper in the Glen is next playing up here."

"Are you over the weirdness with Ian?" I rested my chin on my hand, which rested on the doorjamb.

"Yeah. Also, I mentioned the super-old fiddle to the

professor at Berkeley."

"Does 'the professor' have a name?"

"Oh. Yeah. Brinner. In Ethnomusicology. Know her?"

"No. Though I've had speakers from that department from time to time. It sounds perfect for you."

I watched her for a moment as she bent back to her laptop, then went to the kitchen to turn on the oven.

In the back yard, as I picked rosemary, I thought I saw movement in the hedge.

I thought it might be *Bedw*, in the shadows under Sophie's window, but forgot about the sylph as I set to work on our snack, chopping rosemary and basil to sprinkle on tortillas. I slid them into the oven and mashed avocados for fresh guacamole. I brought the fixings into the yard and wiped down the pollen-dust covered outdoor table and chairs we rarely used, calling to Sophie. When clouds covered the sun, we ran for jackets.

"I've been invited to tea tomorrow with Marget," I told her.

"That's cool. I'll probably still be working on application essays."

As it turned out, she did not stay home next day, hunkered over the computer; Ian invited her on a hike. We walked together to the community gardens. He met us there.

As we approached, I tried to discern the vibe between them.

"Hello, Kay." He held out his hand.

I took it, reluctant. I felt like I had to give him a chance. I watched Sophie's face as they greeted each other. Did she seem attracted to him? There was a comfortable chummi-ness as they walked away.

"Good trip to Boston?" I heard him ask.

"Yeah, great to see my brother."

We hadn't talked about what not to share, about Rous-seau's story. I wondered suddenly at what point she'd fallen asleep. They headed out of the garden, onto the street and toward the hills.

I followed, on my way to Marget's, wondering what she had for me. In her back garden, I took in the potent medley of herb and flowering vine scents. White butterflies flitted, landing on lush mint bordering flowerbeds. One de-tached and brushed by my cheek, startling me.

"Greetings," Marget called from her doorway. "Kiss of a butterfly. Means good luck." She smiled and gestured for me to enter. I climbed the steps and we kissed cheeks.

"Shall we sit in the garden?"

We carried tea and scones to an ornate iron table in a grotto on a patch of thick clover, entering through an arched trellis covered in climbing roses.

"This is delightful," I said as we sat.

Marget laid a gift on the table.

"Should I open it now?" I asked.

Her deep-set eyes gazed at me intently. "I returned briefly to Cornwall," she said. "Also, to the Tower, and Aelfwyn."

At this, my heart skipped a beat. Was it about Rous-seau going to the past?

"Baird was there as well. And Duff. They said Baird promised you a new way to connect with him."

Why was Baird not coming to me himself? "Oh?" was all I could muster. My chest felt tight.

"What they came up with was this." She pushed the

box toward me.

With shaking hands, I untied the ribbon and opened the beautiful box made of a mother-of-pearl type shell. Inside rested a ring the color of the golden crystal. I picked it up from its satin nest. Energy swirled through me, struck the Ing ring, the Brand, the silver pendant until I was buzzing. I slipped it onto my right middle finger and heard voices, many voices, *too* many. I swallowed, unable to sort the thoughts and images darting through my mind.

A gentle touch on my arm brought me around. Marget pushed a warm cup into the curl of my hand. I saw her concern as she urged me to drink. I sipped, then gulped. It was harsh, and settling. I took a deep breath, shuddering. The throng of voices mellowed and receded.

"But I want to hear them. How can I pick out one from the other?" I asked, surprised to find my voice shaky, as if I'd been on the verge of crying.

"You'll be able to. It's a discipline."

I noticed rings and bracelets on her fingers and wrists, as though I'd never registered them before. "Does your jewellery channel things to you?" I asked.

"Some, yes." She took both my hands. "I want to hear about your son."

"Have you read my thoughts? Am I broadcasting worry?"

"You mentioned his trips to the past, the pirate clothes and the amber stone."

"That's right. I get anxious about my lack of discipline, of training."

"You have great skill. You will learn much more. On my most recent journey, I noticed magic is easier in my time, in the past."

"Why do you think that is? The EMFs? Overpopulation?"

"Those are all in discussion in my online forums," she answered.

"Is that why you suggested I be on the dark web?"

"And to encrypt your whereabouts."

"Ah."

We watched an exquisite black and yellow butterfly land on a purple iris, spreading its finely patterned wings. We both smiled.

I told her all my son had shared, and about Ylva taking the amber.

"It's as well," she said.

The voices swelled, making my head vibrate. I gulped more tea, sucking in another deep breath. This time a vision came to me: waves of light, faces, scenes streaming out like threads, with me as epicentre. "Ohhh," I breathed out.

Marget nodded, as though she saw it with me.

This feeling of sharing such a numinous moment touched me. This time, tears did well. Marget's eyes matched mine. I thought about the word *coniunctio* in depth psychology—connecting in such a way with another mirrored in the self as greater wholeness. That's what I felt, a surge of … love? Emotion, at any rate. "Whew. What a gift."

I thought that moment might have been shared with Baird. Was there a rift between us? On another level, I was profoundly moved to have this new ally in my time, to train with, to share concerns.

"I told Rousseau we'd find ways of connecting to him, so that when he's pulled to the past, he can reach out. Do you think that's possible?"

"Yes, of course. We would not have it any other way."

We? "You speak of Aelfwyn?"

"And Kyna. We are forming a new Thirteen. It will also

reach Kyna's time. Branwyn and Gwynedd are a part of it." She pulled her sweater and blouse over her shoulder, enough to show me a healing brand, similar to mine, complex enough to hold sigils of all the ancient runes.

I gasped. "You've been initiated. Shouldn't I have felt it?"

"Not if you didn't know what to look for."

Maybe that was the burn I'd experienced in my Brand. "It's not a heron like mine."

"No, my spirit bird is the kestrel," she said. "The dark web will be essential for this new work stretching across millennia."

I shuddered, unsure about more people sundering the fabric of time. But this was not mine to own or control.

Chapter 11

A t that moment, a cloud passed over, allowing a single shaft of sunlight to angle on the edge of our bower, highlighting a shimmer with rainbows in the air there.

"Are we in a protective sphere?" I asked.

"Yes." She smiled. "Good observation."

Only then did I notice numerous sylphs moving in the deepest shadows of the garden.

"It's a blessing that you drew *Bedw* to our time," she said. "We need her, and her kind."

"They must love your garden. I hope they're not neglecting Mora's clan." After all, I had first seen the sylphs with Mora's clan. But I felt a tiny self-loathing. Was I jealous? No, no, I scolded myself.

"They love the *Silwy*, are always aware of them and shoring up their protection. Ylva also watches over them now."

"I worry about them, without Mora," I said, to try to soften what might have seemed like censure, as if her drawing them here to our time was a wayward act. Truth be told, I'd first gotten Baird to bring them to *me*, after finding Thorgisl in my home.

Marget leaned forward, changing the subject, or actually bringing it back to where we started. "Rousseau is a natural, a great resource. He's not to be allowed harm."

"That's easy to say. But not always preventable," I said.

"There have been failings in the past," Marget said. "They did not know the vigilance needed. After all, Ansgor sat dormant in his cave for decades before renewing his attacks."

"True. But even now, we can't know where threats will come from."

"We have many more eyes, more talents being applied," Marget insisted.

"I don't mean to be skeptical," I said, "but when my son is being dragged into the worst of it ..." I was suddenly very glad Sophie was not able to travel. I thought it meant she couldn't be dragged to the past, either. Was I right? Even now, she walked with Ian in the hills above us. I glanced in that direction and reached for my daughter's mind. Clenching my hands together, I willed the surge of power to rise again. Scanning along the strange tree line of shaggy bull pines and eucalyptus, I felt for Sophie's familiar resonance.

Marget watched me, then took my hands in hers. Her mind joined mine as we surveyed the hillsides. And there, I caught it. Sophie laughing. She and Ian held hands. He grabbed a tasseled grass stock and tickled her cheek, singing.

"Sing in Gaelic," she urged, batting the grass away. They stood near the edge which looked over the Noyo River estuary.

I withdrew my mind. "Seems happy enough." Yet my gut churned to see him with her. I'd seen him put on the charm with others, at the Duck 'n' Hen. I'd also experienced the other side. He wanted—*craved*—my crystal and the drawing of Galfride. His burning lust frightened me.

"They do," Marget agreed. Her eyes, on me, were pensive.

"What did Aelfwyn say about bringing his memories back?" I asked.

Marget twisted a cloth napkin in her hands. "Not yet," she said. "Maybe never." Her gaze dropped to her lap.

Sophie found me in my garden plot at the Green—what we sometimes called the community gardens.

"You and Ian enjoy your time together?" I asked.

Sophie thought. "Yes. I do have fun with him. I'm not sure he's romance material for me. I think it's band mystique. I love when he sings." She gave a self-mocking giggle, covering her mouth.

I tried to detect if there was any undercurrent of unease to her comment.

"Do you think Rousseau will really move out here soon?" she asked, tugging a weed out from under a summer squash vine. "He's been East ten years now."

"He seems to intend to," I said, sitting on my heels from reseeding beets.

"What if he and I both end up back in the East Bay?" She lined the beets on the ground by my cloth bag.

"I'd certainly love it," I said.

"Would you come live there, too? We'd all be together."

I thought about leaving this area where I'd first encountered Baird, where I'd dropped into another millennium. Now I'd discovered Marget. Could Boldo reach me as easily in Berkeley, with its denser population, traffic, noise? Baird had followed me down the rain-soaked streets in the hills north of campus as a squirrel. He'd accompanied me into the UC Berkeley library as a flea. But could sylphs dance in our gardens? "I'd visit. A lot." I tugged at another weed. "But I'm not sure I'm meant for city living anymore."

She puckered her lips. "Yeah, I can see that. I like to come here for a calm nature break. But what about the university? It's hard to imagine you holed away, never teaching again. What do you have in this area? Just Pomo Bluff's dinky community college branch."

I waved a hand. "We have internet. Maybe I'll start a publishing house called Rural Scholar."

Sophie rested her chin on one knee, pointing garden dirt away. "Could you be happy, isolated here?" she asked.

"I'm not sure, sweetness." I scooped soil to tuck in one last beet seed. "I think we come to a time when we have to follow our soul's dictates. Right now, my soul says 'be here'."

"Oh wise one, be here now." Sophie kissed my temple. "I'm glad you remind me to follow my inner voice."

I stroked her cheek with the back of my hand. "I hope your path always appears clear to you, darling. Even if another seems clearer shortly after."

We laughed, helped each other stand, and brushed off.

"Did you find out if Harper in the Glen has a gig here this weekend?" I asked as we gathered harvested beets, chard, and lettuce.

"Yeah. They're playing tomorrow. Sans Shane. He's gone home to Ireland for a visit."

"Nice. For how long?"

"I'm not sure. Maybe a couple of weeks."

"That would change the sound a lot, not to have Shane."

"Yeah, I don't like them as well without him. I mean, they're still great but you know how he adds humour and fun. Ian takes himself more seriously. Thinks he's god's gift and all that." She chuffed a laugh as she accompanied me checking garden plots, gates and office. "I need to make a trip to UC Berkeley. Want to come with me?"

"I'd like to do that soon. Do you mind if I sit this one out, sweetheart?" I was anxious to get back to Marget. The ring was making my head feel chaotic at times. Yet I didn't want to remove it and lose the ground I'd gained adjusting to it. I thought Marget might be able to teach me to control—or at least better monitor—the energies it stimulated.

"Is that a new ring?" Sophie asked, picking up my right hand. It was as though she'd read my thoughts, again.

"Yes." Not wanting her to get fixated on the past, I said, "I picked it up in a shop recently." Then immediately felt ashamed for lying again.

It's to protect her.

How often parents fall back on that one.

She eyed me with a fixed stare.

"Okay. It's from Marget."

"It helps you see from afar, doesn't it? I felt you— when I was in the hills."

"Maybe you're getting more attuned, too." I hugged her, glad to not start a new subterfuge.

"I saw you, in my mind, sitting with Marget at a little table in her yard. And I sensed you seeing me, even though I heard your voices."

"That's just the scene. But probably if I was good at using the ring, you wouldn't feel me seeing you unless I intended that."

"That'd be sneaky," she said, grinning.

"True," I said. "I don't want to spy on you. I want to …"

"…spy on the bad guys?" she asked.

"Yes. Definitely. Or at least keep them from spying on me."

"Wyrd."

We enjoyed a quiet evening by the fire. The clouds had gathered in earnest and a light rain pattered on the roof.

Next morning, I stood by Sophie packing the car.

"Where are you staying?"

"The band's letting me stay at their flat. You don't mind me taking the Prius, do you?"

"Not at all. I like to walk or bike. If I need to go further, I can get a ride."

I had no idea how far I'd really be going.

Once Sophie left, I sat in the front yard practicing with my amber ring. As soon as I turned my energy toward the dark-honey-hued circlet—petrified Tertiary resin, to be precise—I felt a jumble in my head. It was mostly muffled chaos but I feared one of the voices I heard was Thorgisl's— that icy, even tone, more chilling the quieter it got. My head ached.

Almost immediately, Marget's voice came into my mind, and the others quieted. "I meant to give you some of the tea. I can bring it. I need to go by the Green anyway, for one of Shelley's herbs."

"I'll meet you there," I suggested.

In a short while, we were in Shelley's beguiling plot. She'd created a neat European garden of mostly herbs, trailing over objects of mythical fancy. Joaquin was teaching her to carve fauns and dryads, sprites and centaurs, that peeked out from carefully labelled foliage.

I found Marget examining labels and leaves. Seeing me, she straightened, dug in a sweater pocket and handed me a packet. "Steep it five minutes."

I thanked her. Shelley wandered down the path.

"Hey." I gave her a hug. "We're admiring your magical plot, and carvings."

Shelley curtsied, lifting a corner of her skirt. "So nice to see you in the daytime, Marget."

"It's been mostly Duck 'n Hen, han't it?" The older healer took her hand and kissed her cheek, having to reach up.

"Yes. Let's do more. Tea. I'll have you both over. I just have five minutes. Must get back to work but wanted to say 'hi'."

"I'm glad you did. I've been carrying these seeds of my Cornish chamomile for you."

"Soon we'll resemble Cornwall's landscape here." I grinned.

"I'm thrilled." Shelley accepted the tiny packet. "Must run."

"I can share a bite to eat before you go." I held up my cloth sack with snacks in it. I hadn't been sure how long we'd stay.

"Next time. I have a client arriving soon." Shelley kissed us both and trotted away.

"We need to get you to Aelfwyn," Marget said. "She can better teach you to manage your new tool."

"I'm worried that others see me when I zero in on them. Sophie felt when we watched her on the hillside with Ian."

"Her time with Hamelyn may have stimulated her mind powers," she suggested.

I nodded. "Makes sense. Still..." I fingered a velvet leaf with deep burgundy underside. "I should be able to choose. If we're to go back in time, can we also visit your old home, in Cornwall? Was it Saveock Water?"

A sweet light suffused her face. "I'd love to show you my homestead."

She took my hand and, without any warning, we entered darkness.

Chapter 12

Within a moment, we stood facing a town-square. Next to us stood a cottage of white-washed cob with deep green shutters and thatched roof. Children played near it, chanting, then running. By rough-hewn clothing and wattle-and-daub buildings, it was clear we'd gone back a thousand years.

"Oh! You meant right now," I said, taking in a breath as I realized the journey we'd made, without preamble. It was becoming almost seamless for me to step between. I had to wonder what that meant, about the fabric of time, about me.

"I thought I'd brought us to my house," Marget whispered, glancing around warily. "Come."

We started up one side of the town square, next to the green, scurrying past a forbidding row of grey-roofed houses.

"They built these for the smelters," she explained in a low voice. In the narrow gaps between them, wind swept down across fields from the hills beyond. A spatter of rain caught us and we ducked under a tree. The gray overcast sky gave away little about time of day.

A woman, thin and weathered, passed us lugging a basket of produce. She nodded, eyeing us malevolently.

Marget bowed her head in return, then took my arm and we walked on, past low homes of slate, then one a playful greenish hue. Across the square stood a dominating manse. I tried to detect taverns or shops, but with the mist, and Marget tugging me along, anxious to leave the tiny hamlet, I failed to make out any signs of commerce or hostelry.

We came to a rutted lane heading away from the cluster of buildings on the square toward a cliff. Lone cottages dotted the landscape, scattered here and there, farm properties outlined by low walls or hedges.

"Everythin' be made from th' land 'round us," Marget commented. "Stones and slate are dug up for houses and walls, when they clear fields. The reeds for thatch come from estuaries and bogs near the coast." She pointed to the cliff ahead. "That way's the sea."

"Seems like rich growing land," I said.

"Very fertile." She pointed back the way we'd come, at a bridge that must be at the far end of town, which signalled a river, as did willow trees growing in a winding line away from the village. At a far point, I saw a blue bend of water as pale sun peeked through.

I indicated piled debris toward the hills. "Mining?"

"No. No mining here. We just smelt tin in this area. Since the Bronze Age!" She seemed amused to share this.

"Imagine having evidence of such ancient history," I said. "Compared to Pomo Bluff. I think this area is a famous archaeological dig site, in the 21st Century."

"True. In my time, we made pins," she said.

We laughed and walked on.

"And awls, leather borers, loom weights. Spindle whorls made from slate," I offered. These were Kyna's memories of items produced in Cornwall. I checked my mind, wondering if she was with us, in spirit.

I stopped, hand on a slate wall. "Kyna?" I asked in my mind. The other woman smiled and waved a hello.

"What is it?" Marget asked.

"It seems like that might be part of the magic," I said, not mentioning Kyna for the moment. "Everything you make, everything you touch, is from the land around you. With your hands, you make your shelter, your food, the fabrics you wear. It's all natural, from local plants, stones, animals … "After a moment, we walked on. "Did you know that woman?"

"She gathered the vegetables to have an excuse to walk past us," she said. "Aye, I know her."

"Maybe we shouldn't have come. Not visibly any-way," I suggested. "Could she be a danger to you? Do they … are there people she might speak to about—"

"I'm finished running and hiding. That's what I'm working on with the Thirteen. And I have another home."

"Where would you rather be, though? I mean, are you really happy in the twenty-first century?"

She was quiet a moment as we trudged, finding our way among the ruts. She looked thoughtful, eyes sad. "Sometimes I miss it here with an ache that won't stop. But, I'm more contented in our future time since getting to know you."

"I, too," I responded with a smile. "Do you have allies in this time?"

"I do. Few have stayed in Saveock. I have a dear friend in Truro."

"That's close to here, isn't it?"

"Aye. Fair close."

The road grew weedier as we came closer to the loom-ing cliff. Massive stones rose up around us, and the way was barely a cart path, slanting upward. Moss grew on rocks.

We stepped past a few trees, a slight hill rise, and more boulders. And there stood a hut, in a tiny copse, built into the boulders of the cliff foot.

It had an abandoned air to it, yet bluebells and fuschia grew lushly. I stared for a moment at the thatching. I thought I'd seen movement.

"Birds nesting," Marget said. "Robins, wrens, sparrows." We started toward the door, but Marget stopped. "First, I want you to see it as it was. Let's go further back." She took my arm in hers …

She wore a blue silk gown, open at the front to show a quilted petticoat of white satin, half-covered by a muslin apron skilfully embroidered. Over her bright auburn hair, she wore a lace cap like a fairy web. Around her neck hung a string of shells; on her velvet shoes were silver buckles. Having seen the other woman and her dark, plain clothing, I assumed Marget was eccentric for her time.

We stood inside her hut where children, lambs, cats, tame hares and poultry jostled for space. I stepped back against a wall to watch and take it all in.

A spinning wheel, table, high-backed carved oak chair, a few stools comprised the furniture. Shelves held brilliantly colored earthenware, unidentifiable forms both graceful and grotesque, uniquely shaped glass bottles of all hues. On the mantelpiece stood a bright warming-pan, an hourglass, and exotic seashells and corals. Part of the room was raised for a bed and dresser. A curtain, bunched to one side, could be drawn across. In a corner, I spotted a ladder.

"Ian slept up there, in th' attic. And Galfride, fer a while."

A swarm of children ran in and out, chasing ducks, being

chased by puppies. Peat smoke and the sounds of kids shouting, dogs barking and sea gulls crying filled the air.

The younger Marget busied herself with dinner, swatted a boy lightly on the behind when he came too close to the stove. Stew aroma wafted in the air, mingled with musky smells of children, animals and natural materials that made up the home: wattle-&-daub, course fabrics, wood and dried grasses. Shouts and animal sounds—braying, squawking—created a small pandemonium. The Marget with me watched intently. Of course, no one could see us. A tiny piglet ran by so close it could have brushed my boot, had I been there in the flesh.

Then we were back to the silent cottage of Marget's absence. Furniture stood dusty. Besides cobwebs swaying in a breeze from a cracked window, nothing moved.

"You won't want to stay here long, the way it is." She walked to the mantle, touched a shell, blew a web from a statue, which only made it vibrate.

She took my hands. The ice of between engulfed me. Then we stood in a familiar yard.

The door opened. Aelfwyn beckoned us in.

My heart thudded as I anticipated the possibility of seeing Baird. It had been weeks in my time. I wondered how long it had been in his.

We climbed the steps and entered the front room I knew well. A fire burned. Little had changed, at least at first glimpse. At Aelfwyn's invitation, we sat with her at the rustic table, larger than when I'd first time-slipped into Kyna's front room to accommodate Aelfwyn now living there, and Hamelyn and Duff often joining meals.

"Will ye have somethin' hot t' drink?" Aelfwyn offered. She poured from a pot pounded and welded from a variety of metals. "So you're havin' some difficulty with th' new ring, th' amber one?"

"I am. Its power seems marvelous, but at times all the voices and minds swamp me."

"We'll have t' work with you. Everything takes practice. Some requires training."

"Marget's tea quiets the chatter but I want to be able to single one out and hear it clearly. Also, when I'm in that state, I can't be certain if someone is reading me."

She nodded. "O' course. That can't o' ben pleasant."

We three women sat, hands wrapped around steaming mugs. I ventured a sip. The brew had a hearty anise flavor.

Aelfwyn's gaze rested on Marget. "We have further business as well."

Marget nodded. Their eyes held each other in a silent moment. I thought they might be communing without me, and felt a bit left out, shunted to the side.

The curtain at the back of the room moved and Baird ducked through.

I lit up at the sight of him. Yet I had a moment of foreboding, wondering what the greeting would be. After all, he'd not brought the new ring to me himself.

A smile creased his face and he strode to me. I jumped up and hugged him, listening to his heart pound through his quilted vest. My chest rose high, dizzying with elation and heat.

We broke apart.

"Marget, do you know Baird?" I said. Though I knew she'd been in this house very recently, I did not recall her saying she'd met him.

Marget stood. "We have met." She held out her hand.

Baird took it and bowed. "Well met again, *Cymydog Cernyw*." Cornish neighbour, I caught Baird's thought.

"Now my neighbor as well." I felt pride that she was my friend and confidante.

"Oh?" He appeared puzzled.

I glanced around. The other two women seemed to say, with their eyes, "Do the honors. He doesn't know."

"Well," I began, considering what to bring up. "You know the oak you arrived at, in my time?"

He nodded and sat at the table with us.

"And the abandoned-seeming house at the back of the lot?"

"I do," he said as he poured himself tea.

"Marget lives there. Has for years. The front's enchanted to look deserted but she has a lovely home and yard at the back."

"*Gwych!*" he said, delighted. "A sort o' portal, be it?" He looked over at Marget.

"Indeed." She nodded.

"I've just seen Marget's old home in Cornwall," I said. "In this time, I mean. She showed it to me for a moment as it sits now, but we went back and saw it with her still living in it as well."

"Ye have no ill effect from stayin' indefinitely in Kay's time?" Baird asked her.

My heart raced as I studied his face, wondering if he asked for himself, or for Hamelyn.

"None a't'all, though it took some study and experimentation at first," she answered.

Aelfwyn brought a plate of cakes dotted with dried fruits to the table.

"Aren't we lucky," Baird said, winking at the elder as he took the first one and sampled a hale bite. "Most times we get no fruit bits outside of a holiday."

Marget and I helped ourselves and thanked our hostess.

As my hand reached out to the plate, Baird's eyes followed the amber band.

"That be a fine piece. I watched Duff craft it."

"Here? Has he returned?"

"He comes back and forth. I'm not sure we'll see much o' him, though, in future."

"It's serious, then?" I asked. "With him and Ylva?"

"So it seems."

"Have you been to Ylva's home yet?"

"I have not," Baird said, taking another cake with a nod of thanks to Aelfwyn.

Her mouth twitched with amusement but also pleasure, I thought.

"I'll need to take a trip there soon," I said. "I've promised Rousseau a visit."

Baird and Aelfwyn swiveled their heads in unison toward me. All was silent. I thought I saw the side of Marget's mouth pucker, and her thought, "Now you've dropped the cake."

Having stepped in the hornets' nest, I went on, "You see, he's been to this time. You remember the story that came to him about this time?"

Of course they remembered, their expressions said.

"Well, that pull got stronger and suddenly he was ..." I felt a storm of voices in my head, almost nauseating me. "Perhaps we should shore up protections before I go on with this tale."

Chapter 13

The four of us were joined in the Tower by Hamelyn as we prepared for ritual.

As we held hands around the smoking brazier, my Brand tingled, then burned. I saw my heron stalking at the edge of the woods far below.

"This ceremony be t' make yer energy no more 'n smoke, than a breath," explained Aelfwyn, "so we might enter minds as vapor, unfelt. I want ye t' know each part o' yer mind so no one can walk there without yer knowin' or without your express permission."

"I want that, too," I said. Mouths compressed with humor at the passion in my voice.

After perhaps an hour, or more, Aelfwyn tested me. Then each of them entered my mind, and after, I entered theirs. I wobbled within Baird's, as our love sparked. We snickered.

"Enough!" Aelfwyn snapped. "T'is not a game, nor a time for amorous dalliance."

We schooled our faces and hearts with proper contrition. Then Aelfwyn sent the others away.

In the apothecary, she continued to work on my discipline with the access I now had to others' minds, and my defense against their access to mine. At one interval, I heard

Baird invite Marget for a walk with him and Hamelyn by the sea. I longed to join them.

During the grueling process with Aelfwyn, she gleaned details from me of Rousseau's escapades into medieval time, including his encounters with Galfride and Thorgisl.

"Now we will try less friendly territory."

I felt dread. "What territory might that be?" I asked, though I thought I knew.

"Oh, yes. You know," she said. "Be vapor. You should only need your scarification and jewelry, though I have a feeling your *crëyr glas* helps you."

"Really?" I glanced toward the covered window, sending my senses out beyond to the woods, searching for my heron.

"Concentrate," she grumbled.

Obediently, I became as a ghost and braced myself to be in Thorgisl's mind again, where I'd spent too much time held captive, my memories plundered and torn asunder. This time would be different, though. I'd be with Aelfwyn.

Sure enough, the Brand of the Thirteen's bond held our spirits fast together as we successfully breached the man's mind. He sat unaware, in his Jutland tower, gazing out to sea. First, we penetrated the edges to test how much he would detect when we entered together. He was thinking of Otho and his ship. Dread and anger stirred in me as I detected Rousseau in his thoughts. I carefully schooled the feelings, maintaining my smoke-like essence. I felt Aelfwyn's mind grip mine and ease the turmoil.

We moved deeper, seeking, as one, knowledge of Mora's location, foremost.

There were many layers to this man's keenly fortified mind. We spent time on surface levels, catching some strange and disturbing traces of memory that left much to be explored. Exhausted, we withdrew and sat back in our hide-covered chairs, like hammocks on crossed poles. Darkness had fallen.

I had a growing dread. What did Thorgisl know of the ship carrying the power stone? Could Rousseau disappear with the ship?

"Galfride has joined with Thorgisl?" Aelfwyn asked.

"No!" My vehemence surprised me. How had I come to defending this weasel of a man? "He's suspicious of Thorgisl. He's been spending time by the Jutland fort ever since I was taken there, but he would not go inside when Thorgisl invited my son in. I think he's investigating." I still did not know if he had tried to help me when I was captive there.

Aelfwyn's hooded eyes gazed at me, mouth working a series of grimaces. "And your son?" she asked at last.

I stiffened. "Rousseau is … he … well, Thorgisl gave him a stone, an amber, but Ylva took it to keep safe."

"You do not fear that Thorgisl has inserted something in your son's mind?"

"That's why I had Ylva take the amber. I thought he might be watching him with it."

"A good thought." Her eyes penetrated. "And you do not fear Ylva having both ambers?"

"I figure I have to trust somewhere. And Ylva's got great powers that we need. We went into the tunnels in the Brocken to get Duff."

She held up her hand. "I know. I know. And helped break the terrible spell on him. Yet…" She pursed her lips again in thought. "And yet, I would gain more insight into this Nordic priestess. I believe we need to engage our new Thirteen in this. That may require adaptation to your Mark."

The skin around my brand pinched and sickness dropped into my bowels. "If you think so," I squeaked.

We heard voices, then footsteps coming in the back door. Laughter was quickly quelled.

"It's alright," Aelfwyn called. "We be tired."

Marget popped her head in past the doorway drape. "How did it go?"

I waited for Aelfwyn's response, curious what she thought.

"It went well. Ceirwyn has learned to be vapor."

I felt an uncommon swell of pride. A giggle, born of weariness and emotion, shook my stomach.

Aelfwyn pushed herself up in the chair. I leapt to help her stand as the men came in.

"How was the sea?" I asked.

"*Gwych.*" Marget used the Welsh term for fabulous Baird had exclaimed earlier, and all chuckled. "They showed me the castle ruins that stand by the breakwater in your century. We plan to look at the full castle of the 13th century tomorrow, if you wish to join us."

Such tourism we could manage now.

After a late dinner, Baird and I walked behind the house, stopping by the meadow. A brightly painted Traveler wagon stood in the field. Its side was lit by a campfire, illuminating intricate carvings on its ends and along its curved roof. A thick-built horse munched grass a short way off. Music drifted to us.

"Talaith. She stayed behind when her clan moved north for summer. Thought she might be needed." He paused. "Got a family o' her own now."

I thought back to my first memory of Talaith, Boldo's sister, hand-signalling with Kyna at the Winter Faire, then kneeling knee-to-knee with her as she gave her Aelfwyn's amulet. I'd been in Kyna's spirit, before it was so brutally torn out. None of us had been as wise then, even Aelfwyn. *We could have used Ylva's help.*

Baird leaned against a tree and took me in his arms. Feeling our hearts beat against each other, I fought a tumble of thoughts: anger at his meddling with Sophie and time travel, anxiousness to make sure he'd be able to help if Rousseau slipped back in time again, puzzlement at his absence when the ring was delivered.

He stroked hair from my forehead. I looked up and he brought his lips to mine, softly, then more urgently. The beating of our hearts doubled and I let worries go. He pulled back, searching my eyes.

I blurted, "I was upset that you and Hamelyn tried to take Sophie back in time without me knowing."

He nodded. "T'was a foolish notion. How be she?"

"She's fine. She's moved back to the West Coast." I realized in that moment how happy the fact made me. "There's so much to impart. Do you know Ian is Marget's son?" *Wait. Does he know Ian?* I was well aware of Ian's knowing of Baird but couldn't remember if they'd met.

"'Course. We're helpin' her decide whether t' return the blighter's memories," he said.

Blighter. He must know details about what happened before Marget and Ian left Cornwall. I felt unaccountably defensive of the boy, Ian at his young age, when Galfride influenced him. Despite his odd behavior toward me at times, Sophie was enjoying him. He was a part of my modern world. My group of friends loved his band. I only said, "So you've been involved with that. Has any decision been made?"

"Nay. Needs more explorin'. Aelfwyn thinks Ylva may be helpful with her mind-healing skills, but—"

"—she wants to involve the new Thirteen in investigating Ylva," I finished for him.

"That be right. She told ye."

"Not much."

He wrapped an arm around my waist and we walked along the path that approached the Travelers' camp.

I thought about a new Thirteen that involved Kyna and her daughter. That meant closer connections. Probably a positive thing. Then I remembered the planned trip to the 13th century next day, to see the castle when it was complete. Odd to think Baird knew the future, what this area would be like in the twenty-first century. We'd seen it together.

We arrived at the fire. Perched on a hide stool, Talaith strummed a mandolin. A man on a blanket whittled, a child lying, head in his lap.

"*Sastipe,*" Baird greeted them in the Welsh Traveler language.

"*Lachhi tjiri rat,*" Talaith said, getting up and kissing each of us on the cheek.

"Ceirwyn, meet Django," Baird said, indicating the man.

Django grinned and, still seated, held out his hand to shake Baird's, ducked his head toward me. He was a wiry man, with hawkish features. He wore suspenders over a workman's shirt.

"Is this one yours?" Baird pointed toward the child in his lap.

"As much as a child be anyone's." Django smiled. "She's from Talaith's womb and my loin. At least I believe so." He cocked his head toward the woman.

She laughed and settled again with her instrument. "Join us."

We sat on a log.

"No harp?" Django asked, disappointed.

"Not tonight," Baird answered.

"Help yourself," our host offered, pointing to an earthenware jug.

Baird poured us each a horn cup.

I sipped and almost spit out the strong, sour ale. After the first mouthful, I just pretended, touching my lips to it. "Did you all know each other as children?" I asked.

"I was maybe eleven when the Travelers took me in," Baird said. "I saw Talaith a few times a year, sometimes for long stretches."

I yearned to know what his early years were like and wondered if he'd ever get a chance to share with me how he'd come to live with the Travelers.

"Baird was called Tuig when we first knew him," Talaith said.

Baird flicked her a Welsh Traveler hand sign meaning, *Say no more*, but she had a teasing look in her eyes.

I still understood the signs. The last I'd seen them was at the Solstice Faire years before, when I'd been in Kyna's mind. I hoped there'd be more exchange about their past as children with the Travelers, but Talaith only raised a brow as she poked the fire.

"I'm putting this one to bed," Django said. Lifting the three-year old, he climbed the several steps to the beautifully carved and painted door of their horse-drawn living quarters.

"We're going to see Kyna tomorrow," I said. "Aren't we?" I turned to Baird. "We won't go to the castle in her time and not visit her?"

"Most like." Baird smiled at me.

"What fun," Talaith said.

"Will ye join us?" asked Baird.

"I might. Come see me before you go," she said.

"Well." Baird emptied his cup. "We will see you on the morrow. Sleep well." He rose and held out his hand to me.

Back in the house, all the beds were taken, Marget in my usual spot, Aelfwyn across the main room behind her curtain. Baird crooked a brow at me and tilted his head toward his room.

Though the intention of this trip to the past had been to build my abilities with the new amber ring, it seemed to be a harkening to moments of my first medieval foray. I'd never slept with Baird in this bedroom, except inside the spirit of Kyna. And that was one of the most excruciating incidents of my life: lying within the other woman's consciousness as she made love to the man I'd thought about and searched for incessantly, turning my life inside out in the process.

Now I changed into one of her flannel nightgowns, after a quick teeth-brushing with an anise-tasting stick, and slid under the covers.

The thick sheets smelled of fresh heather, probably swatted with it while hanging out to dry. Baird put out the lamp and pulled me close. He wore long johns that smelled fresh as I snuggled to his shoulder. I wanted to hold the moment, not waste it. And I wanted to ask everything I'd wondered.

But Baird's lips met mine, full of passion. We made love with the heat and desire of having waited so long.

Chapter 14

After, we lay entwined, cast in moonlight from the edge of the window hide.

Baird stroked strands of hair from my face, head tilted to look at me. "Rousseau's come t' this time?"

I bunched the pillow to gaze at Baird. "He has. Pulled by one of his stories onto Otho's ship."

"That seems ver' dangerous, Dove. Didn't ye say that ship disappeared as Thorgisl was watchin' it?"

"Do you think we're shielded?" I asked. "Would you know if anyone's listening? I don't feel his presence but I'm not good enough yet with the ring. Every time I activate it, I hear too many voices, feel unsure if someone—if *he's* watching. I feel like if I say his name I might draw him."

"T'is no fun livin' in fear. We've got t' strengthen ye." He paused, as if in thought. Then said, "I'm goin' t' ask Aelfwyn about a gatherin' o' the Thirteen. Ye have the Brand of our coven. Ye need t' have the full power of it."

"I'd like that," I said, but my stomach roiled. "Aelfwyn mentioned adding to my brand." I'm sure I winced.

Baird cupped my cheek in his hand. "Dove, Dove. Tis no' what ye think. No more burnin'."

"What then?"

"You're not t' worry," he said.

"I wonder how powerful we might be with Ylva working in the circle. Do you think Aelfwyn would consider it?"

"It's been Welsh, Travelers, and Kyna and Duff from Germania. Probably a Norwigi's no' out o' the question."

"What kind of test would make her trust Ylva, do you think?" I said somewhat rhetorically. How would he know?

Baird shook his head, shrugged. "I'm no' sure."

"Maybe we could bring it up tomorrow with Kyna and Talaith."

"I imagine that could happen," he said, pulling me closer and snuggling his head into mine.

"I should give you some of the history of Aberystwyth and the castle," I said.

"Hm?" He sounded sleepy.

"Well, for one thing, in 1257, all of Europe was—or will be—covered by a terrible dark cloud, due to a massive volcanic eruption way down in, I think, Indonesia. People will suffer, many die of starvation. I saw a documentary."

"A docu-who?"

"Remember the moving pictures I showed you? A movie?"

He nodded.

"That sort of thing. But it's not a story. It's about real things. History, or science."

"She can come here if that happens," he said, voice drowsy.

"Who? Oh, Kyna. Yes, true. And Branwyn and Gwynedd. But also, there's a lot of fighting through that century when Kyna's living there. On the confluence of two rivers into the sea—no wonder people battle to control the area. Welsh rulers build a castle there. It gets torn down, built again. Then in the 70s and 80s, the castle we see in ruins in my time was built by the English."

"Feckin' usurpers. Kyna's not that close to the castle site, though. Nearer Llanbadarn Fawr, but you're right, we should warn 'er."

I yawned. I had no idea how long it'd been since I awoke in California that morning.

"Mayhap the witches can keep an eye on it in their crystal balls," Baird said, his final waking words.

I heard his breath drift into an even rhythm, and wondered if I'd spend a sleepless night awake and listening. I didn't mind.

In the morning, I woke from a dream and knew I'd slept.

We sat on the front porch, hot drinks in hand: Baird, Hamelyn, Marget, Aelfwyn and I. We discussed the planned outing to the thirteenth century to see the castle, early sun rays slanted onto us, bird calls abundant.

Talaith, Django and Jordy soon joined us, perching on the steps.

"So, we're goin' t' Kyna's time," Talaith said.

"Good, you're joining us." I was glad. Ever since I'd seen her and Kyna together, I'd felt warmth for the woman, and longed to experience more of their camaraderie, not to mention the hand signs. They seemed to fulfill a longing in me from deep in my cells.

"Want to see where I make the fiddles?" Hamelyn asked the four-year-old Jordy.

The girl's eyes brightened. Django and Hamelyn stood.

"Ye won't be joinin' us then?" Baird asked.

Hamelyn shook his head. "I've seen it."

Django said, "The boy's been on the move much o' the time lately. T'will be good to stay put fer a day."

They took their leave.

"Might be just as well not to have a child with us if there's fighting," I said.

"Let's take a look," Aelfwyn said, and we filed to the tower. Once there, we moved the brazier to the side and replaced it with a shallow stone bowl, perhaps a meter across, black as onyx, or obsidian. It had a shiny surface. Talaith fetched an urn filled with water and poured a thin layer into the bowl.

We sat around it on narrow chairs with backs made of twisted and twined reeds that usually sat by the wall of the tower room. Once the water settled the surface was like glass, reflecting our faces and the torches that lit the room dimly. The day, which had started out with some sun, was becoming overcast and gray.

Marget, Aelfwyn and Talaith rested hands on the sides of the bowl, while Baird and I watched. Almost imperceptibly at first, the scene on the surface of the water in the bowl changed from the tower to Kyna's front yard. Gwynedd was there with Branwyn, who played with a young girl, swinging her around.

Kyna came out the front door and joined them, then looked up. *At us?*

"What year is it, love?" Aelfwyn asked.

"1256," Kyna answered. I heard her words in my head, saw her mouth moving, smiling.

Gwynedd looked our way, and Branwyn, too. Her daughter followed her gaze. What did they see? Our faces looking down at them? Branwyn squatted and spoke to her little one, pointing.

"That's the year before the dark cloud will cover all of Europe for months, causing starvation," I said. "And the castle won't be up for decades."

Aelfwyn squinted at me. "We must inform Kyna. What causes this miasma?"

"A mountain explosion – volcano – *llosgfynydd*?" I wasn't sure if the word that came to me was right.

She nodded. "With the red flowing fire?"

"Yes. And when a huge mountain bursts, it sends out a cloud of ash that can cover vast distances. This one is far to the south of Europe. In the Far South East."

At that moment, Ylva and Duff appeared on the surface of the water. Ylva's reflected face turned to me. "We must talk. It's happened. We saw the ship disappear. And Rousseau's on it."

"No!" I cried, standing so abruptly my chair toppled back.

Ylva and Duff then arrived in the room with us.

Seconds later, Kyna and Gwynedd stood with us as well. My twin from ancient time wore an outfit of a future century, a green-gold sheaf over long-sleeved, ivory under-layer, nothing binding. Gwynedd wore similar, of midnight blue, crimson underneath. Their hair was coiffed up, Kyna's in a snood with crystals.

"I'll call Hamelyn," Baird said.

"Django can take Jordy," Talaith said.

Hamelyn bounded up the stone steps of the tower.

Briefly, we tried to see the ship with the scrying bowl, but even with these eleven powerful seers; it had never been visible once it disappeared, and did not reveal itself now. Quickly we moved the bowl to the side again and brought the brazier back into place. Kyna brought out the gold crystal half that I'd loved so well, had worn for months. Seeing it, Baird pulled his from where it hung around his neck. Duff and Aelfwyn went to work preparing to seal the two halves back together.

This was right, I thought, with a pang.

Holding the beautiful gold stone in the pan that hung over the low flame, they chanted. A light seared in a fine line along the sides; with a slight pop, the stone was whole again, unblemished. A sigh went around the room. Ylva watched with fascination.

"What next?" My voice shook.

Baird took my hand, eyes warm, concerned.

"Who wants most to know where that ship went?" Aelfwyn asked.

A groan escaped me.

"That's right. Thorgisl."

"We go to him," Ylva said.

"Just appear in his tower?" I had dreaded this confrontation, yet part of me longed for it. Put us all in one room and get it done.

"My Brand. Does it need to be…embellished in some way?" I asked.

"T'would be best," Aelfwyn said. "Ylva needs it as well. If she wants it." Her eyes turned to the woman with challenge, maybe hope mixed in. Certainly respect.

This must have been a giant decision for her, to include the powerful, foreign woman in the Circle. Yet with the making of the new Thirteen, much *had* to change.

Ylva's eyes gleamed. "I'd be honored."

Duff took two long strides to the built-in rack against the curved wall. It held a wide selection of tools in long narrow compartments and on shelves above. He returned and set the metal end of the brand into the flames. I winced remembering my own branding experience but Ylva looked on without any anxiety whatever. In fact, she seemed to anticipate the experience with glee.

"But …" I didn't really know how I wanted to follow

the single word.

"T'would be best t' bring 'im 'ere, you're thinkin'?" Aelfwyn asked.

"Y-yes," I sputtered. Sure. That or a million other possi- bilities. "Whatever you think, though."

"Kyna?"

"I think we go there," Kyna said. "T'is closer t' where the ship was last seen. We find Mora at last. Let's hope the eleven of us are up t' the task. I've not been able to reach any others."

"Nor I," said Talaith.

"Do you want me to bring help?" asked Ylva.

Aelfwyn studied her a long moment. "Nay. This is as far as I can trust in our workin's together fer now. I hope ye dunno take offence."

Ylva said, "No. I understand."

"Good." Aelfwyn turned to Kyna. "Other than the crystal, which we've experimented with over the years, need we bring ought else?"

Kyna looked around at us, each in turn. Heads shook uncertainly. "We have not done a ceremony with all of Ceirwyn's talismans added to our powers."

"The branding then," Aelfwyn said.

Chapter 15

The old witch busied herself at the curved work table fastened to the stone wall. When she signaled to Ylva, the others clustered to one side of the room, backs turned. I followed their lead, catching a glimpse of Ylva dropping her clothes. I figured she'd have no compunction doing so with full audience.

I turned away, my sweaty hands clasped to my stomach.

Baird slipped an arm around me. "We'll find 'im," he whispered. I gave a short nod, throat too tight to speak.

Marget reached out and touched my ring. "Can ye see if Thorgisl's in his tower?" she asked.

I stared at her, shaking my head. "What if he detects what we're doing and goes into hiding? Especially with my bumbling attempt to reach out."

"Good point. Not that I believe you'd bumble, dear. Let's surprise him."

"Can't you see where he is?"

"I can help ye." A voice vibrated in my mind. *Galfride.*

"How did you know what we're doing?" Why did I even ask? I felt spooked from every direction, especially in my head.

"I watch ye sometimes. Yer life can be ver' entertainin'," he responded with his signature sneer.

"That's not comforting. Are you at the Jutland fort?" I asked.

"Near enough."

"You can get into his tower?" I asked.

"Been there many times. I like his collection." Supercilious.

"But how?" I asked.

"Disguises. Inside and outside."

I thought of Ylva masking her energy as gopher spirit.

"But there are eleven of us. And why would you help us?"

"I don't like Thorgisl. He be a weasel."

That was classic, coming from him. What mattered to Galfride? I wondered. Was there anyone he cared about, would try to protect?

"I'm in yer head, Kyna's cousin. Don't try too hard to work me out. Leastways, no' now. There be no time."

"What do you mean?"

"Ship disappeared. Your son's on it," Galfride stated.

"Rousseau?" I clutched the nearest shelf. "You saw this?"

"Saw it. Heard it. Listen to yer amber ring. All is a-buzz with it."

"How do you—?" I started to ask how he knew about my ring, but broke off. This was not the time.

Baird rested a hand on my side and moved us toward the tower room's center again.

"Ye look peaked," he remarked.

"My—"

Before he could finish, hands pulled us into the circle.

"Has it happened?" I whispered to Baird.

He nodded.

Ylva, in a simple cream-colored gown, looked like nothing untoward had occurred. I thought back to my swoon and drug trip after my branding. She'd said she could have eased my experience. Now I believed her.

We took hands in the circle. The gold stone glowed in its hanging plate at the center, high above the fire. My gut gripped at the sudden memory of being torn from Kyna. Her gaze shifted to mine and we shared memories in a swift healing review.

Boldo spoke into our minds. "I will join you in Thorgisl's tower."

As if he spoke also into Galfride's thoughts, Galfride said to us all, "I will place a similar stone in Thorgisl's tower. He is there now. I will set the resonance between these stones and you will arrive quite without trouble."

"My thanks," Aelfwyn said to him.

I could only hope all of this would save my son.

Then Aelfwyn turned to me, "You must rest your hands together, just so." She showed me, placing one over my heart, the other covering it so my rings matched up, touching the silver talisman. "Now you invoke your heron. *Dewch ataf. Rhowch fenthyg nerth i mi.*" She said more. The words meant something like, "Come to me. Lend me strength, Heron, spirit bird."

I committed them to memory as I'd done in ritual with shamans. To pass tests, memory was everything. That and the power of my desire, which could not have been greater than now.

"Practice," she said. "Test it."

Hands still to my chest, my amber ring was activated and a thousand thoughts, not just of those in the tower room with me, but from what felt like miles around, crowded my head. I closed my eyes and felt the Brand as if it spoke to me, each sigil sparking like stars. I concentrated, following from star to star. And then all stilled. I opened my eyes and looked at Talaith. I felt her warm thoughts and invitation to go further into her mind. I could have, with or without her invitation. Gems from her memories tumbled into my awareness. She gave me a hand sign for sight. I thanked her and went to the next, until each in the circle had imparted one skill or image. I tucked them as if into a bag of tokens, and labeled it.

"Now we must go," Aelfwyn said.

With Boldo and Galfride, we have Thirteen, I thought.

Then we were chanting. The sound built and I kept the feeling of my Brand. Somewhere outside was my spirit bird, my heron.

I felt a strange squeezing, and then we stood in our circle in a golden place, a tear-drop shaped chamber. We floated there, appearing full sized, but we must have been tiny. We summoned our unified, circle awareness for the next step—to jump into Galfride's stone in Thorgisl's tower. I had a frisson of doubt, unsure of this step. What did the stone look like? How would we find our way? But Galfride's spirit was with us in the circle. He seemed to send a personal jolt of assurance through me. Did I feel something else with it? Could it have been called … fondness? As always, my distrust warred with acceptance. What might follow such a feeling?

Then a shift came. My energy was drawn to join the rest and I needed no thought, no image, just to let my heart surge with the others.

Our teardrop-shaped chamber turned emerald green. The shade was so close to the toxic hue when malice dripped from Galfride's eye sockets in his caves, that panic struck and questions shot through my mind: Had there never been an Ansgor? Had all the cruelty come from Galfride with this green power stone?

STRANGE ALLIANCES

We had successfully leapt into Galfride's stone and stood pressed together looking out into Thorgisl's tower room—a place I had come to fear and despise, where he, for weeks, toyed with my memories in search of the one that would lead him to Otho and the amber stone.

We transported ourselves out of the stone and appeared, full-size, in front of Thorgisl where he sat in his hide chair, calm, as if he'd expected us. This was betrayed by a dart of accusation toward me.

You don't own me. I had to say it fiercely to myself, for at the edges of my confidence lay that eternal sense that he could again control me.

I pulled my awareness back to the Thirteen. Boldo stood across from me in the circle. It was my first sight of him in many months. He looked haggard after searching the world for Otho.

Now we hoped to accomplish that standing from here in the tower.

Aelfwyn spoke. "Thorgisl. Ye want t' find Otho's ship. So d' we."

The twelve of us filled the room.

"You come to me with all your force. Even Galfride. And Otho's family. I should be honored." Thorgisl unfolded his long, thin frame to stand. His gaze traveled around our faces with no sign of unease. "What was your plan in coming here with your unified force? I have not yet located the ship. There is nothing to coerce out of me. I'd think you'd be trying to beat me to it."

"We want to help you," Aelfwyn responded.

At this Thorgisl's eyebrows shot up in disbelief and a wry smile grooved the sides of his mouth.

"To put our forces with yours," Aelfwyn amended.

His eyes moved to Ylva and Duff, red giants, heads

touching lower beams of the cone-shaped roof. He seemed to catch Ylva's energy for the first time and recognition dawned.

"Join us," Aelfwyn said, and offered a hand to him.

"Get out of my fort," he said with gritted teeth. "All of you. How dare you invade me here." He turned to Galfride. "Did you set this up?" When Galfride stared at him blankly, he went on, "Do you think me an idiot? That I didn't know you've been in here? That I didn't watch you, here in my sanctum?"

"I didn't really care," Galfride answered.

"Let's drop this petty bickering and form a plan," Aelfwyn said. "We have strong seers among us. There is urgency beyond your longing for a power stone. Ceirwyn's son is on the ship."

"*A* power stone. No, woman. Not just *a* power stone. *The* power amber, stone of all stones. Never has there been one like it."

"Then it is important to consider where it ends up, for all of us," Aelfwyn said with her commanding voice.

"Indeed," Thorgisl answered, but his lacked sincerity. "Rousseau on the ship. Ts, ts, ts." But his eyes took on a more haunted look. Did it contain hunger? "What do you propose, *klog kvinde?*"

I took translation for the Danish from his head—wise woman. Sarcasm also came across to me, though he was fully capable of masking the sentiment. Still, I assumed everyone in the room saw through it.

"We have two powerful crystals here. I don't know what other tools you have for seeing but we should combine our resources and skills." Aelfwyn folded her hands in front of her and I felt a swell of energy connected with the Brand. *Stay aware,* she projected to us. *If he touches any object, be ready to neutralize powers.*

Galfride spoke up. "We need ground rules."

Thorgisl chuckled and started toward the side of the room. His motions stopped mid-movement. His face conveyed annoyance.

"Let me acquaint our esteemed Circle with what's in this room," Galfride said, "while we hold you in stillness." He gave a brief litany of specialized objects: scrying bowl near the window where Thorgisl stared out to sea and other tools. He gestured to amber stones set into the walls that could be triggered to augment Thorgisl's control of those in the chamber. My insides quaked as I remembered their influence on me when I'd been his captive. I became attuned to a wearying in my bones as I, with the others, held a protection spell.

"Have I missed anythin'?" Galfride asked.

Thorgisl laughed. "And I'd tell you, why?" He was clearly seething at being held inert in his own place of power.

"At this moment, we are a team," Aelfwyn said. "Do you not want your precious amber?" She held up a string of carved beads that hung around her neck. "I sense you have interest in Ceirwyn's son as well. We can work together to find both."

Voice steely, Thorgisl responded, "You've already expressed that you don't think I should have the amber stone." Thorgisl's eyes, dark as flint, aimed a glare at the woman.

She stood straight and unwavering in her black robe, edges stitched in powerful sigils.

I watched this interplay, all the while thinking, "My son. My son. Just bring him back. Where is he?"

"How will we be a team if you don't trust me?" Thorgisl's English was near perfect, with a clipped accent.

"We need only come to an agreement, and understand each others' capabilities," Aelfwyn said

Though admiring her well-spoken confidence, I agitated from the sidelines. *Please get on with it.* I shifted my feet in distress.

Baird squeezed my hand and sent me comforting assurances. "Trust her. She'll make this happen."

I nodded, glancing at his face for comfort.

Chapter 16

As if drawn by our exchange, Thorgisl turned to me. His eyes dropped to my hand still in Baird's, where everyone else had dropped theirs as his gaze moved from Baird to Ylva and Boldo. All involved in my escape. His demeanor promised revenge.

You've already had revenge on Boldo's people, I thought. *You bastard. Your men sliced children. And where is Mora?* Anger bubbled in me. His gaze returned to me for just a brief chilling instant. Then he swiveled back to Aelfwyn. "How do you propose we work together as a team?" he enunciated her own words back. I could almost see him making air quotes.

"We've shown we can stop your movements. We can also hear a great deal of your thoughts. Some of us can go undetected, uncannily deep into the recesses. They might be there now."

"Ah. Ye might underestimate my sense of things, Lady."

A crack sliced the air, then I felt a stab of pain. It boomeranged around the circle, some merely wincing, others doubling over. Thorgisl nearly disappeared but a power surged through me. The circle had joined hands.

Thorgisl reappeared. I didn't "know" the spell we'd

imposed on him that held him frozen, yet I contributed to it, felt it in my cells.

"Cease, man," Aelfwyn admonished, exasperated. "We only want t' find th' ship. Ye haven't been able to on yer own. Neither has Ylva, nor have I, with Kyna and Marget helping. Mayhap we can do it t'gether. Join us. Stop yer games. We do this t'gether and we place the stone in a neutral holding where we can discuss its future. Or you can best us on some later day. Fer now, we all want to find the ship. Let us see if we can find a greater power when combined." She sounded reasonable, commanding.

I watched Thorgisl to see if he'd relent.

"Alright. I give up. We can try it." Clearly, he could still move his mouth. His weasley eyes could not hide malingering malice but I thought it was the best we would get. "The bowl is heavy. I'll need help movin' it."

Duff, Baird and Ylva stepped forward. The four slid the carved stone with its wide shallow bowl, like an immense birdbath, and inched it to the center. Thorgisl and the others dragged tables and chests out of the way until we could circle the immense scrying receptacle lined in black stone, the shallow bowl holding a thin layer of water.

Galfride floated a globe-light over the water. Above it, the gold and green crystals hovered. We stood body to body. Thorgisl had at last assented to join hands with us, choosing a spot between Talaith and Kyna, though he appeared reluctant as did they. I swallowed back anxiety seeing him take the two women's hands.

Was this the right decision? Surely, they could keep him out. He could not take over or insert anything into them, especially not in this Circle, with all our brands activated. I watched Aelfwyn's face closely for any sign of unease.

Thorgisl did not frequently work with others, I didn't think; he appeared to push past a well of resistance for every iota of cooperation demanded. "I suggest we set our hands together around the edge. Touch the water with fingertips, then let it settle."

I watched him, leery. Did the water contain something that would send us away or incapacitate us?

As our hands came forward, I realized Galfride had stationed himself on my right. Our hands touched. I cringed at the electricity that shot through me. Unbidden, the bed in his cave, and the imposed sexual response roared into my consciousness. Fight as I might, it seemed to hover inside me. I shot him a sideways glance, resentful. He smirked. Baird came to stand on my left. Sandwiched between the two men, tension broiled in me.

Aelfwyn, Marget, and Ylva kept their eyes on the Jutlander. Ylva could sense anything untoward, in any element. I felt buoyed by that thought as our hands spanned the circumference, Duff's and Ylva's stretching around a generous portion. We stilled our bodies to allow the surface of the water to settle like glass.

Stilling was not easy for me with my heart hammering.

Aelfwyn chanted until the golden crystal glowed. Galfride joined the cadances with a litany that fired his green stone with equal luster so that our faces shone green-gold. Thorgisl observed, sensing, calculating ... lusting. Energy swelled, reminding me of rescuing Gwynedd. As then, my heart strained to carry the load. My Brand called to me and I traced the sigils in my mind until effort distributed itself through me and into those around me, stabilizing me even as electricity gyrated through.

In this augmented state, I took in those in the circle. Their thoughts vibrated in my psyche, almost as my own. I faced out to the distant view, across the marsh flats to the sea, hands pressed to Baird's and Galfride's.

A quarter of the way around the waist-high stone basin, Thorgisl stared out to the same view. Then his head swung in my direction, and his malevelant, proprietary glare sluiced into the stew that was the Thirteen. Others sensed his thoughts and glanced from me to him. We were One. There was no hiding. He looked abashed, and amazed, to share minds with others in this way, so accustomed was he to invading, not being read himself.

Something was building. I felt Ylva leading, she who was adept at seeking in all worlds. We seemed to skim the seas of the globe, and then go further. As I watched, the water at our fingertips thickened. Where it had been green-gold in the reflection of the glowing stones, it now took on its own hue, a glowering orange, as if it had a different sun. An older one? A city appeared with a sea, ships at port, odd buildings, all cast in egg-yolk tones from the foreign sun.

A ship stood anchored far out, near an island.

Past? Future? Other dimension? It did resemble the *Kauli Pishom*, Otho's ship, with its Welsh Romani name meaning Black Bee, that I'd seen in my son's stories. Though it was distant, I could also see it closely, in fine detail, with the sight we all held.

A face burst onto the water's surface. I recognized the jagged scar, the angry sneer. Otho. Yet rather than the harried look I'd seen when he was badgered by Ansgor, the man was triumphant—wildly, madly so.

He burst out laughing, mirthless, hysterical. "I see you pissants, staring, trying to find me." He held an amber stone cupped in his hands and it glared light, jagged pulses I felt even as I watched the phantom vision. "This what you want, Thorgisl? You thought I'd just hand such power to you? It told me where to go, how to elude you, took me here." He shouted insanely. His eyes were bloodshot.

"Where's my son?" I asked.

He shrieked with more laughter. "Yes. He came with me, mother of Rousseau. You want him back? There is one I desire. I will trade."

"Trade." Thorgisl's jaw looked ready to crack, he clenched it so hard. The ice mage who rarely lost his cool, appeared livid. "Trade. For youngsters. That is not what is on the table. You were commissioned to deliver the amber stone. It does not belong to you." Hands gripping the stone edge of the basin, Thorgisl tried to wield the energy of the Thirteen as a weapon. I felt it aimed at the image on the bowl of water. It felt wrong—a different kind of power. I stared at him, thinking of the fever he'd given Duff and Boldo, a sickness that had dragged Duff down almost irretrievably until Ylva saved him, brought his spirit back to us.

Then I felt his effort shift. He was trying to get into the amber stone, take its power for his own. Face in an ugly snarl, he pulled from the crystals, and from us.

Ylva and Aelfwyn countered him, dampering his control until he visibly sagged.

"Who is it you propose to trade for Rousseau?" Aelfwyn asked Otho, the pirate captain in his ragged yet ornate fitted coat and high boots.

"The one who stitches reality," he said, yearning suddenly so intense in his crazed eyes, I thought they'd jump out of his skull.

Kyna and Aelfwyn exchanged a glance. Talaith moved closer to Kyna as if to shore up her strength.

Ylva had to bend from her great height to keep her hands on the stone rim. Her face moved closer to the water and she said, soft but menacing, "We don't trade our family members, great oaf. You'll give us the lad and the amber power stone or lose your wretched little ship."

Suddenly the vessel rocked wildly.

I feared for Rousseau but could only watch and wait. I had the least power of anyone.

Thorgisl's face lit up and his admiration of Ylva, always strong, blazed anew. He licked his lips as if anticipating holding the stone in his hands.

I felt a raging power in my heart. The Thirteen was preparing. All had to remain controlled, for any chaos might lead to Thorgisl's snatching the stone and absconding with it. Who knew what power he might amass then? He was already formidable.

Quickly I lit up the lines of my brand with my mind, trying to share the energy with the others and distribute the electricity that threatened to overcome me. This was all I could do—focus, one sigil at a time, hold the energy, build it with our Circle, as I stared at Ylva's face concentrating on Otho.

As the battle raged to hold the amber stone in a field at the centre above the basin, Rousseau slammed into the room and tumbled to the floor behind us. Not daring to let go of the power, I glanced back at my son. He lay in a heap. With a most terrible effort, I held myself in place, maintaining our part of the struggle, now against Thorgisl, while keeping at bay the mother-urge to hold my son. He was here. He was here. We must keep him that way.

Aelfwyn and Ylva exchanged a look. The circle broke as Ylva and Duff disappeared, taking the most powerful stone known with them.

A growl started in Thorgisl's throat and his face changed to a choleric purple. As the sound mounted in a howl of rage, the ten of us scrambled from the scrying bowl, scooped up Rousseau and left the Jutland tower.

STRANGE ALLIANCES

We had utterly succeeded in our mission. Yet I knew the gruesome form Thorgisl's revenge could take.

We arrived on the flagging floor of Kyna's tower. I sat, Rousseau in my arms. He sagged against me. I stroked his face; the usual luminous latte tone had a worrisome palor.

Aelfwyn knelt by us. "He been torn from another dimension. That can't be easy on anyone." She pressed fingers to his throat.

Ylva reappeared. "Duff's building a structure to contain the stone. I've spelled it. Back at my home. Not near it—on another mountain. It will be guarded night and day." She took in the scene: Rousseau prostrate, Kyna heating a kettle of water, Marget and Gwynedd sorting herbs on the work counter.

Talaith said, "I've called all the Wanderer folk here. They're asking sylphs to help reinforce th' spells 'round us."

"They should all be here anyway," Boldo said, face haunted by Mora's absence.

Galfride, back against the wall, fidgeted with unseen objects in his deep pockets. Hamelyn watched this process from a wary distance. Baird had left on an unknown task.

I felt relief as Ylva dropped to my side, leg pressed to Rousseau. Her great hands surrounded his face. After a moment, she said softly, "He's not yet arrived." Her eyes had a far-off look. "He's still partly in that other realm. We must…" One of her baseball-mitt hands covered his chest, keeping the other on his head. She breathed deep and slow, lids pressed closed. My hand covered hers and Aelfwyn's rested on mine.

We all saw that other world again: the ship near the island, strange egg-yolk tone cast onto the sea, in the distance an otherworldly city.

MARIE JUDSON

"I think he'd fare better in his own time," Ylva whispered.

"It'd be safe to travel with him in this state?" I asked.

"Better than waiting any longer. He's closer to Otho here. And the sea-dog'll not be used t' finding him at your home. He may have more trouble tracking him there."

My son had yet to open his eyes.

I felt nauseous. "Okay, let's do it."

Without waiting for any ceremonial circling or chant, Ylva scooped up Rousseau, easy as a rag doll. I grabbed onto one of her tree-limb arms so as not to be left. I glimpsed Marget rushing to join us as all went black.

We merged out of the between in my living room, and slumped together on the rug. But not for long. Ylva busied herself building a fire — wood appeared in my fireplace and her spread hands lit it. Marget went straight to my hall-closet apothecary; we'd been expanding the variety in the tansu drawers, filling in from Shelley's medicinal garden and Marget's yard.

"There's no vervain," Marget shouted, backing out with an armload. She plunked herself in the middle of the living room rug and sat, eyes closed, hands out, as if searching the air. A packet appeared on her palm. Her eyes opened. "Yes." She wore a self-satisfied smile as she added it to the pile. "Clean cloth. Boiled pot of water," she said to me as she organized.

I ran for a dish cloth and brought it to her, then scurried to get the water boiling.

Meanwhile, Ylva lay Rousseau on my bed and covered him. She chanted over him, cross-legged, hands on his temples, stroking his brows. "Remember fumitory and rue," she called to Marget.

"Of course," said the other witch as she made crumpled

lines of various herbs and root shavings using a knife with carved bone handle. She hummed and I realized the lines were forming a design.

I checked on the water, returned to watch Marget, fascinated, then paced into the bedroom to stand helpless over Ylva and my son.

The front door opened and closed. I turned to the sound of footsteps.

Sophie stood in the bedroom doorway. "What the hell?"

Chapter 17

I hurried to hug my daughter. "You're back early, sweety."

"I decided not to stay overnight in Berkeley. What's wrong with Rousseau?" She took in the hulking, bright-haired woman. Even seated, she towered over her brother, occupying much of the bed.

Marget called, "Water's ready."

"I'll explain," I said, kissing Sophie's cheek as I left to help with the potion.

Marget was already busy in the kitchen. She'd set out a pot for steeping. Carefully, she slid her herb and root design, on its cloth, onto a flat cookie sheet she'd spelunked from a low cupboard. The pattern was intricate, like a Celtic knot but sharper. She spoke and the entire dry concoction rose up, then dropped into the sieve. A faint trace of the design lingered in the air.

Sophie had come in and now stood behind me, staring. She rested her head on my shoulder. I pressed my head to hers.

"Will he be okay?" she whispered, throat thick.

"These are two very strong witches," I said. "Let's have faith."

"But do you?" she spoke low into my ear.

"Yes," I said, mustering courage.

"Okay, hands on," Marget said, carrying the steeping pot into the bedroom.

I brought in a folding tray.

"First, an incantation on the pot itself," Marget ordered.

We lined up, seated, on the side of the bed, backs to Rousseau. Ylva, on the end, swiveled so that her side pressed to Sophie. We all followed Marget's lead, hands over the pot.

"*Losowen, gwreydhen, dri yaghhe…*" she invoked in Cornish.

We hummed a low note to hold the energy.

When she finished, Ylva directed, "You and Sophie on that side," as she sat Rousseau against her oak-tree chest. Marget brought a cup of the now-dark liquid to his lips.

Then began a most startling incantation. Over and over again, first Ylva, then Marget, spoke in their native tongues, back and forth, without breaks, so that the Old Norse ran into Old Cornish. The sounds vibrated in my head as I pressed my hands to Rousseau's chest, Sophie to his thigh and shin. I activated my brand and kept my shoulder to Sophie's so that she could also carry the energy.

Then a magical thing happened. I felt her communication with the sylph whom I now thought of as our housespirit. She was outside the window, singing, and her song ran sweetly through me. Sophie's eyes opened wide as the music threaded between us.

Marget and Ylva stared as all four of us hummed a note that was precisely the vibration of *Bedw's* sound. It was passing through our hands to Rousseau, calling to him.

His eyes opened.

I threw myself on him. "Sweety, sweety, you're back." I started into his eyes, willing him to speak and confirm his mental presence.

Ylva intoned, "Let us know your state of mind, lad. Who are you?"

He gave a weak smile. "Rousseau."

"Where are you?"

"Twenty-first century. Mom's house."

Sophie wiggled her way in and snuggled into him.

"Hey sis. I'm okay."

"What happened?" she asked.

"Let's give him a little time," I suggested.

"I have a god-awful taste in my mouth," he said, smacking his tongue.

I hunted in my bedside drawer for a mint.

Sophie clearly was not happy waiting to hear the story. Concern, suspicion and anger warred on her face.

Marget beckoned to me and Ylva. We moved into the living room, leaving the siblings. I assumed Sophie would continue digging for truth, and hesitated. On the other hand, I too wanted to know what all had occurred.

Ylva said, "Best thing to get him solidly settled is to chatter with his kin, his old playmate."

I glanced once more at the bedroom doorway. They were in deep conversation though Rousseau had sagged back onto the pillow.

"How about a nice hearty stew?" Marget suggested.

"Sounds like the very thing. Let's see what I have," I responded.

Soon the three of us were chopping, sautéing, and stirring. Working around Ylva in the cramped space was a bit of a trick. Marget several times removed herself to the long table in the living room for food prep, or buried herself in the apoth-closet for surprising herbs to add. She gathered rosemary from the yard. Ylva followed, always happy to get outside. I hoped she didn't have gopher in mind for our dish.

Sophie joined me. "He fell asleep."

"Not surprising," I said. "We can wake him to eat when the soup is done. We don't know when he last ate and he'll need to get his strength up."

She slumped her hip against the counter and faced me. "He gets drawn into the past? Then the ship gets pulled into another dimension?" Her voice rose with each word, her expression a tad apopleptic. "What are we doing about this, Mom? How are we going to prevent it from happening again?" Her hands gripped the counter edge, white-knuckled.

"Honey, Ylva is an amazing shamaness, or witch, or whatever. Everyone's working on it. The Thirteen is going to solve it. And I'm sure he's safe here in this home."

"What makes him safe here?" she asked.

"You felt the sylph song," I said. "That's *Bedw* and I think she's adopted our home. Baird first invited her and she and others put a protective sphere around this property."

She looked skeptical.

Ylva and Marget returned from the herb garden in back.

"You're the one who came to Rousseau's apartment in Boston. I'm Sophie."

The red-haired shamaness of Norway engulfed my daughter's slender hand in her huge grasp.

Sophie smiled up at her. "I hope you can help my brother." Tears filmed her eyes.

"I'll cut some artisan bread and toast it to go with this," I said thickly.

"I'll bake up a little dessert if you have flour," Marget offered.

I pointed to the pantry door tucked in one corner of the kitchen.

She perused the shelves, finding all her baking needs.

"When there's more time, I'll make *Kransekake,*" Ylva said.

"That would be wonderful, I'm sure." I figured any Scandinavian cake would be a treat. "Let's go sit." I led the way to the glassed porch with its several comfy wicker chairs. I thought Marget would have an easier time bustling around the kitchen without us in the way.

But as soon as I was seated, I popped up to check on Rousseau, leaving Ylva and my daughter to get acquainted.

In my bedroom, Rousseau lay on his side, sleeping soundly. I sat by him and stroked his face. I'd have to wake him soon anyway to eat. His palor scared me.

"You'll be okay," I murmured. "We have to figure out how to not let you be grabbed." I thought about the possibilities of training. Who could help him best?

When the stew with its diced tomatoes, thickened by potatoes, was ready, we brought a hefty bowl into the bedroom, a thick slice of buttered herb bread beside it. I brought chairs and trays in so all could be together, then sat by Rousseau and shook him gently.

"Sweetie, you need to eat," I said softly.

Rouss woke abruptly, with a gasp, raising up as he looked around, wild-eyed.

"It's okay," I said. "You're here with us. Bad dream?"

He relaxed, though his face still appeared haunted. "Something smells good."

I put a folding tray over him and packed pillows behind him, then set his plate before him.

"I'm famished." He bit into toast.

We brought in our filled bowls and bread and sat

companionably munching, surrounding my son. So many questions tumbled through my mind, begging to be asked, but I let the calm moments stretch. Time enough for sharing and planning. I hoped.

"So, your visit to UC Berkeley went well?" I asked my daughter.

"It did. Really well. I'm pretty certain of getting into the Masters program and I think Professor Brinner would be my advisor. She's great." Sophie chewed thoughtfully. "We talked about a research project I could start this summer. I want to find a place down there now."

"That all sounds great, hon," I said between bites. "Have you checked the housing?"

"As a matter of fact, Brinner knows of a grad student moving away, back to Germany, who might be giving up her room."

"That's so lucky!" I said. "Have you gotten in touch?"

"Not yet. I think I will now." She finished her last bite and stood.

"Good idea. Others might grab it." I patted her back. "It's all exciting, my love."

She pecked my cheek and went out with her bowl. Soon she passed by with her bags from the hallway, heading toward the guest room.

"She's adorable," Ylva said. "I never had a daughter."

"Do you have sons?" I asked, amazed that I'd never known this before.

"Oh yes. Many," she responded.

"I wonder why she decided not to stay in Berkeley," Marget remarked pensively.

"I'm sorry we never got to address getting Ian's memories back while we were in the past," I said, assuming her comment related to Sophie having planned to stay at his

East Bay apartment.

"It can wait," Marget said. "Other more urgent issues arose."

We turned toward Rousseau, who still ate with gusto.

"How are you feeling?" I asked.

"Weird," he answered.

"Weird how?" I wanted to know.

"I don't want to worry you but … in that other place, on Otho's ship, it was like I needed two hearts or something. I didn't feel right, couldn't breathe well."

I blanched. "Did the others feel that way?"

"Most. But Otho was all wild with his new power and you know, didn't maybe notice. Or just was obsessed with other feelings."

Ylva listened closely, leaning toward my son.

"Was it different going there than being pulled out?" I asked.

Ylva looked at me, nodded, waited for Rousseau's answer.

"Way worse coming out. But a huge relief." He took my hand. "Even though I seemed unconscious, I heard your voice." He smiled wanly at me. "Mom, how will we keep this from happening again?"

"We're going to work on it, honey. You're safe here now." I squeezed his hand. "I was so scared, sweetheart. I can't believe I have you back." Then I took Ylva's great hand and laid it on mine and Rousseau's. "It was Ylva who brought you back."

Rousseau turned his eyes on her with wonder. "Really? Wow, thank you. I wasn't sure if I'd ever … come back." Shaking, he closed his eyes, nearing tears.

Ylva scooted onto the bed, pressed her hands to his face, and closed her eyes.

I pictured how we'd helped Duff when inside the

Brocken, the highest peak of Germania. Slipping my spirit-self with hers into Rousseau's mind we moved similarly, I melting into his pineal gland, sending loving energy, as she moved deeper, seeking anything that might obstruct his returning to us fully recovered.

I felt tension dissipate. This would be far easier than when Duff's consciousness had been fully obscured, buried beneath a controlling, dampering spell.

Spreading my awareness, I sought the memories, the images of his time in the other world. Going further back, I experienced with him the sudden absorption of the ship as it moved, as through a membrane, pulled, sucked, then the odd ochre of the sky and sea. The air was different. Too little oxygen? Hard for me to say. Ylva had joined my mind and saw it all with me. She traveled to the ship's cabin and we three watched Otho hunched over the amber stone as if mesmerized. A monkey crouched on his shoulder, shivering close to his ear, like it wished to be elsewhere.

Chapter 18

Finally we flooded him with a bright-soft light that seemed to come from my brand. I felt *Bedw* join us as we brought all our energies to what felt like a perfect harmony, then withdrew carefully from Rousseau's mind.

His face looked joyous, all cares at last cast away. His color had risen to normal. I kissed his forehead. It was warmer for the first time.

"That was sooo cool," he said, the words floating on an outbreath.

"Feel better?" I asked, rhetorically. *I* felt better.

"You two are quite a team," he said. "You have to teach me to do that." At my crooked smile, he said, "One step at a time. I know. Can I have more soup?"

Ylva and I laughed. Best sign of returning health and well-being. We turned and saw that Marget stood at the door smiling.

Sophie came up from behind and seeing her brother at last with healthy color and demeanor, rushed to him. "You're better!" she cried, throwing her arms around him.

"A lot better. Ylva and Mom are… Mom's learning some very awesome stuff. There's also…" He glanced toward the window, "I'm getting some very nice vibes from over there. Is it my imagination or...?" He looked from face to face.

Sophie said, "It's an elemental creature. I've decided to call her Shadow-leaf. She lives in our yard."

"You've seen her?" he asked.

"Yeah, as much as you can look at her. She's like moving dots and I can never see her except where she's different from the background."

I stared at Sophie. Had I known she was aware of the sylphs?

I left Sophie and Rousseau talking about her plans in Berkeley, she asking if he was moving west soon. I wanted to hear his answer but also needed to have some time with Marget and Ylva.

We sat in the living room with mugs of herb tea. The quiet voices of my kids came to us from the bedroom.

"I should check on the amber stone," Ylva said.

"I should also get home," Marget remarked, hands wrapped around her warm cup, blowing on the hot liquid.

"Okay. That makes sense. You do have a life other than here." I smiled despite the sadness and trepidation I felt that they wouldn't be here to continue shoring up Rousseau's healing process. I also selfishly wanted to keep talking about the training he might receive.

"Your family can use some time together," Marget suggested.

"I suppose," I said.

Ylva drank the rest of the steamy tea to the bottom, set aside her cup and stood. She bent over double to hug me. "You'll be fine, *Félagi*."

Partner or chum came to my mind from hers.

"You know you can call to me anytime." She looked around for the heron she'd carved.

"By my bed," I said.

She nodded, pleased. "Then I will go." And she left.

Marget and I sat in a pleasant silence, drinking and looking out at the backyard through the double set of windows.

"I'd like to go back with you and help," I said.

"Let's do it that way then," she answered. "I'd like to have you with me."

"I also want to see more of your Cornish home, and your memories, if you'll let me," I said, setting down my cup.

"I'm happy to share that with you, dear friend," she said.

"Would you want to take some of our soup home?" I offered.

"That would be nice. Then I don't have to make dinner."

We went to the kitchen to pack her a yogurt and snacks. I taped the top and put it in a cloth bag. I loved the companionship, our growing connection.

In the hallway, by the front door, Marget said in a low voice, "Please practice. You can tell me what's happening." She glanced upward to the attic room where we'd installed my scrying bowl.

"I will."

We hugged and she left on foot, saying, "I need the exercise."

I stood at my bedroom doorway, watching my kids.

Sophie turned to me, grinning. "He might move to the East Bay soon."

"We're going to love being close again," I said, moving into the room.

Rouss lifted his arm, inviting me onto the bed with them. I snuggled in at his side. Soph lay against his other shoulder.

I breathed him in, reached across and stroked my daughter's arm. "Wow, imagine you two back in Berkeley, or Oakland, in our old stomping grounds, but grown-ups now."

"And you can come visit," Rouss said, giving me a happy shake.

"'Til you move there." Sophie gave me a teasing nudge.

"We'll see. Or you can come use the guest room anytime here, walk on the beach."

"For sure," said my son. "I've been longing for that. I'd be so happy to get back to the West Coast." He gave us a little hug. "And be near you two. You've been too far away, Soph, in Paris and then Wales. Meanie."

"Well, you were far in Boston." A bit of defensiveness crept in.

I sat up and turned toward them. "I adore the thought of you both being within a few hours' drive. Now you," I rested a hand on my son's leg, "have nothing with you."

He chortled. "I didn't exactly board a plane, bring luggage."

"No, you took a much more difficult route." I made light of the ordeal.

Sophie worried her lower lip.

"I'll rummge for comfy sleeping clothes, a toothbrush and so on," I said.

"Hey Mom, who's the little lady? Was it Margaret?"

"Marget. She lives in the neighborhood beyond the community gardens. We met ... I think we first met at the library."

Sophie helped me clear dishes.

Rouss edged his legs over the side of the bed and tentatively stood, then flung a hand out to steady himself.

I came to him, reaching out.

"I got it." He took a step, hand to the wall.

"Do you think a walk in the fresh air would help?" I asked.

"First the bathroom."

"Go for it," I said, carrying my load from the room.

In the kitchen, Sophie asked, "Are there things I'm not supposed to bring up?"

"At this point, I don't think anything is verboten." I stacked the bowls and ran water in them.

"Okay. But when are you going to explain how you knew where to find Rousseau? And what if you hadn't?" She grabbed a quick breath, ready to continue.

I broke in, "Let's all put on a second layer and walk to the gardens. I need to check on things and we'll catch some sunset. We can go over the details and fill each other in." I hugged her from the side and we both went for sweatshirts.

As I pulled on my boots, I felt Boldo and stepped out onto the front porch. "Is all okay?"

"Aelfwnn and Kyna are keepin' watch on Thorgisl and stayin' connected with Ylva, at least in a fashion. We're doin' our best t' make th' clan safe. I wanted t' make sure you and yer kids be alright as well. That Rousseau's not sufferin' ill effects."

"I'm glad you're all well. Rousseau's better." I paused.

"What's on yer mind?"

"I think I might have detected Mora's location, in Thorgisl's mind."

He took in a quick breath. "Go on."

"It's not clear. I saw a place and felt for an instant he had thought about Mora in relation to it. I wondered if any of you also spotted it when we were in the Circle, in his tower."

"No. I should have been digging in that scorpion's mind but after my imprisonment, I have a great deal of trepidation anywhere near him."

"Of course, after your ordeal. Maybe Talaith sensed it."

"I think she woulda mentioned."

"She may not have perceived it. If I showed her what I saw maybe."

"Some part of the fort we never found?" Boldo seemed disbelieving.

"No. It's some distance away. I know if you'd seen it, you'd have already gotten her away. I might have to get Ylva to search in his mind for it, if I can give her some clue. Hey, I'm glad you're back with us, no longer searching the world. I've..." I hesitated, "missed you."

"I've missed you too, my bonnie angel," Boldo said, switching mood right along with me.

"I'm off on a walk with my kids," I said. "Let's check in soon."

"That I will." He gesticulated and bowed grandly.

I laughed.

"Got some really long sweats?" Rousseau stood in the doorway behind me.

"I have some of your clothes. Let me look." In the office closet I found a bag of comfy items he often wore – the ones he hadn't absconded with at the end of visits. "How about these?" I held up running pants with lines down the sides.

"Those'll work," he said, snickering at the old style.

I added a striped long-sleeved T-shirt, hoody, and tennies to the pile.

Sophie was ready. We stepped out of the house. I tried to remember the last time the three of us had been here together. Not for a few years, at least.

"This feels good," I said.

Clouds on the horizon promised a dramatic sunset as we ambled along toward the gardens.

"So, when you left for Berkeley," I said to Sophie, "Marget and I met up in Shelley's garden and talked about helping Ian with the memory problem."

"Okay, hol-l-ld up." Rousseau put out a hand.

"Marget has a son. She's a witch from medieval Cornwall. They came here to get away from a sticky situation." I figured I'd pull off the bandaid all at once. "He was mixed up with someone we know—Galfride." I looked at my son.

He stared at me.

I barreled on. "Galfride's had some terrible phases. I'm not absolutely sure he's out of them now but he seems different."

Sophie interrupted, "Rousseau knows Galfride?"

"We'll get to that. So, when all of them first got to the British Isles from Germania—"

"All of them? Meaning…" Rousseau whacked a dangling tree branch out of his face as we bunched together along the narrow neighborhood sidewalk.

"Well, Galfride hitched a ride with the Wanderer wagons that brought Duff and Kyna to the British Isles. Though ironically his family was part of burning their village and orphaning them. He parted company with them in Cornwall. Maybe they got fed up with him and sent him packing. Anyway, he was living on the streets of Saevock and Marget took him in."

"It's weird that these people's stories tie together," Rouss said.

"Yes and no. She was sure it was due to magic that he was getting himself into trouble. She thought she could help. Her son Ian, quite sweet back then," I glanced at

Sophie, "was impressionable, being only around twelve. The two of them got into so much mischief in the town that the Craft Guild of Cornwall Witches banished them, or maybe threatened worse—to strip them of their powers—so they got out of town. The most powerful were still able to track them, anywhere they went. That's when Marget found this portal. The one into the oak that Baird and I have traveled through. Have I showed it to you? It's right in front of Marget's house."

"Nope."

"I want to see her home," Sophie said.

"Okay, why do you keep glancing at Sophie when you talk about Ian?" Rousseau asked me.

"Because she met him when she first came back to California, and they've spent some time together. I'm not sure if it's gone further than that?" I aimed lifted brows at her in question.

"No, Mom. Nothing's happened. We kind of sort of kissed one time."

"How does that work?" I asked, teasing.

"Okay. Our lips met. But it was kind of goofy. Turned into tickling or something. Anyway, I'm not sure I'm into him at all."

I remembered her sharing that he'd gotten a bit intense with questions. "I think it's so hard for him not to remember the past," I said, once again bringing more sympathy to the discussion than I really felt.

"Okay, so how old is he now?" Rouss asked.

"He's around thirty-two, I think," said Sophie. "He plays in a band. Harper in the Glen."

We reached the garden and they admired my plot. It was in its summer lushness.

"Want to show us Shelley's plot as well?" Sophie asked.

"Have you met Shelley?" Rousseau asked her.

"She's met pretty much the whole crew. The band, Shelley, Jarl and Joaquin. They and Marget are the extent of my friends here."

Chapter 19

We entered the midwife's impressive herb garden.

"Wow," Sophie said.

Rousseau clearly was taken with it as well.

We sat in the fire circle.

Sophie asked, "So Mom you started to say you and Marget talked about Ian's memories. What's the status on that?"

"Oh, yeah. So we decided to ask Aelfwyn for help. By the way, Marget took me to her home in Cornwall. A thousand years ago."

"Of course." Sophie stuck out her tongue at Rousseau.

I knew the jealousy wasn't going to go away. It'd have to be addressed at some point.

"She even took me further back and showed me her home when Ian was little, before they came here."

"Holy smokes," Rousseau said. "That's amazing, to be able to do that."

"Should'a been my line," Sophie snarked.

I gave her a look. "Then we went on to Kyna's tower in Wales. We hadn't even brought up working with Ian yet. In fact, we were planning a trip forward in time to see the full castle that's ruins now, in Abyrystwyth."

"Aaagh!" Sophie made a sound of protest.

"I know. It all sounds amazing but it's not just fun and games," I said, laying my hand on her wrist. I explained how we'd been gathered around the scrying bowl in Kyna's tower when Ylva and Duff appeared on the surface of the water, saying they'd seen Otho's ship disappear with Rousseau on it.

Both my kids had open mouths.

I summarized the trip to Thorgisl's tower with all the Thirteen, searching for the ship, finding it, and Ylva yanking it back from another world.

"You were in another world?" Sophie asked Rousseau.

"Yeah. It was bad. I couldn't really breathe. So, it was really good that Ylva yanked us out."

"But how did she yank a whole ship? And what does it mean, another world? Where's the ship now?"

"Hey. I don't know."

Rousseau and I shook our heads.

"I've been so absorbed with my own recovery I hadn't wondered about Otho and his men yet. I was suffering. And was so relieved to see Mom in that circle. At the same time, it's shocking to go suddenly from one place to the other. I felt super-sick for a while."

"You were unconscious." Sophie glared at him as though it were his fault.

I stroked both their arms. "Want to walk to Marget's to see the oak? It's not far. We can wait 'til another time to see inside her house. But it's kind of fun to see from the street." With a private grin, I pictured him seeing the dilapidated house front and wondering how someone could live there.

Sure enough, as we approached the great old oak, Rousseau stared to the back of the lot.

"Someone lives there?" His face was all skepticism.

Sophie, too, searched my eyes for clues.

"You'll see. Can I leave it a mystery for now?"

The next few days, I could almost hope Thorgisl's revenge would not happen. Sophie heard back that she could have the room near campus. We drove together to Berkeley.

The house was an older two-story north of University Ave. She had an upstairs room facing the street with its mature trees and similarly vintage homes. Sophie's housemates were away for the moment. We camped out in her empty room with foam pads for bedding until she found an antique brass bed frame on Craigs list. Then she bought new bedding. We spent the days perusing flea markets for fun furnishings and necessities to tide her over 'til her boxes arrived, also enjoying plenty of Indian food.

The second day, we walked to the campus where I'd been professor until recently.

"I'll be in this cluster of buildings," Sophie pointed out. "Music, Performing Arts, Letters and Science."

"What's the Masters you're doing? All I remember is it's a mouthful."

"Ethnomusicology."

"You just had to be fancy, didn't you? First Paris. Then this."

"It's the oldest program of its kind in the country," she quoted proudly. "Come on. You have a Harvard degree."

"I'm jealous. I have no idea what I'm doing," He gazed up at redwoods as we followed Sather's Cross Path.

"Will you try to find a law firm here?" I asked, wanting to leave his next steps wide open.

"I suppose."

We looked online for available apartments. One that seemed promising was rather a dive and he decided to keep searching.

I hoped her summer project would take her mind off of the medieval travels of which she was not a part. It was the third day and we'd so far been able to keep away from the subject. I thought Rousseau might be too shaken up by his recent journey to the past to want to talk about it anyway. Maybe he would open up on our trip back to the north coast.

It was one of those sunny, sparkling water-view crossings of the Bay Bridge. Boats clipped over choppy water, sails tilted with the perfect wind.

We stopped at Sonoma Taco and ate burritos in the car as we continued north. I chose 128, the slightly longer drive, so we could enjoy the emerald Navarro River and hit the dramatic stretch of coast beyond.

Rousseau slept after lunch and woke in time for the dappled redwoods, sprinkled with sunlit ferns.

Drowsy, he said, "Mom, do you think I'll build the skills you have? Do they protect you and help you control your coming and going?"

"You might have to start wearing some jewelry," I said with a crinkly-eyed glance his way.

"Like your rings and the Celtic knot?" he asked. "I'd be down with that."

I didn't mention the Brand, and neither did he. "Yeah. Duff is an amazing silversmith. Do you have something else in mind? Nose studs?"

We laughed as we admired the vista of the sea so wide you could see the earth's curve.

"Maybe brow. Or tongue!"

"Just don't do septum," I said.

We sobered.

"It was amazing, when you and Ylva were in my mind. I felt the world get brighter. It was … I don't know, just so positive. How did you do that?"

"It's been a slow process. First, I didn't even realize I was gathering a kind of intent with language and writing, when I slipped into Kyna's mind in medieval time. I spent five days in another woman's spirit. That was like a crash course, painless learning, gathering her skills and knowledge. I re-accessed those buried memories when I re-turned to the past on Samhain. I thought I was meeting Baird for the first time, but I'd met him before. It's confus-ing because when I was in Kyna's mind, Samhain had just happened, but it was five years before. That's how fluid the time-travel is."

Rousseau looked nearly cross-eyed trying to follow this.

"Anyway, Baird started to train me deliberately to block out or shield harmful minds. Aelfwyn taught me to build an ice wall around memories I want to protect. And much more, how to form a tower that keeps me safe as I return to my time—but I still often need help."

"What did it feel like when you saved Gwynedd?" he asked.

"You remembered," I said.

"Of course."

We looked down at the cove far below as we crossed over the short bridge at Albion. "Have you had any con-nection with her since you saw her in the park?"

"No, I guess she's been safe since then."

"Yes." I stopped myself from saying "Safely in the thir-teenth century." Though I had learned some excellent skills, I still was never sure if the most powerful—Thorgisl, Galfride—could listen in and find out the women were hid-den in another time. "It seems so."

"We're not really protected, driving along here, are we?" he asked.

I took a deep breath. "I think I'll test my ability to sense that." Both hands on the wheel, I let the two powerful rings touch and began charging my brand, breathing slowly. When the points of the brand felt fully empowered, I let my awareness ripple outward from my heart until I felt a vibrating sphere all the way around our car, moving with us.

"Whoo," Rouss said quietly. "You did it, didn't you? I felt that." He had wonder in his eyes when I glanced at him.

"I think I did." The amber ring was nicely alive and I seemed to be sorting mind-voices clearly. My son's was a gentle but open channel to me, the most vibrant of all with his proximity and our close relationship. "I'm pretty sure I could tune into any mind if I focused there, in this state. And I feel sure we cannot be heard or detected by others. But I'll have to have Marget or Ylva test it."

"Are they your main go-to's now?" he asked.

I thought a moment. "I think they are. I feel more comfortable with them than with anyone before who's taught me magic." I thought hard a moment, then added, "It's that they need me, too. I think that's what relationship is about. Reciprocity."

"Nice, Mom. I like that."

We drove silently along the bluffs approaching the cliff-top town of Mendocino. "This protective sphere would take a lot of energy to hold over time. I'll form it only if we need to protect something confidential." I let go of the muffling spell with a whoosh and rocked my head back and forth to loosen my neck.

"I want that so much," Rousseau said.

I felt a glow with his admiration that I'd missed in the past couple of years. In truth, I'd been suffering as my children took in the strange turns of my life lately, noting the paucity of books, the puzzling prevalence of textiles.

"It's urgent that we get you whatever powers we can. I've done English dancing there." I pointed toward the tiny hamlet of Caspar as we passed. "Loads of Celtic musicians play there. I think it's their best venue on the coast. Maybe thirty members."

"How was it?"

"Well, I was a bit of a clod. But it felt super fun pretending I was in a Jane Austen movie."

"I bet. Did you wear all the gear? Flowy dress and stuff?"

"Nope. Just a skirt I made. It was all in the imagining."

"Who'd you go with? By yourself?"

"Jarl. But Ian and the other Harper in the Glen members were there." I remembered the unnerving conversation about my drawing of Galfride and thought I might show it to Rousseau. "We should pick up food at Harvest."

"Yeah, let's."

We discussed what food to buy as we crossed the graceful, arching bridge high over Noyo Harbor and entered Pomo Bluff.

Chapter 20

After supper, I rummaged for the drawing and found it in the drawer by the overstuffed chairs. I brought it to the table.

"Galfride," Rousseau said. "Wow. That's kind of a haunting picture."

"I know. And I don't remember drawing it."

"It's for sure yours, though. It's your style. Really good, Mom."

"Thanks. Talking about English dancing reminded me that Ian had this drawing for a while. Jarl saw it sitting out at his apartment and brought it back to me. Ian is a tad obsessed with it. In fact, he's gotten real growly about a few things. Like my gold crystal, back when I had it. And just the fact that he knows I time-travelled. I think it activates his buried sense that he has a past."

"He remembers nothing before here?" my son asked.

"Nothing. That was the price of separating him from Galfride, when the Cornish Guild came after him and his mom."

"Came after? As in … not like the witch burnings?"

"No, something more like stripping their powers. I'm not sure what all but it didn't sound pleasant."

"So Marget came here with him."

"And when they got here, Ian didn't even remember her, his own mom."

"Ugh. That must be pretty awful."

"You bet. Hey, I'm going to text and ask if she might let us visit tomorrow. Would you want to see her home?"

"Yeah, for sure. I'm extremely curious." He let out a full yawn. "I don't think I slept that well on the foam."

"Me, either. Let's make it an early night." We cleared the dishes, washed up and put clean sheets on in the guest room fold-out.

"This bed is the best," he said.

"We should do wash tomorrow," I said as I saw him drag them out of his new travel bag for a fourth sleep night.

"Sounds good." He kissed my temple, heading for the secondary bathroom with toothbrush.

"Have a good night. Sweet dreams." I blew him a smooch.

In the living room, I settled in a broad chair, cross-legged, and built the power of my brand, then sent tentacles of energy outward to the edges of the sylph-created shield. Breathing slowly, I checked, rings together, pressed to my silver pendant, to see if it felt the same as in the car. Yes, it did but how could I be sure of its impermeability?

I climbed the ladder to the attic, dreaming of when I'd have outside stairs to it. I'd dusted and put down a rug in the area with the scrying bowl. I'd have to figure out how to refresh the water and how often. Get plumbing up here?

Sitting on a puffy pillow, I focused and gently tapped Marget.

Her face appeared. I thought to her my proposal, that I build the sphere around the house and she test it.

We spent the next quarter hour on the project and she pronounced it impenetrable. "You might also have Ylva check. She has some wily ways."

"I will. I also wondered if Rousseau and I might visit you tomorrow."

"I'd love that. I'll make huckleberry scones," she said gleefully.

We settled on a time and I said good night.

As I clambered down the ladder, Rousseau said, behind me, "What's up there?"

"Hey, sweetie, can't sleep?"

"I wanted water," he said.

"Want to see?"

We ascended the stairs and I showed him my impressive *pensieve* for scrying.

"This is getting to be a pretty good space. It's bigger than I thought," he said, though, being nearly 6'4", he had to bend over even in the tallest area, which is where I'd cleared.

"It's way better. I still have improvements to make. I want running water up here, and an outside stairway."

"Good call," he said, rubbing his head from bumping a corner at the skylight.

"You okay?"

"I'm fine."

"Want cocoa, or are you too beat?"

"I never pass on cocoa. You know that."

So, we ended up in the living room chairs with a fire going.

"Marget wants us to come early afternoon tomorrow," I said. "She's making berry scones."

Rouss lifted his brows as he blew on his cup. "Mmm."

"I want to talk to her about training you. We can do that when we work on our plans for Ian."

"Okay. I'm going to leave this up to you," he said. "Since I'm kind of more awake now, I think I'll bring my laptop out and start working on some emails to let my firm know I'm probably leaving. And I'll need to check on getting out of my lease."

"Are you excited? About coming back?"

"I am."

"Are you still in touch with any friends in the East Bay, from college?"

"For sure. Also in San Francisco and Stanford. It'll be a reunion. I'm thinking of sharing a place with a friend near Lake Merritt. I think he still has an empty room."

"That would be superb. It's a cool, active area. You always liked that. I remember."

"I did. I do."

"I don't blame your friend—what's his name?"

"Brandon."

"Oh, yeah, I remember him. I don't blame him for waiting to get the right housemate. That can be a nightmare."

We settled in with our laptops. He had a fancy tray for his. The scene felt natural and I felt grateful for that.

Oz came and tried to insert himself into my lap. I set the computer aside and stroked him, head against the comfy chair, watching the crackling fire. The cat flopped, contented, and I finished my hot chocolate, mulling over the past few weeks. There was a lot to think about and I didn't know where all the answers would come from.

Next afternoon, as we passed Marget's street, skirting to

the back, Rouss said, "I'm so curious about this place."

"Knock, knock," I said in my mind to Marget as we came to the fence along her backyard. I took Rousseau's hand, and we stood in her garden, on the other side of the fence.

He'd travelled to medieval time, yet for me to able to transport us through a simple fence seemed almost as miraculous. He stared at me. I grinned.

Marget opened her bright green door and welcomed us. "Shall we sit outside?"

"Yes, but I promised my son a tour of your house, if it's alright with you."

"He shall have it." She lifted a full tray from the sideboard. "I scryed you coming and prepared a light repast."

Rousseau stepped forward. "Let me help."

She relinquished her load to him. "Over here." She led the way to the bowered alcove with its ornate iron chairs and table.

We sat and enjoyed tea and berry scones.

"Did you pick the huckleberries for these?" Rouss asked.

"Oh, yes. Over by the creek," she said.

"We have some in Mom's backyard. We should make something like this," he said to me. "We also have a blackberry at the very back. Good in pancakes."

"We've been talking about getting Rousseau trained in the mental arts," I said.

Marget nodded, chewing a scone and sipping tea. "I agree. He needs to know when someone is watching or is about to enter his mind. He also must detect if he's close to being drawn elsewhere."

"Perfect. I'm also hoping you might help me test if I'm effective building my own safe sphere using my rings and brand. I tested it on the drive up here but I'm not sure."

Rousseau looked from Marget to me. "Would I need to be branded?"

Marget said, "Has she shown you?"

"Yeah. It looks awesome. But … was it like cattle branding?"

"Basically, yeah."

He looked horrified. "So, it hurt like hell."

"That's about right. Ylva said she could have made it hurt less, and heal faster. It was over pretty quickly and Aelfwyn muffled the pain with some herbal tonic. Anyway, it has sigils from thirteen runes, and forms a heron, my spirit animal. When I trace the points in my mind, it brightens up and gives me power. That increases my strength when I connect with the others of the Thirteen. There's something about the brand that ties us."

"Can I see it again?" he asked.

I unbuttoned my shirt a ways down, and pulled it from my shoulder. He examined the figure.

"It does look amazing." He touched it. "But I'd *keloid* for sure."

"Maybe not with the salves Aelfwyn makes. Ylva's might be better. She says they'll take the pain away immediately."

"Do you think the amber stone Thorgisl gave me could be useful?"

I looked at Marget.

"If we attuned you to it," she said. "And trained you to use it so it doesn't use you."

"Well put." He chuckled.

"Are you still drawn to write the story? Did that happen before you were pulled this time?" I asked him.

"No. Not this time. In fact, I was asleep. I think something might have come into my dream but I don't remember what. And I certainly had no precursor or warning. Not consciously anyway."

"We can set traps," Marget said. "Ylva's tasted Otho now. I'm sure she can put a warning system into your psyche."

"We should go to her then," I said. "This might be a good time, when Sophie is staying in her new place. She's coming back at the weekend. She wants to see if she can find cool things for her new room here at yard sales."

"When shall we go?"

"I think we want to bundle up for Norway. Even in summer, she's at a high altitude."

Marget brushed crumbs from her fingertips. "Well, you wanted to see the house from the inside."

"Yes!" Rousseau popped a last bite of a second scone into his mouth and we cleared the table.

Rouss looked around at the old-fashioned kitchen with interest. "Wood-burning stove. Cool," he said.

"Come." Marget led us to the living room. Halfway through, a sort of gray vapor divided the normal half from the deserted-house part. We gazed out the front window at the decrepit yard and massive old tree.

"And no one can see in?" Rousseau asked.

"No," Marget answered.

"Do you ever sit in here?" he wondered.

Marget laughed, then pondered, grew sad. "When I first came here, I sat and watched for Ian to wander back, maybe even subconsciously remembering where we'd first arrived."

We sat in chairs, one soft, the others stiff with upright backs and striped satin covering, lights off.

"Did he ever?" Rouss asked.

Chapter 21

No. Never did."

There was such deep sadness in her voice, a lump grew in my throat. "We're going to figure out a solution."

"I wonder what he'll be like now," Marget said. "Once he remembers. I go over and over it in my mind. Will he want to return to Cornwall? Seek Galfiride out? Or will he want to just hold onto his life here?"

"I told you how attracted he was to the portrait of Galfride," I said, glancing at my son. His look acknowledged awareness of seeing it the night before.

"Did he ever make comments about it?" Marget asked.

"Not to me. But he was livid that I got it back."

"Even though he stole it in the first place." Marget's tone was amused but a crease in her brow hinted she might be seeing the incident as a sign he could go back to darker tendencies.

"What was the big thing he and Galfride did that got you chased out?" Rousseau asked.

From the mouths of babes. I'd never dared ask.

"Oh." Marget let out a breathy chuckle. She seemed to mull over how to begin the story. "They were boys. They couldn't know how their antics could really be cruel. Even ruin lives. I have not checked to see all that came of it. I also don't know the whole tale." She paused, working her hands in her lap. "I was afraid to ask for any more detail."

Rouss and I quietly waited for more.

"There was a girl. A teen. Galfride knew his friend was in love with her. He did some matchmaking."

I mouthed, "Matchmaking?" That didn't sound like Galfride.

"That doesn't sound so bad," she quickly went on. "That's not all." She sighed. "You know how he can manipulate minds," she said to me.

"Indeed I do."

"And you know Galfride?" She asked my son, seeming to have just remembered.

"I know him a little. He's been kind to me. Helpful. Even, dare I say, protective?"

Marget nodded, watching his face, pensive. Then she looked at me. "Do you think Galfride's changed much?"

I said, "I can't be sure. It was only months ago that he treated me cruelly, in his caverns."

Rousseau sat up straight, eyes grilling me. "What did he do to you?"

How to frame it all? "I've been in his caves a few times. He's snatched me there in various ways." I hated to say his mother had endured torment, yet I wanted him to be fully aware of Galfride's capabilities, and proclivities. "He said at first he thought I was Kyna. He snatched me from the castle, held me paralyzed. I was able to break the spell by tracing runes on the dress I wore, one of Gwynedd's." I gave them a picture.

"You look beautiful," Rousseau said. "I like the crystals in your hair."

"Marvelous seamstress," Marget remarked.

"But he raked my mind as I got away. I was afraid he'd torn memories from me. The other time, he snatched me out of the air over Kyna's home as I was transporting. We ended up battling and I sent myself to outer-space. The Thirteen found me and brought me back before I suffocated. That was when I felt mountain-love for the first time."

"Mom, you're scaring me. But I'm also really impressed. You're the bomb."

"He can be frightening."

"How did you fight him?"

"It was when I first had the Ing ring." I showed him the slender silver band with Ing runes looping it. "I built a spear of sharp diamond shapes. And shouted commands I didn't know I knew. Sent him flying against the wall of the cave."

"I can't believe that." My son stared at me.

"That's not the most amazing part. The mountain loved me. The peak of the cavern parted and I shot up through. I think it closed behind me so he couldn't follow."

"I so want to do that."

"Yeah, that part was great. Up to then, he'd had me pinned and roughed me up a bit."

Rousseau scowled.

"But when I got out into the blackness, I couldn't breathe. I saw only stars."

"The Thirteen somehow knew you were there?"

"I played the flute and it seemed to call them. Only I played it in spirit. I couldn't actually breathe so couldn't play notes, but I imagined the flute in my pocket—the one Hamelyn made—floating up to my lips and me playing it. That imagining was what my friends heard, in Kyna's tower. They brought me back. That was when I first shared your story with them about Otho's ship and Gwynedd escaping using her stitchery."

"I'm getting some new parts of the story," Marget said.

"It's incredible how many times we can share and something new comes out," Rousseau said, holding me with a steady, meaningful gaze.

"I didn't let the kids know about any of this for a long time and it felt like betrayal," I explained to Marget.

"I know that feeling well," she said.

I nodded. "It's been coming out bit by bit. You can't keep big secrets from loved ones forever. They're going to reveal themselves, and the longer you wait, the more catastrophic they can be."

"I have no doubt. What first forced the truth out?" Marget leaned forward, hands clutched in her lap.

"When the dangers started closing in, Hamelyn couldn't be found. Sophie had a dream of a flute-playing lover. Next thing you know, she's moving to Aberystwyth, and talks about a guy she calls Ham. He sounds like Baird's son. Baird and I go to Wales and there he is."

"That's astounding. And when did you come out to Rousseau?"

"We didn't know he'd been to the past until Sophie and I went to Boston. He was being cryptic. I think he didn't want to worry me."

"Just like you didn't want to worry us."

I rested my hand on his. "I found an old pirate coat—medieval style and material. He told us he'd been pulled back—"

"To the same time and people you'd been visiting," Marget said. "It's very web-like. I think there's no accident to any of it. Your bloodline is tied to them. They were going to reach all of you, sooner or later,"

"You certainly give the whole thing shape." I stood. "Let's look at the rest of the house before I dislocate something in this adorable but brutal chair."

"Probably good for your back." Marget chuckled as she led us to the second floor and down a narrow hall. "This is my busy room." The cozy den had a project table holding a sewing machine, a writing desk, packed shelves, plus a comfy chair and cushioned stools.

Rousseau and I took in the view over the yard and park at the back.

"I like this." Rousseau's head nearly touched the ceiling.

Marget pivoted. Back in the hall, she pointed. "Bedroom." Then she opened a door to more stairs and we climbed to an attic room that put mine to shame. Its high ceilings met at the center in a peak running from front to back, with dormer windows.

"Awesome." Rousseau approached the long altar one the far side. There were alcoves with pillows, some low shelves with books. A desk held an open book with writing and drawings looking like DaVinci's notes. "Oooh," he breathed as he stared down at the unreadable text and symbols.

Something was happening in my son. I'd seen it at my house and on our drive up here.

"Is this what you call a scrying bowl?" he asked, peeking behind a heavy curtain.

I joined him and saw an area with thick pillows surrounding the shallow bowl on a low pedestal. Tables at the side held candles, incense, and various accoutrements.

He didn't hesitate, poking around. I had to love his candor.

Marget watched with indulgent amusement and I thought she must be missing sharing her life with her own son, who was close in age.

"You look at whatever you want," she said, seeming to confirm my guess. "We'll be training you so we don't want to keep you out of anything."

I recalled Galfride hunting through her apothecary, finding some of the secrets he'd turned into dark arts. "I guess it's all how you're trained."

Marget had caught my thought. "Galfride did use craft in destructive ways. Any craft can be beneficial or harmful, depending on the intent."

"He'd been through some ghastly experiences: family guilty of burning Kyna and Duff's village, himself orphaned perhaps, leaving everyone he knew to travel with the Wanderers to the British Isles, living on the streets of Cornwall as a young lad. Today I think we'd say he had PTSD. Maybe that led to his craving for riches and elegance, performing magic for royalty."

"It'd be interesting to talk to him about those times," my son said.

"Indeed it would," I said. "Well, Marget, I think we've pushed your hospitality to the rim."

"It's been a great pleasure," she said with feeling. "I need to get to the library. Shall we walk some of the way together?"

Chapter 22

At the active local library, I found a book on gardens of the U.K. It was old and packed with photos. What intrigued me were folkloric notes on herbs' properties. The volume had been pushed behind others on a bottom shelf. I perceived its presence and searched for it.

Drawing it out, I scanned the pages. I sensed Marget come up behind me.

"I've had that one before. Look at this." She took the book from me and flipped through to an illustration that depicted one part of a cottage garden. I could swear I saw a sylph fluttering among the lowest shadows.

I held Marget's gaze. "This author had 'the sight'."

"You might have interesting experiences if you borrow it," she said.

I tucked it under my arm. Rousseau picked out a few novels.

We parted ways out front, planning to meet by scry in the evening, and travel next day.

Walking toward home, Rouss said, "Ya know, even though Otho dragged me along unwilling, I'm feeling worried. If I was suffocating, he must be, too. And his crew. Can he even get his ship back without the amber stone?"

He looked at me. "I know we probably don't even want them back in this world. I mean, he kidnapped Gwynedd. But it's weird, not to know."

Just to be safe, I built a protected cone around us before I said, "You're right. Let's check with Ylva. She's the one with the stone."

When we arrived at home, I sat on my bed holding the carved heron, stroking her smooth surfaces. Oz flopped beside me. "Okay, I'll stroke you, too."

Ylva appeared in my mind. "Quite a summons, from heron and cat familiar."

"Greetings," I said. "How goes it?"

"It goes well. My beloved chops wood. One of my sons has brought grandchildren to visit. What compels you to my spirit?"

I saw a girl in a red cloak, cheeks flushed rosy, run up to Ylva and pat her side. The spoke in Old Norse, Ylva leaning down to her. I oberved their mannerisms, mystified to view a scene of a thousand years ago. "Your granddaughter is adorable."

"This is Bergljot." Ylva beamed.

"I should let you go—be with your family."

"I will. But what made you call to me?"

"Rousseau worries that Otho might not be able to return without the stone. The world they were in has low oxygen. They might not survive."

"He's worried about the sea-scoundrel, is he? His kidnapper, as well. Big heart, your son. I already thought of it and brought them back."

"Were they in bad shape?"

"Quite dismal. I spent some time reviving them."

"You are something."

"Does that phrase have actual meaning?" Ylva asked.

"I never thought I was nothing."

I laughed. "I guess it means the person lacks adequate words. Anyway, it was good of you to help those men. I'd forgotten they might be suffocating. I don't know how thrilled the others will be to know you rescued them. Did you spend much time in that strange world?"

"Not much. Would you like to go there?" she asked.

"We'd have to solve the oxygen issue."

"I think the stone is from there. That's what pulled them. So, your son had a good instinct, that they might not be able to come and go without it."

"What makes you think so?"

"I think the stone told me. And it may hold the answer to the breathing problem."

"I wonder how it came to this world." Bergljot tugged on Ylva's coat.

"I'll leave you to your family. We can talk more when we get there."

"We will speak more soon."

"Can I bring my son and Marget to you tomorrow?" I asked.

"That would please me." Ylva flashed a bright smile.

"Me, too. Until then." Our connection ended.

I wandered out to find Rousseau. He sat at the picnic table in the backyard, under a colorful umbrella, starting one of his library books.

"Is it good?" I asked, joining him.

"Sequel to *DaVinci Code*. I'm not liking it as well. But it's interesting, about the symbols in Washington DC buildings. I wonder if they're really there."

"Maybe we can go and find out."

"You've read *The Lost Symbol*?"

"Yep. Can't keep me away from symbol books."

"That's true. Did you reach Ylva?"

"Yeah. She already brought them back."

He stared at me. "Otho and his crew? How quickly? Were they alright?"

"Soon enough. She revived them."

Rousseau huffed a sigh. "That lifts a weight off me. Even though they might be scum of the earth."

"It's the right thing. But conscience is tricky."

"Yeah, it is. What now?"

"We go to medieval Norway tomorrow," I said. "Marget, too. It's beautiful. Ylva has grandchildren visiting so I don't know how much of an imposition it'll be. But Duff's there. Maybe you can get to know him a little."

"Big guy? Red ponytail, chopped bangs?"

"That's the one." I recalled he'd seen him in the circle in Thorgisl's tower.

"I've only seen him," he said. "I'd like to meet him."

"Good. I'm trying to think what we have for warm clothes. There are the beach-walk coats. I left my down jacket in medieval Germania. Hope that doesn't change history somehow."

"That's a worry, isn't it? Where'd you leave it?"

"Back of a cave. I should get it, if I can find the place. I'd kind of like to see the place again. What a crazy time. I bet Duff could get us there. It's where he hid when Thorgisl made him sick with a spell."

"Not very nice," my son said, though I sensed his opinion of Thorgisl was far different from mine. The man had never been cruel to him. In fact, they all—Galfride, Thorgisl, Otho—seemed partial to my son.

Back at the house, we rummaged in the closet. I sniffed a wool pea coat, made a face. "Musty." I held out a thick, Scottish pullover sweater.

"Nice," Rouss said, lifting the patterned sleeve and feeling the texture of the wool. "I'd be quite dapper for Scandinavia in this."

"Let's go with it, then," I said, taking it off its hanger. "Hungry for an early dinner?"

"Famished," he said.

In the kitchen, we made pasta and salad.

Rousseau minced garlic. "I've been mulling over why Otho compelled me to write his story, if that was what was happening, or why he pulled me to him. He seems to sense me as his chronicler. How he found me, I have no idea."

"I suspect the Wanderers are our kin as well."

Rousseau brushed the garlic into hot olive oil. "It's weird that Gwynedd came to me for help. She'd been abducted by Otho and then he started sending his stories into my mind. Almost like she drew his attention to me. If that doesn't sound too farfetched." He guffawed.

"Yeah, why did he choose you to write his story?"

"It's mysterious. But when they were young, they were all together, right? Otho and Boldo were with the Wanderers, so they knew Kyna and Baird and Duff."

"Must have." I handed him more to chop. "It might be impossible to explain every aspect, but I hope we'll have chances to try to work out the answers."

"Thorgisl's the biggest threat now."

"As far as the stone. But we don't really know what Galfride is up to. I'm pretty sure we're safe in this house but I want Marget to check."

"Is she coming here?"

"No. She thinks getting practice with our scrying bowl is important."

"She'll be in her attic room and we'll be in ours?" Rousseau put a hand on my shoulder. "Mom, I love that room of hers. I want to make ours like it. I know it's not as big but—"

"Maybe we can build ours out. I've been thinking the same."

We finished cooking and served.

"I'm feeling bad about Sophie." Rousseau carried full dishes to the table.

"I am, too," I said. "Something will work out. Maybe it'll just take time."

"I bet you're glad she's not being grabbed into the past, though."

"That I am."

I brought garlic toast from under the broiler and we settled into eating.

"When she was first drawn to Aberystwyth, I felt terrified, and guilty," I said.

"Back then, did you really think it might be related?"

"Well, it was too strange. A fiddler in her dream, and then she happens to travel to his town, but in our time. Star-crossed love, to the max." I quirked a look at him, guilty, sheepish.

"It forced the truth out." He tasted the sauce.

"It did, though your situation would have made that happen soon enough." I got up to make more garlic toast. "She doesn't seem to be pining away that much over Hamelyn."

"She found Ian quickly once she got here. I think he's at least a good distraction. Of course, a lot of the attraction is the music they share."

"It didn't hurt that he has an apartment in the East Bay."

"Ha. True."

"She knows about the connection to Marget and all that?" Rousseau asked, fork halfway to his mouth.

I nodded. "Yeah, she's all filled in."

We ate quietly for a bit. When the silence stretched, I asked, "Are you thinking about our trip tomorrow?"

"Kind of. Wondering about the lessons."

"Let's go to Marget's instead. I can get her to check the protections later. Or maybe she could check when we're here and she's there." I guessed he wanted to be in her marvelous attic room again. I picked up my empty bowl and stood. "I have brownies in the freezer."

"Great!"

"We can warm them up and put coconut-milk vanilla ice cream on them."

"I'm in," he said, bringing his dirty dishes.

"While we're waiting for them to heat, I'll ask Ylva to check our perimeter."

"Sounds very military." He dropped into a comfy chair in the living room and picked up his book.

"Ten-four. Over and out."

He snickered as I left for the bedroom.

Sitting at the head of my bed, I held the heron. I didn't really need it to connect with her but liked the feeling, the *way* it connected us.

"I already caught your thought," Ylva responded. "It's tempting to check in on my patient."

"Rousseau's doing great."

"So he seems. You want me to test the sphere around your home."

"Yes, please." I straightened, getting ready.

After a moment, she said, "It's still strong. I could get in but no one else I know of could."

I chuckled at her arrogance, but it was not ill-placed. "What about now. Wait a second." I did my new spreading of the power-sphere from my Brand. "Does it feel more secure?" I waited.

"Depends on how hard someone is willing to work. I mean, someone like me...I'm a force. Who are you worrying about? Thorgisl?" Ylva asked.

"Yes."

"Don't lose sleep on his account. That worm can control minds but he's gotten used to ones he can access in his ordinary ways."

"That reminds me. You're sure the Jutland fort doesn't hold Mora, right? You checked."

"That's true."

"When we were in the circle with the Thirteen, I felt Thorgisl's mind briefly show Mora's location, a place away from the fort. Did you sense that?"

"No. But I wasn't thinking there."

"Well, you were much more key to the main operation with the ship than I was."

"I can go back into his mind and search."

"Please do."

"Kay, explain to me. Mora is leader of her clan?"

"Yes. That's right." It was strange to hear Ylva say my name. They all had so many nicknames for me.

"What relation is Boldo to her?"

"Nephew."

"Does she have children?"

I heard Duff's voice near her. When she turned her attention back to me, her voice rose in surprise. "Otho is her son? Does he know she is missing?"

Duff joined our mind connection. "Otho cut himself from the family long ago. Something with a murder. A clan murder. It was never proven but he was ostracized by the main clan."

"That's why he took to piracy," I said.

"And who is now the leader of the Silwy?" Ylva asked.

Duff answered, "Boldo. They've gone time after time to find Mora. I'm afraid… Boldo be sure she be still alive. But I'm no' so certain. Why would none of ye find her? Even my sweet consort, wi' her gopher shapeshiftin' an' all." He turned his admiring eyes on me.

"Galfride's told me about strange stones, amulets, other objects Thorgisl has in his tower." Rousseau had come into my room and joined in our mind-meld. "He thinks there are some that, set around a place, can mask even the best of … I don't know what you'd call it. Detectors?"

I wondered then what else my son had picked up.

"That is helpful, lad. We must go, but I will find a time to search."

"They want to meet you and your son," Ylva said. "I'll say goodnight. It's late here."

"See you tomorrow."

We parted.

Chapter 23

O ur place or Marget's?" I asked Rousseau who was buried in his novel.

He chose the witch's home, and we walked there in the balmy evening.

"Nice night." Rousseau remarked. "Doesn't seem like Pomo Bluff."

Crickets chirping, filling the night air, suddenly stopped. Started again. Frogs joined in as we neared the creek in the park.

Marget welcomed us and offered cookies. Rousseau grabbed a few.

"After brownie and ice cream?" I winked.

We carried hot herb tea to the attic.

"Have you named your house?" I asked her.

"Not yet. Thinking about it. Back home, we always did."

"Is the front going to rot away?" Rousseau asked. "I mean, it looks like it's … shredding."

I snorted tea up my nose.

Marget snickered at me. "I keep it up very well. It just looks dilapidated."

"Do neighbors get mad? Like watch groups or something?" he asked.

"I'm almost certain they don't see it. Like it doesn't

exist," she said. "I'm not even sure there's a space between houses."

"I brought Harper in the Glen here," I said. "All that gang. Shelley, Jarl, Joaquin. I showed them the oak where Baird appeared. They saw the yard and house."

"Ian was with you. I remember it well. I opened his sight to it long ago. Hoping."

"So, you think it got through to him, on some unconscious level?" I asked.

"Even without memory, he still had the magic of sight."

We worked for several hours. I call it work but it was exhilarating, even beautiful at times. Marget slipped into our minds, taught us to notice her presence, then how to repel her. Some of it was as Baird had taught me, but she went much further, educating us to sense any kind of new energy. She could mimic malevolence, which was startling at first, but then became a sort of game. Rousseau was thrilled, I sensed.

All was not wicked or attack-oriented. Some involved the bonding we did with the Thirteen. This part was similar to Baird's therapy-like training, where any touchy spots that might serve as vulnerable triggers were brought to the surface, shared and healed. Rousseau's recent ordeal with Otho could become such a weakness to be exploited.

"I want you to have something like the brand, Rousseau," Marget said. "Once we've trained you further, I'm sure you'll receive the real thing. But for now, I have a few ideas. Ylva may have more."

I saw his mind working on possibilities. "Sounds interesting," he said.

Marget went on, "We should have Ylva come at you with an energy like Otho's. He's the one who most recently pulled you to him. But let's don't neglect Thorgisl's. He could be next."

"She might need to replicate being drawn by the stone as well," I suggested.

"Good thought." Marget tapped her lip. "It's nearly midnight. Let's sleep. Tomorrow might be an arduous day. I want us to be as strong as we can be."

"I agree," I said.

We hugged. Marget gripped Rousseau hard in a hug, reaching up from her tiny perspective.

Walking through the night air, Rouss and I talked about what we wanted to accomplish the next day.

"Go to Ylva first and shore up these skills and protections," I said.

"Then, with our superpowers, find out where Mora is and free her," Rousseau pronounced.

"I like that. Superpowers." I laughed and hooked my son's arm.

"We'll try to find that cave, too, right? And get your down jacket?" he asked.

"For that, we might want to bring Duff. I don't think I could find the cave on my own. "

"And Boldo. Was he ever there?"

"No. But there's another reason to have him come. Remember the tavern you went to from Otho's ship?"

Rousseau brushed his hands on a branch dipping toward us in the shadows, like he wanted to do a pull-up on it but decided against it. "Yeah. I remember. He turned invisible and went out the back with the giant and the dwarf."

"Ulf was thinking about that same tavern."

"The creepy jailor you slept with?" He guffawed.

"I did not sleep *with* him. I was inside his mind overnight." I slapped his arm playfully. "I think the town might be *Geestendorf*. Ulf had the hots for a waitress who worked there."

"The one with the amber beads."

"Did you see her?"

"Yeah, she's the one who served Otho." Rousseau tried to see my face in the near-moonless night. "What are you thinking?"

"It might help us understand what that stone is about, if we can trace the source. Understand its properties, what Thorgisl could do with it if he obtains it."

"What are you thinking?" he asked.

"Ylva says it might be from that other world. To make you safe, we need to know what influence the stone had on Otho."

"I see what you mean. Do you think Ylva can figure it out? What if it's a danger to her?"

"I hadn't thought of that," I said. "I think of her as all-powerful."

He chuckled. "Yeah, she's pretty darn talented. Hey, why don't you ask Boldo if that was *Geestendorf*?"

"Right now?"

"Sure. You're wearing your boots, aren't you?"

"I don't want to be rude."

"I don't mind. Remember cell phones, Mom? People do that all the time."

"I know. My point exactly." Smiling, I sent my thoughts toward Boldo.

"I'm here," the Wanderer responded. He sat at a workbench in a wagon, fashioning a tool out of leather and metal. "Saving Angel, how doth thee fare?"

"I'm well, thanks," I said. "I have my son, Rousseau, beside me."

"How be he?"

"Doing fine. Fully recovered." I held onto Rousseau's arm and made a three-way connection. Rousseau and Boldo greeted each other.

"He seems fit and hale, as you say."

"And you? How do you fare?" I asked.

"Thank you for inquiring. I travel with my clan on our summer journey."

"Where are you now?"

"In the north of Angle land."

"Could they spare you for a short time? Tomorrow, Rousseau, Marget and I are visiting Ylva for training."

"That is good."

"I'll ask Ylva for help searching Thorgisl's mind for Mora's location. I wondered if you would want to join us. I think that would help."

"You need to ask, my friend?"

"Fantastic. I also have a question. Were you in *Geestendorf* when Thorgisl snatched you?"

"Yes. Why d'ye ask?"

"Maybe we can meet near that tavern? Then I'll explain. I'll let you know when we're there."

"I will feel your boots' travel that way. Safe journeys, Rousseau."

My son turned to me. "Say thanks for me."

"Tell me yerself," Boldo said.

He was in my son's mind.

Rouss tightened his arm on my hand. I sensed him opening, receiving, with a first keen effort. Tentatively, he spoke. "Safe travels to you as well." Our minds were melded, as in the circle. We saw Boldo grin.

"Have you followed our conversation?" Boldo asked him.

"I did. Most of it. Mom told me you we're going to Ylva's tomorrow and then asked you to meet us in *Geestendorf.*"

"Excellent, young pup," Boldo said.

I felt Rousseau beam despite being called a pup. "I'm glad you can join us," he said.

We saw Boldo's bow and said goodnight to the Wanderer.

"I hope I get a chance to ask him what was making," Rousseau said. "It looked intriguing."

We were almost home. "I was curious about that, too."

As we turned onto our front walk, Rouss said, "At this point, I feel more like staying up here than moving to the East Bay."

"You're drawn to Marget's house, that amazing room and all the magic around the place."

"And the learning," he said, shoving his shoes onto shelves by the door.

I slipped off my boots, dropping in lavender and rosemary packets to make sure they stayed fresh.

Rousseau laughed. "Got some of those for mine?"

"You can help me make some. My lavender's finally taking off."

"I'd get my own place, of course."

"Up here? Wouldn't you miss the lively culture of Oakland? Occupy movements, and the like?"

"I might," he said, pondering as we locked up for sleep. "Maybe I could take some time before moving there. Look for work around here."

"Seems the wisest thing. Maybe there are some human-rights jobs you could also do part of the month. Make your own schedule. There's a Mayan population that could use your help."

"I like that idea," my son said, bending to kiss my cheek. "Night, Mom."

"Night, sweetheart. I hope the anticipation of tomorrow doesn't keep me awake."

"Me, too!" He scratched Oz's head on his way through the living room.

Chapter 24

I considered a relaxing bath but decided I'd better just put head to pillow and maximize sleep time.

My slumber was deep when it at last came to me. I woke with the morning light, startled to remember our plans. I pattered sleepily to the kitchen and made coffee. Other than putting on warm jackets and boots, there was little to prepare. I'd gathered harvest from the garden, including unusual herbs from Shelley's plot, and put them in a cloth bag to bring to Ylva.

As I added half-and-half to rich, brewed French roast, I felt Marget in my mind.

"Why don't I just join you when you're ready to go to Aelfwyn," she said.

"Of course." I sometimes had the feeling she and Ylva felt in competition. Was that what made her avoid going to Norway, or something else?

Rousseau appeared, yawning and rubbing his eyes. He made herb tea for himself, not being a caffeine type. He made his usual granola with fruit. I toasted us hearty raisin-nut bread.

Gulping the last of my coffee, I donned a thick Welsh winter cape. Cloth bag over one shoulder, I stood, ready.

Rousseau cleaned his dishes and pulled on the sweater

we'd picked out. "What do we do now? Do we need to put out extra food for Oz."

"We'll only be gone maybe twenty minutes in this time, even if we stay there five days. That's usually been my limit."

"Wow. That's … hard to fathom."

"I think I'll ask Ylva to help make sure we get there, though." I gave her a mental call.

She appeared in our hallway, head brushing the ceiling.

"Oh, you actually came!" I said.

Rousseau's mouth dropped open.

"Come." She spread her arms and encompassed us both in a hug.

We entered the *beyond*, briefly, with its utter darkness, then stood on her hillside.

Three children of differing heights ran to us and buried themselves in Ylva's long red coat, peeking out at Rousseau who gazed at the high-peaked houses backed by dramatic mountains.

Duff ambled downhill toward us. I'd never seen him look so contented. In the past, he'd appeared lonely, angry, sometimes jovial. Now he just seemed at home. He hugged me, then rested a hand on Rousseau's shoulder. "Glad t' see ye feelin' better," he said with sincerity.

"Thanks for helping me get back." Rousseau's eyes were bright with the travel and alpine air as he looked up at the immense red-haired man.

The residents of Ylva's village came and went between houses in layered clothing, dark with red or green accents, fur hoods, broad belts, legs wrapped. And for the moment, we felt safe.

"Will you come into my home?" Ylva asked. "I have a hot drink ready. We can plan."

Rousseau stepped forward, anxious to see inside the intriguing houses with their flares and peaks. We followed her and Duff into the narrower column at the base. My son stared around at the combined workroom and storage at this first level before we climbed the central stairway into the clean, spacious living quarters. More windows were uncovered so that summer light rayed in, forming laser-lines on the floor.

"I love this place," Rousseau said, gently touching carved animals on a sideboard.

Ylva looked pleased as she brought a steaming pot from the fireplace and set it on the high table. Duff distributed mugs.

The furniture, built for tall people, would add to the home's attraction for my 6'4" son.

Ylva poured a dark liquid.

"Roasted grains?" I asked.

"Yes," she nodded. "Barley and rye. I discovered chicory in Normandy and always add that. I need seeds or seedlings to try to grow it in my shade house."

"I'd like to see that." I wondered how she overcame the unique challenges of these alpine heights to grow plants. "Where is it?"

Ylva pointed upslope behind the house. "I'll show you."

I tasted a pastry from a brightly glazed plate. "Mm. Buttery."

Rousseau tried one and waxed complimentary.

Then I got to the point. "We worked with Marget last night. She had thoughts about training Rousseau might also need, if you're willing. And some testing."

"Sounds intriguing." Ylva got up to refill the plate of rich goodies, then took her seat in the substantial wood chair, back colorfully painted, with a woven seat.

Rousseau picked up the narrative, "Marget thought if you could replicate Otho's mind, I might be able to stop him from pulling me to this time. Though even if I knew he was in my mind, I'm not sure how I'd stop him."

So humble. So charming. I beamed at my adorable son.

"If it can be taught, Ylva can help ye." Duff pushed an entire pastry into his mouth.

I asked Ylva, "Have you had a chance to further search Thorgisl's mind for Mora's location?"

Duff flinched hearing the name, and turned his blue-gray eyes on me.

"No. I considered using the amber stone for it. But I don't have enough sense of it yet to attempt that."

I explained to Duff, "I thought I caught an image of a place in Thorgisl's mind, connected to Mora. I'm pretty sure it wasn't in or around the fort. Ylva searched everywhere so Mora's not likely to be there. Boldo said he'd meet us and help, if we get any new clues."

"No one else sensed this location in his mind?"

"I don't think so. But they were all focused on finding the ship and the stone."

"We should ask Talaith."

"I've never connected with her outside of the Thirteen."

"We could find her easily enough. She's most like with her clan in their summer grounds."

I sent out a tentacle of thought to Boldo.

"Been feelin' my name bandied about," he said.

"Not surprising," I said. "Hope I didn't interrupt anything,"

"Nothing that can't take a pause," he said, standing and stretching.

I felt Rousseau join our minds. "What were you making yesterday?"

"When we last spoke? Boot makin' tools, from deer bone and melted-down copper. I can show you sometime."

"Thanks. I'd love that."

"Is Talaith with you?" I asked.

"She and Django be here with their child, aye."

"Have you asked her if she got a glimpse of Mora's location in Thorgisl's mind?" An odd thought came to me. Why would only I have seen it? Had he given it to me as a trap? He was used to being in my mind. "Maybe he was luring me somewhere? He might want another hostage as leverage for retrieving the power stone."

"You *are* having dark thoughts," Boldo said. "I did ask. Talaith caught no such memory in the Jutlander's mind. I'll see you soon." He parted from us.

"I wonder if it's unsafe to draw him away from his people, since he's clan leader now," I said.

"We need not worry about Thorgisl and his men attacking them. They are headed to our shores," Ylva said, without expression.

"What?" I said. "Coming here?"

"Of course. He seeks the stone. He has been testing my protections. He will not be content until he pursues it."

"They're approaching?" Rousseau asked, staring at her. "In boats? Across the water from Jutland? How long does that take?"

"A single longboat," Ylva said. "He has great confidence in his abilities and has perhaps fifteen men."

"What are you going to do?"

"Let's continue with our plans. They will not reach the shore and climb the mountain in less than a day."

"Okay," I said tentatively, unsure about that. "You don't think he might make winds to push the boat faster? Fly his men up the mountainside?"

"I will keep watch," Ylva said, and stood.

Duff descended to his workshop while Ylva led us upstairs. For the first time, I saw a comfortable bed chamber but couldn't see beyond it. A top room, walls covered in talismans of bone, metal, feathers, beads and stones. "We will work here briefly. We must go to the stone for the rest. I think Marget is right about that."

She used a dazzling repertoire of shielding and seeking methods on us. Some would require a deeper level of training, and ordeals, I sensed. Perhaps some initiations and toughening up, time spent in the wilderness with wild animals. For now, she imitated Otho's energy, then Thorgisl's, having my son and me each practice sensing their presence, then shutting them out, blasting them away if necessary.

Afterward, I felt much better about my boundaries. She took down a few objects from shelves and packed them in a satchel. We put on jackets and left her home.

"Where are we going?" Rousseau asked.

"Where I have the stones."

A cone of silence moved with us and was glad to have Ylva's strength providing it. My skills being new, it still exhausted me to hold a protective sphere for long.

When we reached the back of her house, she pointed out a shade-house structure built into a slight gulley. I longed to go inside and explore but that could wait.

We climbed. The high altitude dizzied me so that a few times I rested my hand on a rock or tree to regain equilibrium.

"You okay?" Rouss asked.

I nodded and pushed on, giving him a wan smile.

A half hour took us over a rise—I was fairly sure they'd move much faster without me. Ahead, an enormous slab of granite formed a steep drop at the edge of a wooded glade.

STRANGE ALLIANCES

A narrow waterfall cascaded from a stone outcrop high above. We stepped onto the granite shelf at the far end from the falls. Ylva lifted an ivy curtain, revealing a cave.

Inside, in the blackness, she felt for a torch shoved into the wall and lit it with her mind. She led Rousseau and me into a tunnel that at first slanted downward, then climbed. We wound around and split paths until I was sure that without her, I'd never find my way out. We turned sideways and slid ten feet, scraping along a narrow space between walls. She and my son had to duck their heads to enter the room at the end.

A stone oval towered at the center of the cavern. Ylva wedged the torch into a crack, then stopped before the monolith, chanting. She cut her hand and wiped the blood on the side over carved symbols. An opening appeared. In a crevice rested the amber-colored power stone, the size of a football.

She drew a finger along the cut on her palm and it instantly healed.

Rouss watched in awe.

"While here, we'll test as you suggested, as though Otho wielded the stone—though it more likely wields him." She sniggered. "Then we're taking it with us."

"Out of its protection here? Do you think that's wise?"

"He will not expect it to be back near his fort," she said. "Your planned journey to Jutland to rescue Mora gave me the idea."

"He'll be here coming after it and we'll be back in his home territory with it," I said, frightened at his possible reaction, yet relishing the picture of his disappointment. "Do you think he'll sense it being moved?"

"Duff constructed a container that will muffle the stone's energy. We will have a ceremony tonight."

"You'll come with us?" I felt childishly dependent, hoping she'd say yes.

"I will. Of course." She removed a strange leather pouch, thickly layered and firmly constructed in a sort of hat shape. She enclosed the stone in it, fastening a wooden clasp so that it now resembled a ball for some primitive sport. This she set carefully into the backpack and reslung it on her back.

"We go," she said, ducking and sliding quickly along the slice of cavern.

Chapter 25

After that, her strides were so long I had to trot to keep up. Rousseau ambled behind me, quiet, contemplative, I thought. Nervous? He'd had a terrifying experience related to the stone.

The return trip to Ylva's home took much less time. It was downhill and we knew where we were going. We climbed to her roost and sat on thick-folded mats. She drew the stone from its casing and quietly held it for a moment, mumbling, before reverently uncovering it.

I dared not brush the stone and hoped Rousseau wouldn't either. Having it in the room made me uneasy; a strange energy came off of it, dripping nervousness into my intestines. A subtle play of light and shadow moved within it.

She murmured, "This room has been mightily shielded, over decades. Yet the stone has not yet been introduced here. I want to take in its energy properly so as not to introduce dangerous new elements." She spoke Old Norse as Rousseau and I watched. Her eyes rolled back so that only the whites showed.

I glanced at my son. He gave a slight nod, keeping his eyes on her, fascinated. I wanted to take his hand but hated to interrupt.

"*Ætlan*—hold the intent," Ylva remonstrated in an out-of-body voice.

Then I knew she wanted my help. I ignited my brand, my rings pressed together in my lap. I felt swept into a void.

Tall, masked beings chanted, stepping high around a fire. Some wore headgear resembling animals. I circled the bonfire with them, moving with the flow of the dance, humming low. Rousseau, in front of me, did the same. My heart jumped to see my son there with us. We marched under a night sky packed with stars. One fell, then another. I had to force myself to breathe deep and steady, it was so unearthly.

Sparks rose into blackness. The fire crackled in loud snaps. The Otherworld beings emitted hoarse, guttural chants.

In another instant, we sat once more in Ylva's eyrie.

"Good." She nodded. "The spirits have accepted you both."

I sat wordless, breathless.

She set the stone into a leather hammock and lit incense. "Rousseau, imagine yourself in your daily life. In Boston?"

"I'm moving to the West."

"But you return there soon?"

"Yes. To pack."

"Let's start there. That's where you were taken. Close your eyes, breathe slow and deep. Imagine yourself in that apartment, going about your normal business."

Rousseau did as he was told, resting his hands loosely on his thighs.

"I will enter your mind in a way I think will resemble Otho. Be aware."

Rouss' expression changed to a frown.

"What does it feel like?"

"Like Otho," he said. "I don't think I noticed before. Just maybe thought it was weird. Now it feels invasive. But I could swear he was nearby."

"Now I'm going to enter with the intention of bringing you to me," she said. "I will not be in that other world but I will make you feel its atmosphere."

Rouss looked worried. Nausea stirred in my gut. He would be imagining suffocation.

"Okay," he said, barely audible.

"Could you detect that?" Ylva asked.

"I did. It feels like a new part of my mind is opening. Are you helping me?" he asked.

"Yes," she said. "I'm stirring those thought places to encourage awareness."

"Thank you."

"You're welcome. Now, get very solid in yourself."

He wiggled his back and set his shoulders.

She touched the stone. I saw struggle on his face.

"You felt it. I might have drawn you then. I'm going to teach you to keep from being pulled against your will. You will have to throw the intrusion out. We must build a powerful image that you will use. What is the strongest force you can imagine?"

"Um. Maybe a catapult? And then a gate dropping. Like a fast one. A sort of guillotine-gate?"

"It will have to drop all the way around you. I'm going to help give it reality."

They worked. I did not enter my son's mind, reluctant to disrupt the training in any way. I would have to learn this at another time.

First he scowled, then grimaced. Once he depressed his shoulders, yanked his neck to the side. I gripped my hands until they ached.

At last, Ylva sat, releasing my son.

Rousseau opened his eyes. He seemed distant until he settled into our presence.

"You've done well, Kayson."

I realized, after a moment of thought, that she'd called him Kay's son. I liked it. I longed to gather him in my arms; he looked ragged, but a proud spark had formed in his eyes.

"Can you sense where Thorgisl and his men are?" I asked.

She touched a finger to the stone. "It's almost an insult to an object of this power to use it for such elementary divining." But her eyes shone with the contact. "They're approaching our shore. We're a long march from there, once they hit land."

"He can't transport the men up here? What *are* his abilities?" my son asked.

"Mind control. Depleting someone's powers if he has them captive. Giving disease spells," Ylva named. "He's working on knowing the objects he's collected. Portation takes a great deal of energy. It cannot be done alone. And he will not work with others. He does not trust others who have magic. They have to secure their boat. Thrizzle will need to put an incantation spell. Taking memories."

A narrow window faced down on the single street of her village. Preparations were being made: barricades set up at the ends of the road, windows boarded. Ylva's people were dressed for war.

"I'd lose no time in making the planks of the boat pull apart and not seal back together by any power he knows, but I believe we need to face him or we will only put off what is inevitable. Here he has less soldiers than at his own fort."

I tried to smile but felt the corners of my mouth pulling down. Here was my son, in the middle of a war.

"Don't worry, *Fraendi*," she said. "I have no concern about this lot. Now, Rousseau, I will imitate Thrizzle entering your mind."

"You call Thorgisl Thrizzle?" Rousseau quirked a smile. He looked tired, but prepared himself, loosening his neck and shoulders.

With increased daring, I put myself in the periphery of his mind as Ylva sent a simulation of Thorgisl's mind, then Otho, then Otho-plus-stone, for him to detect and ward off.

"Whoa." Ylva threw herself backward. "That packed a good punch, lad." She beamed as she got up. "I'll test you unexpectedly now and then during our trip." She left the room, thumping down the stairs.

We stood. I wrapped my arms around Rouss for a quick squeeze. He brushed my hair with his cheek. Then we followed Ylva down the stairs and outside.

Duff, in the front, held out his hand. "I'll carry it for now." Ylva handed him a carryall with the carefully stowed stone. He slid the straps onto his shoulders and settled it.

"How are you with its energy?" she asked.

"You know I'm immune to most things," he said gruffly. *Just not the Ronglut*, I thought.

"A rock on a rock." Ylva squeezed his arm fondly. "I'll get our coats and a bag of food."

"I brought you some fresh vegetables and herbs," I said, remembering.

"I wondered what was in that sack." She climbed ahead of us to the first floor. "Thought I smelled chives."

She picked up and rummaged through my cloth bag that had lain in a corner by the coats.

"Do you think Rousseau'll be warm enough tonight in this sweater?"

Ylva slid her fingers beneath one cuff of the knitted garment. "Good outerwear. I will give him a high-necked shirt and long johns to wear under. You might want some, too." She clomped up to her bedroom.

It seemed wise. "What about bedding, on our trip?" I called.

"We'll improvise, if we stay that long," she said, coming down the stairs with an armload of warm clothing.

Rousseau and I outfitted ourselves with mittens, knit hats, and thick socks. We came back down to the ground floor.

Duff wore an overcoat draping nearly to his ankles. "There are boots in here. One of Ylva's youngest son's should do the trick." He handed some to Rousseau.

I joined Ylva in the thinning sunlight.

"Did you get any answer from Talaith?" she asked.

I checked for Boldo in my mind and asked about Talaith. Then I felt Talaith enter my mind. "Greetings. Aelfwyn, Kyna and I have searched Thorgisl's mind and tickled a thread but can't get quite deep enough. Me thinks mayhap the Norwigi can go some-ought deeper."

Ylva slipped into our conversation. Talaith showed her the area. We were in Thorgisl's mind as he stood on shore. When with Ylva's spirit, I only felt able to tiptoe there undetected.

She and I slowly, softly, melted through the icy wall, feeling his malevolence, his anger toward the woman who could shield him from the whereabouts of the stone. Now he knew who had the stone and where it was, and his hatred lingered. And there it was. A forested place. I could not know the exact coordinates but Ylva did.

We slipped out as smoothly as we'd entered and gave the location to the others: Talaith, Boldo, Duff.

"Do you think he sensed us?" I asked. "He might move Mora."

"No."

Duff and Rousseau joined us.

"I've given the location to the Ronglut," Ylva said, flooring me.

"What? After their trickery? Duff hasn't told you?"

"I think we might need them. You don't think the Ronglut are too much for me, do you?" Ylva asked. "I know them. They owe me a favor."

"I don't trust them," I said.

Duff said, "They have long ties to Mora."

"Then why did they treat you the way they did?" I felt my emotions rising.

Duff laid a huge warm hand on my shoulder. "Let's talk more about it."

"We'll meet ye there," Talaith said.

"You're coming?" I asked.

"Boldo and I. Of course."

The Ronglut had tricked us. But I liked the size and strength of our group if Thorgisl followed us. Ylva's reasoning was sinking in. "You expect Thrizzle there?"

Ylva announced, "The stone will draw him."

I opened my mouth to protest but she went on, "I've duplicated the vibrations of the stone in another object, which I will send elsewhere to throw him off. Shall we?"

We held hands, the four of us—two red-haired giants, my tall son, and my 5'7" self.

Chapter 26

The location was in Southern Jutland, not far from *Geestendorf*; I knew this from Ylva's mind. We stood in a copse at twilight. I felt sure it was the right place but saw no clue of where Mora might be hidden.

Talaith and Boldo appeared. We searched. Soon Ylva gave a low whistle like a bird call, and pointed through the trees toward a slanted, wood door so overgrown I never would have detected it.

Suddenly, we were surrounded by Ronglut, adorned in elaborate weaponry. One burly man stepped forward. "I greet you," he said formally. He'd been among the group of men who'd carried Duff into the Brocken.

"*Haila.*" Ylva spoke in the Goth tongue. "Well met."

I stared at her. "Like hell they are," I thought.

"Have you investigated the area?" Ylva asked, taking charge. "Has Thortisl posted guards? I see none."

A Runglut with pierced bangle in one ear, the front of his black hair slicked into a topknot, spat. "He believe them ornament keep y'out."

"Did it keep you out?" Ylva looked bemused.

"A-ya. Can't go in that circle 'round th' door," he said, rolling his r's.

I stepped closer. Sure enough, a barrier stopped me

several trees away from the door, which appeared to seal off a mine shaft. I glanced at Ylva. She disappeared.

Duff frowned, looking around. Talaith and Boldo agitated, feeling their way along the invisible barrier, all the while eying the Ronglut suspiciously.

"I'm sure Ylva will figure it out," I mind-spoke to Boldo.

The air stirred behind us. Thorgisl appeared with several of his men—burly, wearing weaponry strapped over furs.

"Thought to trick us." His ominous eyes pinned on Duff's pack.

Ylva reappeared. "We go now." She sent the message into our minds.

The Ronglut moved between us and Thorgisl's thugs. They were long-time enemies. I caught this thought from several on both sides.

I did not see Mora. Boldo and Talaith crouched for action. Ylva grasped my hand and Duff's. I grabbed Rousseau's. Seeing this, Boldo held onto his sister and Rousseau.

In that instant, pain struck me and I dropped to my knees. I saw a flash from Ylva toward the Jutlanders before we disappeared in a shimmering field of light.

Seconds later, we fell in a heap on Ylva's mountainside, gripping our bodies in pain. I checked Rousseau. He gave me a thumbs-up though he remained doubled over.

"I thought Thrizz couldn't transport people," he gasped out, to Ylva.

"Must have learned a new toy," she grumbled, rubbing her side.

No one seemed bloodied. I checked under my shirt and found an ugly burn mark. I straightened up, testing.

"What about Mora?"

"She is in my home," Ylva responded. "I sent her there. Thrizzle thought no one could find her, or get in, or take her out."

"I want to see her," Talaith said.

Ylva checked the beach, many miles away. We saw what she saw. Ylva's countrymen and -women surrounded him and his soldiers.

We ran to Ylva's home.

Still sharing Ylva's sight on the beach scene, a clash of weapons, combined with explosions of magic, rent the air. Ylva's folk, of the Jotunheimen mountain range, were powerful. But something else was happening on that shore. Fire came from above, pouring down around Thorgisl and his men, ushering them to their boat. Thrizzle couldn't seem to combat the fire. It shot in gouts at him and the others with him, singeing clothes, hair. The Jutlanders jumped into their longboat and pushed off.

Thorgisl's face, narrow, smoothly shaven to a goatee at the tip of his chin, shoved its way into our vision. "This is far from over," he growled.

Ylva shut him from her mind and he disappeared from ours as well.

I knew he'd be back, with the stone and Mora in our possession. Ylva knew as well, and people set watch posts from the sea to their mountain village.

"Will you make their boat come apart?" I asked.

"Probably," Ylva said. "He'll have enough magic to get them to their shore, I imagine, though not happily." Her mouth twitched.

"Where is she?" Boldo asked.

Ylva led the way up the stairs. Seeing the direction, Boldo and Talaith dashed ahead to the eyrie. Ylva left us and went to speak to her townsfolk.

In the top floor room, the Wanderers dropped to their knees.

Mora lay, a fragile figure barely bulging a blanket. Her clothing stank, her hair was knotted in dreadlocks.

Talaith lay by Mora, crying. Boldo reached to touch the sallow cheeks. Mora's eyes remained closed. Her breaths came in shallow rattles and rasps.

I cried, too, as Rousseau and I watched the three Wanderers of the Silwy clan reunited. I backed out of the room. "I'll get hot water." I started down the stairs.

"I'll help," Rousseau said. "Do you think we should get Marget here? Or other healers? Aelfwyn?"

"I think Talaith's also a healer," I said.

On the main floor, Ylva was gathering clean rags. She handed Rousseau a covered pot held with an oven mitt. I went ahead up the stairs carrying the cloths and a cleaning bowl.

Rousseau stepped outside as Talaith removed Mora's filthy clothing, forced to cut some off. I set the clean cloths by her and gathered the wretched heap of apparel. Rousseau followed me downstairs.

Boldo crooned to his clan leader, tears in his eyes as Mora lay, eyes closed, rasping for air.

Ylva passed us carrying a nightgown and salve.

"Where should I put these?" I asked Duff, holding out the filthy rags that had been Mora's clothing. He led me to a back room near the bottom stairs, clearly for washing.

"How is she?" he asked.

I gave him a picture from my mind as I dumped the heap on a counter.

We sat in the living area. Duff buried his face in his hands, then exploded to his feet and paced. "The bastard."

"I don't know what we can do to help," I said.

"We mun prepare t' fight. She were his bargainin' chip for th' power stone."

"Why didn't he try to make the trade sooner?" I asked, voice hoarse. "She was there so long. I can't imagine."

"Ylva regrets not finding her. She can usually locate anything. Anyone."

My son sat by me, worried.

I took his hand. "I think I'll go back up and see if I can help."

"Should I come?" he asked.

"I may not stay long. Why don't you try to rest here. It's crowded up there."

Duff sat by Rousseau. I heard them speaking quietly as I started up the stairs.

Talaith stroked Mora's face with a wet cloth and worked on washing the rest of her. Unclean clothing and lack of bathing had left sores all over the old woman. Ylva administered salve that had astringent smell, helping to replace other less appealing odors.

She looked up at me. "I don't know how long she's been feverish. It's not good."

Mora lay limp, as though deflated, skin over bones.

"I'm going to call to Marget," I said.

"We should get Kyna and Aelfwyn as well," Talaith said.

I heard voices downstairs. Soon the room was filled with witches. I scooted to the wall to make way.

Ylva had formed a fire that hovered over a heavy metal plate. Rousseau appeared in the doorway and crept into the corner near me and Boldo.

Marget had brought a pouch packed with herbs. Kyna and Aelfwyn, likewise, bore bulging cloth bags slung over their shoulders.

Having finished washing and tending Mora's raw spots, then covering them with clean cloths Marget put the fresh nightgown on her, propping her against Talaith like a ragdoll.

Ylva returned and folded her body to squeeze in near Mora's head.

Aelfwyn asked, "Are the sores from neglect? Or torture?"

To my surprise, Mora cleared her throat weakly and answered in a croaky voice, barely audible, "Both." She reached out a crab-like hand and Aelfwyn, her long-time partner in magic, took it. "At first he tried to …" she whispered, "get information I did not have. At … last—" She coughed weakly. "At last, he gave up and sent me to the mine shaft, to die, I suppose."

"Why did he not try to make the trade for the stone sooner?" I asked, looking from Ylva to Mora.

Ylva looked stricken. "He did try. I was so sure I could find her."

"That's only been days, though, that you've had the Stone. She's been captured for months. He thought she could draw Otho or find the Stone."

"It hasn't been months, Ceirwen." Aelfwyn turned her hawk-eyes to me. "It be only weeks since ye were his hostage. Ye be thinkin' o' yer own time."

"I'll give her broth." Marget took a jar from her voluminous bag, dolloped some in a cup and held it to Mora's lips. The old woman sucked some in, coughed.

"They've been feeding you?" I asked.

"Someone brought food," she said hoarsely. "My thanks. Don't believe I know you."

Marget introduced herself.

I asked Ylva, "What was it like in the mine shaft?"

"Dark, drafty." She gave me a mental picture of a pallet with a tattered blanket, a fetid pot for waste.

Boldo picked up the image from me and grimaced. He crawled to his aunt and stroked her hair.

Talaith patted her legs, tears rolling and dropping. "Aunt, he had you at the fort at first?"

"Way deep, under the catacombs." She breathed the words.

Ylva frowned. "I searched everywhere. I don't usually miss what's hidden."

"He had it walled with stones of a strange vibration," Mora said weakly. "Or it might ha' been in a different dimension, one with a terrible quality about it. Much as I hated the bitter cold mine shaft, I was relieved to leave the place under the fort where I could sense it." Mora's eyelids dropped shut, her mouth slack.

"I know many worlds," Ylva mumbled.

Aelfwyn said, "We need to make plans. Thorgisl won't leave this alone. He wants the Stone. I fear he'll harm your people, Ylva. I'm sorry we've got ye involved."

"It affects us all, one such as him. He must not have a power like the Stone. It yanked Otho to another world, ship and all, made him crazy with greed. The trouble belongs to everyone."

Marget drew a clear crystal ball from her bag and peered into it. "They have returned. They're sneaking along the shoreline."

"We need to truce," I said. "Are you sure we shouldn't give him the Stone?"

Rousseau spoke up. "Why did we take the Stone with us? Why didn't we just leave it where it was hidden?"

"I thought to draw Thrizzle away. I did not know he'd mastered transporting himself and others."

"If he has, why isn't he sending himself and his men up here?" my son asked, reasonably. "He can feel the Stone wherever it is?"

"I think he only sees it sometimes," I said. "Like when he saw the ship disappear. He'd been furious not knowing where Otho was. Then he saw his ship approaching. And suddenly it disappeared."

Ylva unfolded her seven-foot frame and stood. "He does not leave the shore because I have something guarding the air from there to here."

"The fires?" Rousseau asked.

"Yes, lad."

"Where's the Stone now?"

"Duff has returned it to its keep."

I remembered how it was the blood on her hand that opened the compartment in the rock monolith. "He can get to it, too."

"Only he," Ylva said, stepping to the doorway.

Talaith took her place at Mora's head. "Let's let her sleep. Perhaps when she wakes, I can get more broth into her."

Kyna and Marget remained while Boldo, Rousseau, and I trooped downstairs after Ylva. When we reached the landing, I saw Galfride standing with Duff in the center of the room.

I stared. He gave me a nod, then Rousseau.

"Ah, a new guest." Ylva straightened to her full height, frowning.

I didn't realize Aelfwyn had followed us until I heard a low growl in her throat behind me.

"I come in peace," he said.

Once acknowledged, Ylva ignored Galfride. "Let us gather and discuss now. I will also need to meet with my people."

The room, boarded, had a fort-like feeling. Lanterns were lit. We sat on cushions around the main room. Together we built a column that protected and silenced our words and thoughts from outside.

"What would this truce entail, Kay?" Ylva asked.

"A neutral zone for the Stone?" I asked. "Maybe with a guard made up of members from each of the ... peoples?" I looked around for opinions.

There were thoughtful nods, scowls of concentration.

"I need to find the source of the stone," said Ylva. "Then I might start to know its nature. Until I know that, I do not trust its influence. I feel it has a pull on anyone who comes under its power."

"Including Otho," Rousseau said.

"Yes, or me, or you," Ylva said to my son. "I will speak to Thorgisl and ask for some time. Then we will come to an agreement."

"He will want something in return," I said.

"We will see."

We released the protective column and stood.

"We can use these." Galfride brought out his gadgets—the ones he'd used to make Ansgor into a hologram, to show his location. They'd also transported an entire Traveler caravan. Those had been occasions when she'd been grateful for their power. But for whatever reason might he use them?

Ylva nodded approval. He set them up around her.

We watched as she appeared as a hologram on the beach near Thorgisl while also standing in the flesh by us.

"We wish for you to leave these lands. We ask for seven days. Then we come to an agreement regarding the Stone."

"Why should I not merely take it from you?" The tall,

thin mage wore his usual dramatic black and gray clothing under a perfectly crafted cloak. He wore no weapons; he did not do his own fighting. He could apparently achieve a sort of glamour for he appeared almost as tall as Ylva.

"This land is guarded, as you have seen," Ylva said. "But I dislike bloodshed. I find warfare a tedious and wasteful enterprise."

"You cannot guard all places at all times. There are others I can take." I felt his serpent eyes on me, even though I was far from them, in Ylva's home. Then he seemed to reconsider. "Very well. On one condition."

"And what is that?" Ylva asked, wary.

"I hold Rousseau as long as you hold the Stone."

Ylva said, "That is out of the question."

"I'm told you have Mora." A tic twitched by Thorgisl's eye, revealing the extent of his irritation that he'd been outtricked.

"We are ministering to her after your atrocious treatment, yes," Ylva hissed.

Thorgisl waved this off as though she were insignificant as a sand flea. "You have stolen my bargaining piece. You will give me another."

"You are a trying little man. You should be glad I don't destroy your fort and all in it. I have allies in more realms than this." Ylva's voice had taken on an ominous, threatening tone. She stood imperious in her long red coat, its metal symbols clanking when she moved. She studied Thorgisl like a repellent bug she might decide to squash.

I like bugs better than this eitr-ormr, she thought to me. Poisonous serpent.

Rousseau spoke. "I will stand as collateral."

Chapter 27

I stared, sick to my stomach, and shook my head vehemently.

He will not go without me," Galfride said.

A terrible dread struck me then. How convenient, that Galfride had shown up. Was he in this with Thorgisl?

"This is absurd. We will not contemplate such a barter," Aelfwyn hissed.

"It *is* best," Rousseau said. "Let me do this. So they won't hurt anyone else." He spoke directly to Thorgisl. "You promise to hurt no one if I come to you now?" I realized he'd made himself visible to the Jutland mage.

"We have to shorten the time," I whispered to my son. "Four days. We shouldn't try to stay in this time longer."

Ylva said to Thorgisl, "We will shorten the time to four days. You will harm no one. You will treat Kayson as royalty, as your own if you had begotten children. Galfride will remain with you and in sight of Rousseau at all times. Those are our terms."

Thorgisl's lips twisted, his eyes pinched.

What does he intend for my son? I did not want this. It was not the deal I'd pictured.

"Done. Give me the boy now." He seemed to value my son as much as the Stone. What did he perceive in him?

Rousseau bestowed a long hug on me. "It'll be okay," he whispered. I shook my head against his chest, willing him to change his mind.

Marget came down the stairs and slipped her crystal ball into his hand. He put it in his sweater pocket, nodding thanks to her.

Galfride gathered his instruments and threw an arm around Rousseau's shoulders. The two men disappeared, and reappeared on the beach.

My throat clenched as I now watched with Rousseau's sight.

"I love you, Mom. I'll stay connected as much as I can," he thought to me.

"Don't let him fool with your memories," I said. To Ylva, "Make sure Thorgisl knows that no harm includes not fooling with his mind."

She relayed this to the vile wizard.

With my brand charged, I connected with Galfride.

"Yes, Kay?" he said, snarky.

"Thorgisl likes to mess with people's memories. Can you keep him from doing anything like that? Are you able to ... keep watch, really?"

"I am capable of this, Rousseau's Mother," he responded with a smirk.

Around them, preparations were being made to leave. Men marched from both ends of the beach.

"I thought you didn't like going into Thorgisl's fort," I said to him.

"Not when he's there," was his answer.

"But you'll do it for my son?" I didn't want to push my luck in having a guardian for Rousseau, but felt suspicious of his intentions, as always. *Was it possible Thorgisl and Galfride were in league, after all?* I had to stop this line of thinking. "Please be careful," I ended with, hoping sincerity would be the best last message.

"And you," he said, surprised and sardonic.

Ylva shook my arm. I tasted the salt of tears on my lips. The Nordic woman pulled me into a bear hug and I soaked the front of her cloak. "We will keep close watch at all times. I did not bluster weightlessly when I said I have allies in more realms than this. I have a dragon quite close to his fort, cloaked, undetectable."

"Seriously?"

"Yes. There are forests on the east side of Jutland. Now, for planning to go to that other world. I did not want to take your son after his recent ordeal, but might you want to accompany me?"

"I had promised to help Marget with Ian's memories, to work with them at Kyna's Tower." I had planned to get my down jacket from the cave as well, and to try to sleuth how the stone got traded, investigating the tavern of the amber-necklaced waitress.

"We can help with Ian's recall later," Ylva said.

I looked around the room. Touching Ylva's wrist, I said, "Can we walk a bit?" I wanted her to know about Otho and the cove, the giant and the dwarf. She had said it was important to understand the origins of the stone. I thought this might be where to start.

As we stepped from the base of her home, people removed barricades and unboarded windows. There was an air of relief. But I could not share it. I reached for my son's mind. He stood on board the ship, over dark seas.

We strolled along the narrow road that ran between homes. Ylva nodded at her folk.

A woman waved from a doorway. Ylva nodded to her in recognition, or assurance. "Go on," she said to me.

"One of my son's stories took Otho to a cove where he rowed to shore with two men. They entered a tavern; the same one I saw in Ulf's mind." I described the woman with the amber beads.

She chuckled as I shared Ulf's sex fantasy with the amber-bead woman.

"Otho and his men sat together for a short while, then I think Otho made himself invisible because the other men don't even seem to see him go."

"You sound like you saw the scene."

"When I read my son's writing of these tales, I do see them. I experience them as if I'm there—the sounds, the smells."

"No ordinary tales, then."

"Unlike any others. Otho exited the back. A sort of…" I squinted up at her in the dim moonlight, trying to gauge her height against the man I'd considered a giant. "…a very tall man, bigger than you, and a dwarf joined him. The three walked down the dark alley. I've suspected that Otho was accepting the stone there. The town, I'm pretty sure, by some of their thoughts, is *Geestendorf*, where Germania meets the south part of Jutland."

"Would you recognize the tavern?" she asked.

"Yes, I think so. I've seen it clearly. I can go over the letter with you, too. Maybe you'll see everything as I do."

"You brought it with you?"

I make such assumptions about having phones and electronics available. "Oh. No. I'll have to get it. It might also be good to have Rousseau with us."

"And Otho."

I stared at her. *Was she joking?*

"Don't be so surprised. I administered to him and his men. They think quite fondly of me now."

"I'm sure they do. But…"

"Best to hear it from the horse's mouth? Isn't that what you say?" She paused. "I've wondered why you say that?"

"Maybe because if horses could talk, they'd talk about the torment people put them through."

She nodded soberly.

"Do you know where Otho is now?" I asked.

"I could find him easily."

"Do you think the Stone is safe?" I asked

"My apprentice is nearly my equal now. He is in charge of guarding the Stone. I have several other safeguards around the cave that I will not go into in detail."

"Someday I'd like to know all those details, but as you say, not now." I imagined being under her tutelage, as apprentice, or any underling. I liked the idea. "Will we call to Otho? Or go to him?"

"I think we will go to *Geestendorf* and call him to us there."

"Why do you think he drew my son to him when he had the Stone? Have you gotten any sense of that?" I had little hope.

We arrived at the end of a road that dipped abruptly downward. On the upslope to our right were several conical structures around a clearing with a fire pit.

"Is that where you carry out your ceremonies? I believe this is where I first saw you."

"Yes. And where I first saw *you*, at least up close," Ylva acknowledged. "I still remember the sight of you, on the Brocken. I had to pull you to me, to get a better look." She smiled, seeming pleased with herself. "I like having you in my life."

I swelled with happiness. "I seem to take a lot of your attention, though," I apologized.

"It is important work. There are many answers we need. Are you ready to go to Jutland again?"

"Yes," I said, a glimmer of hope rising. The idea of being close to where my son was held hostage brought my spirits up considerably.

"Then we will prepare," she said, and we started back toward her home.

I took in crisp alpine breaths and tried to massage away the ache in my chest that threatened to bring tears at any moment, worrying about Rousseau.

Before we entered her house, she put a hand on my arm. "He will be alright. I can feel your heavy heart."

I sighed. "Thank you." I bumped my head to her arm.

Duff was back at work outside, constructing something on a board across sawhorses. In the main room, Marget, Kyna, Aelfwyn, and Gwynydd partook in tea and snacks at the table.

We climbed the stairs. At the landing, we saw that Mora had been moved to the bedroom. Talaith and Boldo sat tending to her. Though her face still looked ghastly, she slept soundly, breathing better, under a thick stack of down quilts. I hoped tender ministrations, nourishing broth and sleep would get the healing started.

We descended back to the main room. I stepped to the window just as Hamelyn and Baird arrived. They glanced up, saw me and waved. I ran down to greet them.

Baird wrapped his arms around me. "Sorry I never came sooner, Dove."

I breathed in his scent, mixed with alpine air, my head resting on his chest. "No need to be sorry." But my throat knotted. Not being able to see him, separated by a thousand years, I seemed to have hardened myself to the longing that had plagued me a year before. But as soon as I was with him, the feelings overcame me.

"What's happened? I know some of it. They've taken your son hostage." He touched my chin, peered into my eyes.

I gave his waist a squeeze, nodded. Not wanting to burst into tears, I shifted to Hamelyn. We cheek-kissed. "Hello. Good to see you." A lump formed in my throat, unaccountable, maybe because he was Rousseau's age and height, resembling him slightly.

"Are the others inside?" he asked Duff who'd come up behind me. They hugged, brusque and fond.

"They are," I said. "We're amassing quite a crowd."

Duff gestured for us to proceed. Acting the host, he said, "Ylva will be happy you've come."

In the main room, all traded greetings.

Talaith and Boldo descended to join us. ""Marget's with Mora," Talaith explained.

After more greetings, Baird asked, "How'd this happen with Rousseau?"

"He went willingly," I said, throat tight. "Galfride's gone with them."

Baird looked baffled.

Aelfwyn sniffed. Kyna grimaced. Boldo shook his head.

I tried to explain. "Galfride offered. It seemed wise to have someone there, but no one else who could become hostage to Thorgisl."

Chapter 28

Ylva said, from the kitchen area, "Never give a foul tick like him the satisfaction of hearing his name spoken."

Baird huffed a laugh. "Wise."

I amended, "Ylva got a promise from *Thrizzle* to treat my son well. At least Galfride's a witness, maybe a help. I—" I stopped myself from naming my concern that Thorgisl and Galfride might be in league to get the Stone. What good would it do? Everyone there suspected the possibility. "Ylva has the fort watched night and day."

"We're all watching," Aelfwyn snarled.

I thought I detected a competitive tone. "Can I bring you tea?" I asked Aelfwyn.

Ylva held out a hot, full cup and I took it to the Welsh elder. She accepted, approving but never one to fawn.

"It's just for four days," I said, trying to shore up my own confidence, as I went on serving around the circle. Others served snacks that Ylva brought out; she'd made puffy cheese pastries alerted an appetite I didn't think I was capable of at the moment.

"Rousseau's gotten some training, with Marget and Ylva," I said. "I think he can sense unwanted entry into his mind and repel it pretty well now."

Aelfwyn and Kyna nodded approval, tasting the food and drink. I sat with my own.

Baird took one of my hands. "He'll be alright. We know where he be, and there be a great deal o' watchin'."

I had to smile at that, a one-sided tuck of the mouth.

"Ylva says she has—" I stopped. "Maybe I shouldn't say. He doesn't know it's there." I looked at Ylva.

"Best not," she said, popping a pale-yellow pastry neatly into her mouth.

We heard the sound of flutes from above and I realized Hamelyn and Boldo must have gone up.

"Healing music," Baird said. "Just the ticket. I'm going up and see Mora." He squeezed my hand and stood. Of course he'd brought his harp. Its bag stood by the entry. He lifted it and took the stairs by twos, calling behind him, "Are you coming?"

"I'll come soon."

Marget emerged onto the landing and whispered with Baird.

Ylva brought cheese and bread to the table and sat. I took a stool beside her. Marget joined us.

"Ylva and I need to do a bit of work in South Jutland," I said quietly to the Cornish witch.

"You go. Do what you must," Marget responded. "These are urgent matters."

Kyna, Aelfwyn and Talaith sat huddled together, talking in earnest whispers in the sitting area.

I squeezed Marget's hand across the table.

"If Mora's well enough, I'll return with Aelfwyn and Kyna," she said.

"To talk about returning Ian's memories?" I asked quietly, glancing at the other women. They were deep in conversation. "Judging from how she heals others' minds, I'm sure Ylva can work well with Ian's memory. Let's check on Mora."

We got up and started for the stairs.

"You're thinking I should hold off, not have Kyna and Aelfwyn's help?" she asked, as we climbed.

"Ylva could come and do it in our time. It would avoid the Cornish guild. And … maybe coming to his memories in the 21st Century, he'd have a better chance of adjusting. Even keep from Galfride's influence."

At the landing, we peered into the bedroom. Ylva sat by a sleeping Mora. We heard music from the room above: Boldo, Hamelyn and Baird.

"Want to walk?" Marget whispered.

We donned warm cloaks, trotted down the stairs, and stepped into the night.

Marget took my hand as we started up to the knoll next to the house. "I can't say how much I appreciate—how deeply I cherish your having given this such serious thought. I couldn't wish for a brighter, more well-reasoning friend."

The hills below were dark. I grinned as we stood gazing out from the hillock at myriad stars. We hugged, to be sharing this sight. I'd needed such a relieving moment.

Ylva smiled in my mind, as if she felt the affection, and joined it.

"I will do that, then," she said. "I will wait. Do you need me in Jutland?"

"I don't think so. Maybe just Ylva and I should go. Though of course I need you everywhere."

We started back toward the house.

"I'll tend to Mora as long as she needs," Marget said.

Ylva stood at the window looking down at us as we approached the house.

When we arrived on the main floor, the three of us went upstairs. I heard Baird's melodic voice singing a low, soft ballad. Hamelyn brought in harmony and, at the chorus, Boldo added his sweet tenor to the mix. I climbed to the eyrie to find them seated on soft folded pads in a circle. A magical fire burned at the center above the lead plate.

Baird made room for me and set aside his instrument, beckoning to the others to keep playing.

I whispered, "Ylva and I are going to Jutland soon."

"I must come," he said.

"I think we'll just slip there, the two of us, to go unnoticed."

"That great woman, go undetected?" he asked with a crooked smile, but he frowned. "Duff must go."

"I think we'll be … meeting one other person. I shouldn't perhaps say who."

His scowl deepened. "Such secrecy. Dove, we've had so little time."

"Let's have more of it. As soon as this business is done with." I squeezed his hand, rested mine on his leg.

In that moment, I felt that all was about to be resolved. That we would be safely settled, no one yanking anyone across time, my kids starting new lives on the West Coast. I kissed Baird's cheek and got up to check on the healing process.

"I believe she's strong enough for the next step—a full-on healing." Ylva had her hands on Mora's face.

We held hands and chanted. In mindspeak, Ylva requested that I put my hands on her shoulders and trigger my brand. Together we entered Mora's mind, the rest supporting us with their energy. Ylva began by exploring her blood. I slid along with her, now accustomed to this practice. I gave her strength without knowing exactly what she needed.

When we at last moved out of her, I thought I detected a slight glow in her complexion. Ylva got up slowly. Even she had tapped her resources to the limit. We left Mora sleeping again.

All gathered in the main room for more refreshments and a dark, restoring drink. Ylva and I made our good-byes. We stowed food in knapsacks. We piled on warm clothes, Ylva fastening on her long-hooded cloak with the animal appliques. We went outside.

"I have to get a few things." Ylva strode toward her ritual ground at the far end of town.

Baird ran down the stairs and joined me, straggling behind Ylva's tall figure, grabbing a few smooches along the way. Several others came out of the house and followed behind to see us off.

"I'll come t' ye in yer time after this," he said. "I know nothin' o' yer life now. I want t' feel us connected again."

"Both of my kids are moving back to the West Coast. I'll be able to see them much more often."

"That must make you happy," he said, pulling me close, arm around my shoulders.

"It does."

"You've had some adventures with yer son lately."

"That I have." I slumped, wanting to avoid thinking about him in danger. Thorgisl could be very cruel when he wanted something.

"You must be glad Sophie cannot be drawn to this time." He checked my face for agreement in the faint light of torches placed along the road.

"Yes and no," I said. "She's so envious. It's strange when a family is yanked apart, not being able to share the same experiences."

"You never know what the future holds," he said.

"That's true." I wondered if he now knew something that could be done for Sophie.

We caught up with Ylva. She had a cabinet open, part of a cone-shaped shelter standing on a wood pillar. Inside were talismans and tools. She pocketed several objects as Baird and I watched.

"I love this," Baird said, admiring the symbols carved and painted on the storage. "I want one of my own."

She closed the door and ran her hand in the air over it. "*Sitja læsa.* Thank you, bard of most magnificent music-making. We will leave from here." She bowed formally.

Baird bowed back, eyes amused and sad. I gave him a quick kiss, then stood by the woman, slipping my arm into hers and waved to the others, who'd stayed some distance away.

Ylva and I arrived in deep forest. I was glad for the shelter obscuring us. "Where will we meet Otho?" I asked. "You already arranged it?"

"Yes. Behind the tavern. It's not a long walk."

We started through the woods. She seemed to have a homing device within her for soon the trees thinned. We arrived at scattered houses along a rough road. Buildings grew tighter packed toward town. Ylva provided a globe of light, floating ahead, showing houses of wood, painted brick and thatching. When we heard the sounds of docks and the sea closeby, the raucus laughter of drinking men. We came to an alley and I recognized the tavern's back steps.

"So much for me being the one who needed to recognize the tavern," I said. "You brought us straight here."

Otho stood by the stairs, leaning against the wall, picking his teeth with something sharp. It was strange to see the scarred face in the flesh, having only encountered him from a safe distance, reading my son's stories.

He pushed from the wall. As he neared, threat wafted off of him, along with the briny smell of the sea. "So." He tucked the sharpened tooth-picker into a pocket. "My doctor." He held out his hand to Ylva, lifting only his eyes to her face, not wanting to crane his neck, I thought. "Is it me who will help you now?"

"I hope so." She took his hand and he bowed toward hers.

We moved up the alley.

"Can you show us where you got the Stone for Thorgisl? And who sold it to you?"

Otho stopped, sea-legs planted wide and obstinate. "I'll tell ye no such thang." He groped at his waist and rested his hand on a dagger hilt.

Ylva moved close to him, having no fear of the blade. "Sea captain, I have no interest in competing with your trade, nor in giving up your information to any other. I only need to find out essential information about that other realm."

"Ye can't go there. Air's no good," he said with finality.

Ylva took a deep, patient breath, then let it out. "I am not an ordinary person, Welsh Wanderer. I can adjust to bad air, along with many other things."

He lowered his voice. "Ye're no' thinkin…"

Ylva's brows lifted. She took me with her, deep into his mind. Together, we saw quickly that Thorgisl had set a trap for certain memory areas, in case anyone did just what we were doing. This would alert the Jutland mage. She had to act fast.

Chapter 29

Swiftly Ylva expunged the thoughts, any memory of her questions. Otho's face took on an expression of puzzlement. We detected no Thorgisl presence in his mind. So the mage had not been alerted. Yet.

"Hey, what are you doing here?" he asked, grinning. "How does it come t' pass that you're on these streets, Doctorin' Magic Worker? Ye belong in Norway, don't ye?"

"I do. I'm visiting. It's good to see you looking so fit and hearty. What might your business be here?"

Otho thought a moment. "I came t' —" His brow furrowed. He glanced at me. "Who be this?"

I had my hood up, shadowing my face, and stood slightly behind Ylva's shoulder, though he'd never actually seen me, as far as I knew; I knew *him* from my son's stories.

"She's my friend." *No one to worry about,* she thought into his mind. *Were you here to collect money, perhaps owed you by the giant and the dwarf?* she asked into his mind. *Somewhere along this alley?*

"That's it," he said. "Still have some … something t' exchange. Gotta …" He checked his pockets and a few leather bags that hung from his waist, clearly struggling to piece together his reason for being there. We continued down the alley with him. He stopped at a murky, odorous gap between buildings.

"Well, I'll bid ye ladies good day," he said. He pictured the door he'd enter. We saw it clearly.

"Good day, then," Ylva said.

I nodded politely, remaining as obscure as possible.

He picked his way along the furrow, retreating from us. Ylva stepped into shadows and turned us into spirit-mites. We caught up with Otho as he pounded on a door barely attached to its moorings, and landed on his coat.

A child-sized man opened the door a crack and peered out. "We expectin' yee?" he asked, squinting up.

Ylva automatically translated languages, partly by reading minds; we understood the stranger, whatever tongue he spoke.

"I have a proposition." Otho was a merchant and probably never lacked for bargaining ideas.

"Wait." The door shut and we heard a bolt slide to. Voices.

The opening widened for Otho to enter.

The inside was nearly as dark as out. The smell was worse.

In a packing room, lighted only by a guttering lamp, the giant man occupied a creaking chair that listed to one side. "Watcha got?" he growled, his voice a strangled sound, oddly high for his great size.

"I'll speak with the Trader, if ye don' mind," Otho said, planting his legs wide in that characteristic stance of stubborn resolve.

A voice, high, almost falsetto, drifted in from an unseen room to one side. "Yah come t' cheat me, sea-scoundrel?"

A crooked grin, foul and scheming, crept onto Otho's face, livening the scar as it twisted, bulging at the base near his mouth. He ambled into the adjacent space.

I suspected the smell here would have been unendurable had I not been a mite. Slowly a shape—was it a man?—formed in the light of a few candles, nearly melted away.

"Ye look like shit, sea-dog," said a mound of flesh with something resembling a face at the top.

"I'm humbled by your noticing, Worthy One," Otho said, giving a bow.

"Always were ugly as cuss." The mammoth creature spit into a can. "Why d' y' darken my door? Did I invite yah? I don't recall that."

Her voice had a strange burr—for I was leaning toward female now. In the dim light, it was hard to make out features but a hand reached back to scratch some unnamable place.

Ylva whispered, "Do not follow. I will be back."

Then I was a lone mite, clinging to a threadbare, velvet coat. The two bartered over a vile object unfamiliar to me by name or concept. A weapon, to be sure, but no ordinary knife.

Soon I felt Ylva's spirit return next to me. We rode Otho out of the dank, dreary hovel, and down the breezeway. Just before he entered the alley, we jumped onto muck-encrusted boards and hopped into a shadowy area. Obscured from eyes, we took our normal shapes. Ylva craned her head around the opening to see Otho re-entering the back of the tavern. We walked in the opposite direction.

"Did you go into her mind?"

Ylva was silent a moment, taking her long strides as I tried to keep up. "It was a strange mind, *Friendi*. Difficult to pick up thoughts. After some time, I found the part that knows the stone. She was made uneasy by my presence so

I left quickly. Her name is Shagfen. I found that much out."

"So, she was the trader of the stone?" I asked.

"She had some part in it," Ylva said soberly. "I found out something else."

"What was that?" I asked.

"She's been to the other world."

We passed along an opulent block, encountering serv-ants lugging baskets, and a few sellers who barked their wares. A man strode by, money bag jingling. His long robes of dark and light cloth, belted at the waist, reached his boots. A hat like a thin bread round perched on his head. Ladies with cloth head-coverings draping down to their shoulders chatted in a cluster. I had a feeling Ylva hid us with a glamour, for no one seemed to notice us. Then we were back to rickety shacks put together with scrap wood and hides. A woodcutter in rugged hide clothing passed with his ax. Ragged children raced by, dirty faced, yelling with their games. Back streets took us to the edge of town where buildings thinned into sparse forest and scattered dwellings.

"Could she be from there, do you think? Maybe she brought the stone here."

"It's possible. Your son might have been right about the oxygen. I thought I detected two hearts beating in Shagfen, but I wasn't there long and was focused on her knowledge of the stone. She's ill, though."

"Did you find out how to get back there?" I asked.

"I know how."

"Oh." Of course she did. "What about me being able to breathe? You said you could manage it. How? Give your-self a second heart?"

Ylva laughed. "I don't actually know yet. I planned to ask the stone. But now I might be able to find out from

Shagfen. Are you ready to check on Rousseau?"

"Yes. Of course." That was what I wanted more than anything at the moment, but I hesitated. "We were going to call Boldo here. I guess maybe we don't need him anymore. We found the stone merchant. But—"

"There's something else, isn't there? What is it?"

"It seems kind of paltry, and we don't have to take care of it now. It's just that—I left a very modern jacket in the cave where Duff was ill. I'm worried that such a thing shouldn't be here in the past to be discovered. I'd thought, if we were getting Boldo and Duff here anyway, they could help me find the cave and retrieve it."

Ylva put a hand on my head and smiled down at me. Her eyes went misty and Duff appeared in our hidden copse.

"Duff." I squeezed his fingers in greeting since we hadn't been apart all that long.

He gave me a sideways hug. "Ceirwen."

"Do you think you can find the cave you were in when I came to you, when you were sick? We're near the town where you and Boldo stayed?"

"*Geestendorf*. This is the place, is it? Hmm." He stepped through the trees. From the slight rise, we saw down over the town. "I might have t' get t' the waterfront, to the flea hole of an inn we stayed at. Then I could retrace my path out o' town."

I closed my eyes, hand on a tree to stay balanced, and searched for Galfride's mind. After the way he'd treated me in his cavern in the French Alps, I hated the thought that its resonance now came easily to me. But he was Rousseau's only guardian in this world right now. I felt Ylva with me and was comforted. She had more force.

She asked Galfride, "How are things going there in Jutland?"

"Thorgisl's enjoyin' yer son's company," he addressed me.

"Are you with him at all times?" I asked.

"Let th' boy crap in peace," he said, sardonic.

"Do you know what I could do to your wee gadgets?" Ylva asked testily.

Galfride sobered. "I'm wi' him whenever he's with Thorgisl. And know where he is, where either of them are, at all times. Does that ease your minds?" Even in thought-speak, the clipped, resentful tone came across.

"Thank you, Galfride," I said. Then I couldn't resist slipping into Rousseau's mind. "Are you okay?"

He thought back, "Yes, I'm fine, Mom. Don't worry."

I felt him straining to concentrate on whatever Thorgisl said without giving away our connection. Through his eyes, I saw Galfride and Thorgisl lounging as if they were all enjoying a pleasant natter. "Kiss, kiss," I said. "I'll see you soon," and crept out, Ylva retreating as well from Galfride's mind.

I tapped on Boldo. "Can you join us now?"

"Have been waitin' fer yer call." And then he stood before us. Duff slapped his shoulder. They hugged. Boldo greeted Ylva, then twinkled his eyes at me and gave both my cheeks kisses.

"We're goin' t' find the roomin' house we stayed in." Duff indicated the distant water. From our look out a' the woods' edge, we could make out boats and bustling movement.

"Not good memories," Boldo remarked. "Why d' ye want t' go there?"

"They want me t' trace my route to the hills and the cave where I hid," Duff explained. "Thought y' c'd help wi' this part."

"Ah," Boldo nodded understanding. "There be a lot o' eyes in this town. Mayhap the two o' us should go there, take a look-see, and return."

"I want to see it," I said. "And Ylva should go. She might pick up something."

"What are ye tryin' t' learn?" he asked me and Ylva.

"More about Thorgisl's motives," I explained.

His clan had been badly hurt by the Jutland mage. He, of anyone, understood the danger of not knowing what Thorgisl had in mind.

Ylva said, "I'll make us undetectable. We needn't pass through the town. Give me a sense of the rooming house location and I'll try to take us there." She stretched her arms around Duff and me.

I pulled Boldo in on my other side.

"I know a lonely, derelict wharf nearby." He sent us a picture, then took us there.

We stood in shadows, surrounded by pillars and the wash of the sea, or whatever waterway this was, leading out to the North Sea. The beginning of sunset gave us both light and shadow. The smell of seaweed, some rotting, carried powerfully on the salt air. Sea gulls cried shrilly. A pair fought over a crab near rocks covered in mussels.

"Let's keep in th' dark," Boldo suggested, leading the way toward a seafront road. "Ye've all shielded yerselves?"

We nodded, though I thought Ylva carried the bulk of that load.

Boldo stopped on the lee-side of a fisherman's shack. We skirted stacked crab traps and other detritus of the shore trades. Stepping onto the frontage road, we kept close to walls. As we rounded a bend, activity increased. Sellers called out wares, women with baskets shopped. Taverns lined the land-side.

STRANGE ALLIANCES

At a rough building with peeling paint, we stopped. I read the sign, *Meri Scûm* and looked around at the others, ready to laugh.

"I'm told it translates 'seafoam'," Boldo said with a snigger. "This be it. Now can we go?"

Chapter 30

Ylva, invisible, stepped onto the rough-planed porch of the *Meri Scûm* tavern, then entered through the front door. Her message came loud and clear in my head, and to the others: "Show me."

Reluctant, Boldo followed. I checked to make sure I was also transparent. I was. We scooted into the inn.

The noise of a full-swing tavern, with lively bar scene, assailed us. The rooms, with worn décor, reeked of old spilled beer and layers of sweat. Boldo floated, in spirit form and invisible, down a hall and up some stairs, grumbling into my head along the way. "Got t' come here t' this miserable place…"

"Sorry," I thought to him. "I guess Ylva wants to search for something."

"I can feel the Jutland arse-hole lurkin' and sensin' me here."

I gasped. *Might that be so?*

Boldo stopped in front of a door. Kick-in dents shredded the wood. We floated through the door like a pack of ghosts. A couple fornicated loud and lusty on the sagging bed. We snickered silently. Ylva floated around the room, taking in every scent, touching surfaces, as though no one else was there.

The woman on the bed, dress hiked up, turned her head in our direction, and said something to the hairy-butted fellow on top of her as if she might detect our presence. Ylva took her time, taking in some sensory details of which I had no clue. I urged her to hurry though neither of the sex partners seemed to noticed us.

"Is this the room where you and Duff stayed?" she asked Boldo.

"Aye. T'is," he answered, agitating to leave.

"Your blood was here." She pointed to a bare wall. "Three men," she said, as if she saw the scene as she touched the invisible stain. "Ronglut are involved."

"Ronglut?" Boldo asked, shaken.

"Are you sure?" Duff stared at his companion.

She nodded and indicated that she was finished. We left the room and descended back stairs to an alley behind. Trash dumped from overhanging balconies heaped. I was glad my spirit form only took in smells if I concentrated on that.

"I wouldn't ha' found th' room," Duff said to Boldo. "Wasn't sure which one, even which inn."

"Your bloodhound wife would'a," Boldo said, still twitchy from the whole encounter with memory lane.

"You lead now, love," Ylva said to Duff. "Try to remember how you got to the cave from here."

"I ran along this way." Duff strode with his tree-trunk legs to the end of the alley. A lane crossed, heading to the docks to our right. He turned that way. We followed. "I was sick and…" he pressed a hand against a warehouse as though imagining himself struggling with fever. Then he straightened, turning away from the water. "There." He pointed toward hills, studded with forest.

We could see hills, some farms in the distance.

Duff shook his head. "Thought I saw. But I dunno."

Ylva put her hands on either side of his head. She drew me along in thought. Boldo tagged with us. We caught sight of a hawk in the sky above there and saw from its viewpoint, the detailed landscape below.

"That's it," Duff said, pinpointing the entrance to the cave.

We followed with the hawk's sight, scanning the surroundings. Ylva held onto me and Duff. I hugged Boldo's waist and then we stood, side by side, on the shelf outside the cave where Duff had lain sick under a spell. Duff's and Ylva's heads came up far higher than the top of the cave opening. Boldo and I ducked in before them. Ylva followed with a glowing globe floating above her hand. Duff came in last, kneeling near the entrance.

"Can I have one of those?" I asked Ylva for a globe of my own, holding out my hand.

"You'll have to give it energy." She put her hand on mine and a ball of light appeared over my palm. I felt her in my mind, showing me how to feed the illumination. I sucked in a happy breath as a sparkling rush ran along my arm.

Carefully I moved to the back of the cave, crawling on one hand to hold up the light on the other, searching for my jacket. I found it, crammed under sticks and dried moss in the deepest cleft. I set the light to hover over me as I jammed the down jacket into my knapsack, borrowed from Ylva.

"What are ye doin' 'ere?" Galfride asked, from the entrance.

I turned to see his outline against the reddening sky.

"Getting my jacket. Why are you here? You're supposed to be—"

"Save th' remonstrance," Galfride said, squatting and peering around at the others. "I was lookin' fer ye."

"Is something wrong?" I crab-crawled until I could duck-stand. "What is it?"

"Nothin's wrong, worry worm. Thought ye'd like a daily report."

"Of course I would." I stepped over Duff's legs—he sat against the wall, right where his bed had been through the fever—and onto the ledge outside the cave where Galfride joined me. "You could have mind-spoke to me though. Is all okay then?"

"Thrizzle… isn't that what Ylva named him? That's good."

It was as if he purposely tormented me. I waited.

"He likes to try to get us apart."

"As you are now."

He rolled his eyes.

"Have you detected foul play?" Dread clenched my heart.

"No' as such. I hang 'round them 's much as possible. But 'e sends me fer things."

"Like what?"

"Food."

"He has servants for that."

"Indeed."

I turned into the cave. "Can we go to the fort?"

As Duff ducked out, he shot Galfride a hearty scowl. Boldo emerged and then Ylva. Galfride sent us a clear image of where to arrive, in a shadowed side of the fort, near the woods. We grasped hands, all but Galfride, who smirked and went ahead. The rest of us joined him in the forest by the Jutland fort where my heron had been when I'd escaped Thorgisl.

"Why're ye comin' here now, wi' only three days left?"

"I want to see my son," I said.

Galfride sighed. "Well, if y'er determined to be in there … I c'n show ye the best way t' go undetected."

I dreaded re-entering the place of misery but wanted to check on Rousseau with my own eyes.

"Ye know yer way around as well, don't ye, Ceirwen?" Boldo chafed his hands, nervous, his thoughts dark, on cells and chains.

Galfride said to Boldo, "Ye know only the dungeons, am I right?"

Boldo glared at him.

"But me thinks Ylva may ha' explored the under-halls more e'en than me. I get distracted by—"

"Thrizzle's toys?" I suggested.

"Might be." Galfride stepped toward the stone wall of the fort.

"Do you know where Rousseau's chamber is?" Ylva asked.

"O' course I do. I told ye I'm keepin' an eye on 'im. My bedchamber's next t' his."

"How will we go undetected?" I asked.

Ylva suggested, "Mice."

As mice, our human vibrations would not be detected by Thorgisl. "We have to kill mice?" I asked, grimacing.

"I only killed the gopher because I didn't feel as … sure … in your time. The magic is different."

"Missing, you mean?" I asked.

"Perhaps lessened. Not altogether gone."

Hm. That was interesting. It had to be true, for Marget and I were able to tap into powers.

"Ah, I hadn't thought o' that way o' bringin' ye in," Galfride commented.

Ylva made me and Boldo into brown mice, herself and Duff reddish. Galfride slipped us into his capacious pockets, along with his jumble of baubles and gadgets. I sniffed my way to a birdwing, then scuttled next to Ylva and stayed there.

We felt the sway of Galfride's strides as he climbed stairs and clomped along flagstone hallways.

"I've brought ye a surprise," I heard his voice.

His hands reached in and lifted us out.

Rousseau lay reading an enormous old book with thick parchment pages, in a bedchamber much like the one I occupied when imprisoned here.

He looked up and smiled. "You brought me four mice? That was kind."

Galfride set us on the bed.

I crawled onto his leg.

"Wanted t' check on ye," Galfride said aloud.

Rousseau's eyebrows rose as my mind touched his.

I ached to take human shape and hug my son.

The Ylva mouse disappeared.

I thought, to Rouss, "I think she wants to do a few things in Thorgisl's chamber. Has he treated you well?"

"Yes. He's been fine." He put out his hand and I crawled onto it. "Though foul-tempered most of the time. Is everything going okay with you? What are you guys up to?"

"I'd better fill you in later. I just wanted to see you."

"Yeah, we don't want any cats to find you." Rousseau smiled, sad. "Wish I could come with you, but it's not much longer."

I nuzzled his hand. "Have you sensed why he wanted you here? Does he ask you questions or put thoughts in your mind?"

He stroked my head with a fingertip.

I gave a mind giggle. "That's something I never would have imagined happening."

"Me, either," he said with a smile.

Boldo and Duff sniffed around on the blanket.

"No, he hasn't been asking questions, just talking, about life in general. It's actually interesting. I don't have information he needs. I guess he did ask me how I got onto Otho's ship and what I saw there. I think I've been able to stay aware and he's never pushed any thoughts in or taken any away." He pondered a moment. "I have wondered if he might put me in a trance, plant something so I'll spy for him later. I guess Ylva will have to inspect in my head after it's all over."

"You bet she will," I said, as Ylva appeared again on the bed. "We'd better go."

I nibbled lightly on my son's hand, a tickling of whiskers.

Galfride brought us back to the woods, where we took human form, keeping a protective shield around us.

"Boldo, will you come with us to *Galdhøpiggen*?" Ylva asked.

"Yes. If Mora is well enough, Talaith and I can bring her home."

"Very well, then." She gave a slight bend of the head toward Galfride. "Thank you for your help."

He gave a supercilious genuflection. "Here to serve."

Oh, so not true, I thought. It's not his nature. Yet he had. With one glance at me, he was gone.

As I felt him walking along a hall inside the fort, I thought to him, "I'm still not sure why you came to us and didn't just report to me by thought."

"I wanted to see the cave again. I felt you there. Funny, how a combination of person and place get imprinted. Good day, Ceirwyn."

He continued on to the steps to Thorgisl's tower.

"You two getting chummy?" I asked when I saw that he hadn't gone back to Rousseau. My suspicions rose.

"He's not in his tower room." His tone was surly.

"Ah." He'd take the opportunity to explore.

The four of us returned to the mountain across the North Sea. Upon arrival, Ylva headed for the stone.

I trotted after her. "Should I come with you?" I asked.

"I am not sure. I don't want you near the stone. I feel your unease with it. But I must ask it questions."

"Can you teach me to protect myself from it?"

"I would have to learn that as well. We will approach slowly, in order to learn what protections are needed."

We made our way through the tunnels to the inner sanctum where Ylva pressed her hand to the symbols on the obelisk that held the powerful amber—if amber it was—in its bowels. When the opening appeared, Ylva tenderly, reverently, lifted it out. She did not shed blood this time.

"Why can you get in now without your blood?" I asked.

"That was a particular incantation I'd put on it. You wait in here." She pointed to an adjoining room. With a wave of her arm, globe-lights appeared there, floating over a comfortable space with rugs and pillows.

I entered and settled against one wall. I'd been pulling my thick cape tight against the caverns' icy air, even put on mittens, but in here the globe-lights also seemed to warm the air. I relaxed into a sort of meditation as I waited.

Ylva's voice spoke in my head. "Come."

I sensed where she was and, bringing a globe-light with me, ventured into a deeper cell in the labyrinth. She sat in an elaborate chamber that could fit at least twenty people. She gestured from the center, seated on a mound of pillows.

The stone, out of its casement, on a cushion, glowed a sullen rusty tone.

I crept toward her and the stone. It sent glowering energy.

When I was still ten feet away, she said, "Stop," holding up her imposing hand in warning.

Chapter 31

She laid her hands on the eight-inch oval stone. Its insides roiled visibly. She communed with it, sending me bits of thought.

I knelt on a pillow, keeping distance. Breathing slowly, I tried to sense what she imparted from the stone. Visions of the other world, bathed in its egg-yolk tones, came to me.

Suddenly Ylva and I stood before a temple. Short trees with rounded gold foliage lined the walk. We stepped onto shallow stairs. In some ways, this place resembled an Earth city, but there was a difference in the atmosphere, in the mood, nothing like Earth in its colors or atmosphere, plants, shapes of dwellings.

I seemed only able to focus on the temple, as if drawn, though I longed to look to my right and left, behind me, to see more of the place. I wondered if it was the same for Ylva.

Step by step, we ascended toward massive doors, then crossed a mosaicked landing. I felt wary, on the lookout for inhabitants, unsure if we were visible.

The doors opened. Was this all a mind-game? Since I was there in spirit, or this place was in our minds, I was not affected by low oxygen. We stepped into a shadowy entry hall.

I jumped as an extremely tall being, taller than Ylva, in ornate robes, with a tall domed head, reached a double-hand to me.

Which should I take?

"Don't touch her," Ylva thought.

"Did the stone send us here?" I asked Ylva.

"I'm not sure."

The smooth, conical head held disturbing eyes half covered in bulging blue-brown skin though the hue was hard to identify considering the sun's orangish tinge.

Had Shagfen been the same shade? It had been too dark to see, in the hovel.

"I am Arlong." The priestess brushed my fingertips, sending a chill down my arm. She turned and led us through a second grand set of doors into a sanctuary where pale light filtered through thick, mottled glass, giving the place an underwater appearance.

Foreboding engulfed me, as though malevolent thoughts emanated from the wall alcoves.

"Let's leave," Ylva said.

"You are mine now," the being said, leading us between rows of benches.

"Are you the voice of the stone?" I asked.

"Stop speaking to her," Ylva said. "I'm pulling us back."

"But should we find out more?" I asked Ylva, in our minds.

Ylva took my hand. "How did we get here? Did you call us? Have you drawn us here? Are you trying to hold us?"

The creature tilted her head, seeming to listen. "I will teach you. You are ours now."

"I am no collector's item," Ylva said. "And we leave when we decide."

Arlong did not answer. Her neck, sperpent like, stretched forward. A force seemed to pull us toward an altar.

"Kneel," she said.

Against my will, I knelt obediently on a low, cushioned shelf.

Ylva frowned at this, then looked around. "What are we worshipping here?"

"The stone must be returned," the priestess said.

"Why?" Ylva asked. "Says who?"

"There is one of ours stuck in your world," Arlong said. "She must return."

I didn't get the sense that it was concern for her health.

"She and the stone are missing. She must answer for herself and her father. Others must have the stone back."

"You're accusing Shagfen of stealing the stone?" Ylva asked.

A rasping noise seemed to be laughter. "She could not carry the stone."

"But her father could. Yet he is dead. You want Shagfen to answer for her father's actions?" Ylva had stayed standing, a hand on my shoulder as I remained on my knees. "This one is under my protection. I am not to be trifled with. I have been to this world before, to remove a ship and its men who held your stone."

"We know of the ship. We were about to punish the men when you took them. This makes you a criminal."

Ylva bridled. "What do I know of your laws?"

"They must be captured and brought to justice. You meddled."

"They obtained the stone from Shagfen. How did she get it? You say she could not hold it."

"She cannot survive in your world. The gravity is strange. The food is not right."

"She did seem ill. You have sympathy for her then? And if she returns here, she will be punished?"

"You must return the men who stole the stone, and Shagfen."

"They did not steal it. They purchased it. They were merely delivering it when their ship was diverted, perhaps by you or your priests. If that's the case, it could be said you stole a ship and its men from earth."

"We must solve these matters. You must all come here to stand trial. We cannot come to your world. You must bring all the men from the ship, and this one who purchased the stone, as well as Shagfen."

"How do you propose I do that?" Ylva asked...*if I were so inclined.*

"You must find a way or we will send other, less cherished but more damaging objects into your world."

"If you can't enter our world, how will you send objects into it?" Ylva asked, reasonably.

"We have mages, like Shagfen's father. They will know how."

"I will hold council with others," Ylva said. "What was it you proposed to teach us?"

I stood at last. Despite being there only in spirit, I felt my limbs aching from the prolonged kneeling.

Ylva took my arm and, in that instant, we were back in her mountain chamber.

I breathed in the crisp air, grateful at the return to freedom. "I was afraid she'd hold us there. Did you feel compelled at all or were you just staying long enough to get information? Could you have left at any time?"

"Of course I could," she said. "I'm sorry I did not communicate that to you. I'm still not sure if the stone sent us, or those of that temple drew us, but they could not keep us there." She spread her hands on her thighs, gazing at the stone. It roiled gold within.

I stretched my legs pleasurably.

"I must erase that creature from my mind—" She lit a pile of powdered incense in a rounded stone bowl— "and cut all connection to that world before I speak again with the stone.

I scooted the cushion against a wall and settled back, another cushion behind me.

Had they made the ship crew short of breath, including my son, to punish them? Just the idea that the world contained low oxygen made me feel strained breathing but I was there in spirit and couldn't be sure. I tried to imagine what harmful objects they might send if the men did not stand trial. How would they get back there? What force had pulled them in the first place?

I still wore my mittens. In the other world, I'd seemed to have bare hands when Arlong touched me. I had so much whirling through my mind and wanted to talk it all over with Ylva but she seemed in a trance. With relief, I felt the threads of that world slip away from my consciousness as well.

At last, Ylva spoke. "We will try to understand who is in power there, and how this stone relates." She closed her eyes a moment, then opened them. "I am told that mountains love your energy. Call upon that now to lend the strength of the mountain to our work and to make the stone approachable for you."

I felt startled by this. "I did feel that from the French Alps, when I escaped from Galfride."

"I want to learn more about that. For now, *Félagi*, let us draw the mountain's strength in."

She came away from the stone and settled next to me.

Pulling the mittens from my hands, she enclosed them in hers, which exuded warmth.

I closed my eyes, charged my brand, and felt my spirit blend with Ylva's. I detected the deep recesses of the mountain around us as the spirit of the metals, rocks, and rich ancient earth entered my veins, filling my heart, rushing with my breath. As before, I felt mountain-love and mountain-energy as part of me.

Ylva's eyes glowed with approval. "Now." She pulled me up and we sat by the amber stone.

I asked *Galdhøpiggen*, the highest peak in Norway, "Is it safe? Can you help me?" I felt myself part mountain—old, patient, immovable yet also yielding to gradual forces—and received my answer. Moving rock-hands toward the unearthly stone, I spread my fingers on its surface until my palms were one with it. Ylva laid hers on mine. She held my gaze.

The stone explored this energy, in us as well as in the mountain, perhaps in all the planet. It no longer felt malevolent. Its force and ability to draw terrified me. This power could break a mind, I was sure. But I was knowing it in another way now.

"We must not stay long at one time," Ylva said to me.

The energy was hard to hold. I would not be able to counteract it, even with the mountain's help, if it shifted away from the current benevolence.

"Can we speak directly to you?" Ylva asked—an elemental thought, not language.

"I am," the stone retorted.

"What do you want of us?" She conveyed the idea of desire. Will.

"*My* mountain. Not this one, though I am glad to have tasted it," it answered clearly.

"In the other world?" Ylva shot an image of the egg-yolk-colored lands.

"That is the realm of me. You are not seeing my mountain, though," Amber-stone said.

"You will show us? Can you help us breathe in your land, if we bring you there?"

Affirmative. "Then things will be in balance again."

"Did you draw Otho's ship to your world?" she asked.

"Yes."

"Will you be safe there, though? The priestess in the temple—" Again Ylva formed the image. "They want you back. They said Shagfen's father stole you away to Earth. Will they allow you to go to your mountain? What will guard you from being captured again?"

"I don't know. I have power to draw, not arms to resist or repell."

The powerful stone seemed, nevertheless, vulnerable.

"I will see if any of my dragons like your mountain," Ylva said. "I know them in many realms. A dragon should be capable of protecting you."

The stone brightened until lights swirled within, paler in tone than the smoldering tones before.

"It is settled then. For now, I will return you to your compartment, for your own safety. I have only two days to accomplish this."

Love, clear as a mountain stream, flooded into us from the stone.

Tears welled with the rush of momentous emotion.

Ylva stowed the glowing stone and we put the cave chambers in order. I kept heaving sighs, knowing I'd never be the same after such a monumental shared emotion. I thanked the mountain and it thanked me for having included it in the love as well.

Ylva paused at the entry to each chamber. "I seal the air to keep moisture at bay," she said.

"I wondered about those nice fresh pillows."

Chapter 32

As we walked to the house in growing darkness, I almost floated, remembering the powerful love of the mountain under my feet. Wanting to talk about it, I glanced at Ylva beside me. An immense timber wolf, its back the height of my shoulder, trotted at my side. I'd taken heron form and stalked next to the wolf in the wild bird's shape.

Does it make the feelings the mountain gave us more full, or easier, to absorb, to take these forms? I asked her.

Perhaps, she responded. The eery wolf eyes turned to me, bright in the growing dark. A wolf smile formed, tongue hanging out.

The past three years seemed to make a new sense as I melded minds with my heron spirit.

We stayed in that form until we reached the summit above Ylva's home. Then we reverted to human and strolled downslope.

The love-high couldn't last forever. I sent shielding around us from my brand and rings. "How are we going to deal with that other world and its plans?"

"The stone must be returned to its mountain," Ylva said firmly.

"I agree. But not while Thrizz has my son," I said just

as vehemently.

"No one is safe until we figure out what the priesthood in that other world has against ours," Ylva pointed out. "But I'm going to handle Thrizz. Just haven't come up with an answer yet. I have very crafty counsellors."

As we approached her home, boots crunching on the path, the last of the sunset tones glowed.

"Tonight, we will do all we can to make sure Mora is fully recovered. I brought Thrizzle's amber wafer—the one we used with Duff—back from the caves."

"Great idea," I said, remembering Ylva sliding through it in her tiny witch form.

"I'm sure it has powerful healing properties. And the illness of spirit that drains her body may well be the same spell Thrizz put on Duff."

"He used it as a homing device but may never have known its other properties."

Ylva gave me a smug sideways smile. "Perhaps it attunes to one person in a way that might heal the soul, while only as a homing beacon to another."

"True."

We climbed the stairs to Ylva's main floor. Boldo, Hamelyn and Baird played fiddle, flute and mandolin in the front room now, where they could look out over the sunset-lit peaks.

Duff sat enjoying the concert and whittling.

Ylva and I ran upstairs to where Talaith and Marget tended to Mora. She was piled atop more pillows to ease congestion in her lungs. Marget had a fae-fire—just as warming but needing no fuel—under a pot of steaming aromatic herbs.

I knelt by the bed and touched Mora's forehead with the back of my hand. She was too cool. "How is she?" I asked the healers.

"Not much better," Talaith answered. "Aelfwyn and Kyna are upstairs working a spell. Gwynedd is stitching magic."

"Gwynedd has come?" I asked.

Ylva unbuttoned Mora's nightshirt where poultices lay thick, folded into flannel cloth. "I can remove this?" she asked.

Marget nodded.

Ylva set it aside. "Call everyone."

The group filed in, from upstairs and down. When the bedroom was packed shoulder to shoulder, Ylva took the amber from her pocket. She miniaturized herself and slipped through the red-gold stone, landing on Mora's chest, then disappearing. We held hands and chanted low. She called me into her mind. We slipped along within Mora, settling near her heart. I still had some of the mountain-love in me from the otherworld stone; Ylva had said it was not amber but another fossil of that world. Combined with Ylva's jump through the amber, we brought potent earth magic. I felt the amber stone holding the vibrations with us.

After a time, a subtle shifting began.

We were one with the cells and tissues. We slipped up into Mora's mind. Ylva seemed to go everywhere and I tagged along, sending out healing. At last, we felt certain that she was on the road to recovery. We slipped from her, back into our bodies. Ylva again stood by the bed. I re-entered my kneeling self and got up.

Mora's eyes opened. Her skin tone had gone from grey to creamy. She smiled and nodded, first at Ylva, then at me. "I felt you in there," she said, still weak. "Such a pretty sensation. I'll rest now." She closed her eyes and turned on her side. I heard less rasping and rattling in her breath.

We'd done what we could with the congestion though it was thick. Herbs would need to do the rest.

As her breathing deepened into slow steady sleep-breaths, everyone filed out. I touched her head, smoothed the white hair. A flicker of smile tugged at one side of her mouth.

In the main hall, we decided dinner was in order. Duff started frying fish. Ylva went below and returned with an armload of root vegetables: parsnips, beets, onions. She handed me some to chop. "I've called to my clan elders. We need to meet tonight. I would like you there, Kay."

She'd taken to calling me Friend or Heron-Woman most of the time, in her Old Norse so I was surprised to hear my 21st Century name.

"Of course I will."

"We'll have a ceremony."

"Can we all come?" asked Baird.

I knew he was curious, especially after seeing her cabinet full of talismans.

She thought a moment as she peeled and cut vegetables. "Let me ask." Her hands grew still, her eyelids lowered. At last, she said, "You may all come. You must keep your minds as quiet as possible, your energies neutral."

Everyone nodded. Talaith said, "I'll stay with Mora."

Boldo said, "I'll keep you company."

"I'm too old for these late-night affairs in frosted mountain peaks," Aelfwyn said. "You two go. Learn. I'll be with Mora."

Baird came over to me and reached out a hand. "Walk a bit?"

I said to Ylva, "I'm just going outside for a moment."

They could finish food prep without me. As Baird and I ran down the stairs and exited the earth-floored storage level onto the road, I felt tired. We strolled in the dark to a boulder wode enough for us both to sit. Despite my warm cloak and thermal underclothes, my teeth chattered. He wrapped me in his cape for extra warmth.

I thought my shivering might be a reaction to all that had happened that day: spirit travel, changing form several times, fright in the otherworld. Then there was the sheer energy of working with the mountain and the stone. Might there be residue of the otherworld in me, draining my energy? The priestess had said, "You are mine." What had it meant?

"What're ye thinkin' of?" Baird asked.

"So much has happened today." I took a deep breath.

"D'ye want t' tell me about it?"

"Let's just enjoy the moment for now," I suggested. The thought of recounting it all sapped me.

"Wish I could' ha' shared it with ye, that I could share more o' life with ye." He kissed the side of my head, then worked his lips around to my mouth.

We tangled in close. I ended up wound against his chest, legs curled onto his lap.

"Have you been barding lately? I know so little of your life as well."

"Much is th' same as before." His long, silver streaked hair played in a quick gusty breeze.

I breathed in the scent of his cape. "It seems like life just settles down and then we're tumbling along."

"Tumblin', yeah," he said, mouth hovering over mine tantalizingly. "Where d' ye think we'll sleep. Are we all beddin' down here?" His breath came fast and heavy.

Mine matched his. "After the ceremony? I don't know. I guess we'll have to see what results from Ylva's consultation with her advisors. We may not sleep at all tonight. We only have a couple of days to solve things and get my son back."

The reminder of what was at stake dampered the heat of the moment. I pushed reluctantly away. "Maybe we should join the meal."

As I stood, Baird caught my hand, but I pulled him to standing. He gave way with a half-playful huff. We walked arm-in-arm, breath puffing white in the cold night air. We were silent as we trekked back to Ylva's steps.

I'd told him little—nothing of the fact that we didn't plan to trade the stone for Rousseau, as Thorgisl expected. I dared not even hold that information in my head, much less say it.

As we climbed the stairs, the clatter of dishes signaled dinner being set. We joined the warm, lively atmosphere. The board-and-sawhorse arrangement had been brought up and covered with a couple of cloths for a long table.

I served myself—parsnip mash, grains, an unknown winter green and sweet pudding—and sat where Duff had made room for us.

Duff's immense hand patted my back, making me feel like I'd received shiatsu. I smiled at him, nudged his shoulder with mine.

"Was it awful to return to *Geestendorf* today, and the cave where you were sick?" I asked.

"Strange, yes," he said when he'd finished swallowing.

He bit into bread and chewed thoughtfully. "Gave me the willies, rememberin'. The sickness, and worryin' 'bout Boldo." He nodded across at the other man.

Boldo sighed. "Not good days, those. But Ceirwyn saved me." He nodded around, making sure all gave recognition, before he dug back into his dinner.

Talaith, passing by at that moment, brushed his shoulder

with her hand. She must have been terrified when he was in Thorgisl's dungeons, undetectable. If it hadn't been for my boot connection that seemed to bypass the dampering spells, and metals …

I turned to Ylva. "Are our thoughts and speaking shielded within the house?"

She nodded, full fork on the way to her mouth. "Yes, well protected. You may speak."

I said, "What were you doing in Thorgisl's fort when you left us?"

She said, "I manifested ways of watching and listening."

"That's good," I said. "What have you heard?"

"I haven't had much time to concentrate." She took a bite and chewed, smiled at at me.

"The food is wonderful," I said. "Thank you to all who helped."

Conversation regarding growing and obtaining foods in winter followed. I tried to relax but my mind kept going to the fort where my son was held. What was Ylva thinking? If we sent the stone to its mountain, what would Thorgisl do?

My thoughts reverted to the strange priestess in the other world. Did they have any influence on our world? Her touch had left me in her power, feeling weak.

I pulled my thoughts away, not wanting to draw any mind-powers to me from that other place.

The stone remained in my soul, shoring up my strength. I felt it as love now, despite the first feelings of anger with which it had originally assaulted me. Would I still be tied to it when we returned it? I felt bereft at the thought.

Soon, all were clearing plates, helping to clean, bundling for the cold. We trooped down the street, Aelfwyn and Marget staying behind to tend to Mora.

Townsfolk joined us, in their layered clothing, with furred edges. Men's tunics draped over thick woven leggings. Several were in ceremonial garb, shamanic talismans clinking, sewn onto robes.

We neared the ritual hillside; immense guards were posted there.

So Ylva did fear Thorgisl's trickery despite her assurances that he could be handled. Had she heard something and not told me?

Slowing my steps, I searched for Rousseau's mind, testing our new abilities to connect. I queried—like pinging— "Rouss, do you hear me?" I tripped on a boulder.

Baird caught my arm.

"I'm fine, Mom," came Rousseau's voice in my head. He did sound okay.

"I love you," I said.

"I love you, too," he said back.

"I'm going to help with a ceremony now. Are you able to sense when he's in your mind and shut thoughts and memories into those protected places like we practiced with Marget?"

"Yes. That's going well. I'm getting lots of practice."

I felt him chuckle and so hoped it was true.

"Don't hesitate to get Galfride's help if you need it."

"He's been great, Mom. I'm safe."

"Okay. I'll see you soon." I put all the faith I could muster into my words.

"Yes, you will." He sounded completely sure.

"Bye for now, honey."

"Bye."

I brought my attention back to those around me, amazed that I'd walked to the ceremonial ground, hardly seeing.

Ylva, eyes on me, nodded.

I hurried to her, near the bonfire.

"Tonight I do realm travel," she said. "I do this best with all my fellow magic-workers. You will go with us tonight. First, we dance."

Drumming had begun and vibrated in the air.

I was glad I'd had a hearty meal as we stomped our feet in a shared rhythm around the blaze, building a synchronized force of will. I launched my brand to see how it added to the energy. I immediately felt the Thirteen who were present on the hill and in the house.

Ylva's spirit rose, taking mine with her.

Chapter 33

The Thirteen sent us off, and guardians of Ylva's people watched over our seated bodies as we soared away; I saw a man with a rattle standing tall, thrumming low, circling.

We flashed in and out of star-strewn nights, dawn mornings, nights again. In one world, serpents flew like dragonflies, iridescent wings backed by double-moons. In others, suns were of strange hues. Ylva searched far and wide until we came to a world with a violet sky, the forest so green it could not be called mere color but full of green-light in the leaves. Ylva landed lightly beside a dragon-creature. They sent up a song together that sounded like pure love. It swirled in the air, and I felt it touching my heart. This went on for some time. I could not read the messages but felt their joy.

When we left, she told me, "Amgath knows that world. She can help us enter, and stay with the stone for a time. She'll arrange a constant watch. There is much she can eat there."

At my expression, she said, "Amgath eats plants mostly, some fish."

"Oh. That all sounds good. Now to deal with Thorgisl?"

"I think that'd better be after the transfer is complete."

"What about my son?"

"Not to worry, *Félagi,*" Ylva assured me, as we returned swiftly to our own world and settled back into our bodies.

Not to worry, I thought. That was far more easily said than done, though. Elated from our astounding tour of other worlds, I was equally exhausted. I wondered if we'd discovered worm holes in space, or were other worlds clustered in parallel universes next to ours?

Baird squatted at my side. I laid my hand in his, giving him a pallid, disoriented smile. As he pulled me up, Ylva pushed from behind. She thought to me, "We will discuss this soon. Get sleep." Aloud she said, "We will find bedding for all."

The rest of the crowd seemed too excited to settle, energy raised by the dancing, chanting and whatever else they'd done while we were away from our bodies. I shuffled along, pressed against others, back up the road.

At Ylva's we made rows of beds—thick padding and quilts. All I wanted to do was flop down and fall into exhausted slumber. But I felt dusty. Ylva brought me a flannel gown and I did some washing up in a room with buckets and benches.

Sometime around dawn, I felt Ylva shaking my arm. "We must go."

I got up, splashed water on my face, layered on winter clothes and cape, and tugged on my boots. Ylva handed me a roasted grain drink along with hard cheese on hearty bread. I chewed, washed it down, in a daze. In almost no time, we were crunching out of the downstairs room onto the road.

"Where are we going?" I asked.

"*Geestendorf.* Talk to Shagfen."

"I see." Above the hill that led to the caves with the stone, I saw something iridescent. It might have been a play of dawn light, but had the shape of a dragon's wing, hunched.

Ylva pulled me close and we went *between*, arriving instantly in the forest of South Jutland. Or was it Denmark? I knew from my research years, as professor of ancient languages, that the area had changed hands multiple times, with new borders established.

No one was about as we entered the streets of *Geestendorf* and traced our way back to that foul alley, with its fouler byway to the traders' lair.

"Will we go in as ourselves?" I asked.

"I've been thinking about that," Ylva said. "What's your opinion?"

"I haven't a clue," I said.

"Then let's be unobtrusive to start."

We stood on a low table in ink black. No one stirred. Ylva made us tiny globes of light that floated over our heads. The smell was intolerable. She sent more globes out around the room. We were near a sleeping figure on a bed low to the ground. The rumbling sounds of difficult breathing turned into coughs.

"I think you got us into the right room," I thought to Ylva.

"I believe I did."

A toot might have been a fart. Ylva took herself to the pillow of the massive toadlike shape. "Shagfen," she said into the otherworld being's mind.

She snorted, pushed herself half up.

Ylva made herself visible though still miniaturized, standing on a side table, a tiny globe hovering over her head.

"What are you, tiny person?" Shagfen mumbled groggily. "What you plan do to me? I'll swat you. Who sent you?" She seemed ready to grab Ylva, who froze her.

"I want to speak to you. Listen. I have been to your world, to a temple with a two-handed priestess. They have unpleasant plans for you there. But you are ill in this world. I think you must return to your own."

"What the … what business is it of yours?" The creature hocked and spat loud into a tin.

I worked my way to the far edge of the table, looking for elsewhere to perch.

"Do you think to get money from me to take me back? I see you're a magician. You've made me freeze. At least let me sit up."

Ylva released her enough for her to push up a pillow behind her and work her heavy mass to sitting.

Ylva sighed. "We've spoken with the stone." She glanced toward me.

Shagfen looked around and spotted me on the rim of her table. "So, there's two of you rats. This one a wizard too?"

"Of sorts. Now listen."

Suddenly Shag let out a screech and wheezed, "I have guards."

"Now you've made me paralyze you again." Ylva searched for others awake, ready to enter, and imitated Shagfen's mind, "Only a dream, rest easy." She said to the inert, spread-out creature on the bed, "As I was saying, I spoke with the stone. It wants to return to the mountain from whence it came. How did it get to this world?"

"Why should I tell you?"

She could still speak, just couldn't grab or scream. I felt Ylva weary of the conversation. She pulled me with her into the creature's strange mind. Thought centers had entirely different patterns.

Ylva gave up, leaving the dizzying foreign realm of Shagfen's unconscious and compelled her to speak instead.

Shagfen began, as in a trance, "My father was a wizard in our world, Sartren."

When she said the name, I saw the egg-yolk-colored planet and knew it was the same one we'd visited, with the tall priestess, where Otho's ship had been pulled. So that was its name. Or her name for it.

"He was drawn to the stone during one of his spell-journeys. Similarly, he discovered this world. He found greed here and became tempted by the notion. He thought he'd make a fortune, live well back in our world. In Sartren, power is about abilities. And there's barter, exchange. Not money as you use here."

"And power-hungry priesthoods?" I suggested.

"There's that. A definite hierarchy. My father found it hard to return to Sartren, as have I. His powers worked differently here. Finally, he died here. But not before selling me." She coughed out phlegm onto rag, then went on, "I was unusual in my world. Despised by some. Here I could be rented out. Or sold."

Ylva and I felt sick listening to this story.

"I see," Ylva said. "And Thorgisl? How did he learn of the stone?"

The creature shook her head. "I don't know this name."

"The stone desires to return to its mountain home, in your world, in Sartren. I believe that's why it pulled the ship there."

"What is this to me?" Shagfen slumped, as if trying to return to sleep.

"What if you could get back there, to your world? You could become healthy again, couldn't you?"

We were both suffering from the stench in the air.

Shagfen wiggled her flaccid spread to a more upright position, appearing more attentive.

"Do you have a place to go there?"

Shagfen grunted. "I have no one, knew no one like me."

"Perhaps you could live close to the stone, watch over it."

I wasn't positive that was a great idea. It had a strange effect on some people.

In the dim light from our tiny globes, her strange elongated eyes seem to flicker toward Ylva.

"But I have other defenders for it," Ylva hastened to say. "If I release you from the compelling, will you desist from screaming? I have no intention of hurting you."

"Fine. You seem to wish to help me, for some reason. I'm not used to that. Do you propose to send me with the scarred one, on his ship?" Shagfen coughed hoarsely. "What reward would you expect?"

"I seek no reward. I'm not a mercenary or a trader."

"In my world, nothing is done without a price," Shagfen said. "But as you say, there are those who want the power of the stone. How do you know I wouldn't bargain with them in order to make myself rich, if I were back in my world?"

"From what the priestess told us, you would be put on trial there for its theft," Ylva reasoned. "It would be risky for you to make yourself known." She seated herself on a table.

I wasn't sure about Ylva, but keeping dinky was wearing me out. On the other hand, I didn't want the reek of the place to assail me in my human size. I settled next to her.

"I'll be honest with you," Ylva said. "I care about the stone. It does not want to be used in the way the powerful of your land want to use it. It wants to be on its mountain. It seems fair to me that it should have its wish."

"How do you speak to the stone?" the creature asked.

"It is not hard, for some, I suppose."

"Why does your friend say nothing?" she asked.

"Do you wish for her to speak?"

Shagfen shrugged. "Why not?"

"We offer to return you to your realm," I said. "With great risk to ourselves."

"Why?"

"Because we love the stone. And we don't see why you should continue to suffer," I said.

Ylva beamed approval.

"What's the risk for you?" Shagfen asked.

"A powerful mage here—the one who purchased the stone through Otho—wants it back. He's holding my son hostage. He's not going to be pleased if he finds out we've returned the stone to your world." As I said it, the dreaded reality sank painfully into my stomach.

"I once had a child," Shagfen said, surprising us both.

"What happened to it?" I asked.

"I did not want my father to get hold of her. He liked to be … experimental. So, I gave her to someone who said he could get her back to Sartren. I have no idea if she made it there, or where she is."

I felt deep sadness in the shapeless creature.

"Will you work with us?" Ylva asked. "Perhaps you can rediscover your daughter. If I can help, I will."

"I suppose." Shagfen shrugged a shoulder barely discernable from the rest of her. Futility had seemed to set in.

"You need only gather what you will take. I'm afraid there's no time for good-byes," Ylva said.

Shagfen hacked a laugh. "There's nothing here I want. Who should I say good-bye to? These oafs who fulfill my needs for a price?"

With that, Ylva made her miniscule and we returned with her to the forest.

Chapter 34

Shagfen lay on the ground. A mound of greyish flesh in a shapeless shift stretched to its limit, she gazed up at the dragon filling the meadow far out in the hills.

"Shagfen, meet Amgath," Ylva said, looking pleased.

Amgath sent Shagfen a mental greeting, accompanied by a fluting sound, entrancing her further.

Amgath had the stone's case that Duff made strapped to her. Ylva sent Shagfen onto the thirty-foot creature's back, settling her between dragon wings where she clutched fleshy nobs.

"Ready?" Ylva asked.

"We won't go, then?" I'd been assuming we'd see the stone to its rightful place.

"I think not, *Félagi*. We have things to settle here. We can visit later."

I nodded, tears threatening as I awaited the stone's departure, wondering if I'd experience its love again. It sent me a pulsing throb, just like the welter of emotion we'd shared in the Norwegian caves. I returned it, relieved it had not been a one-time sensation.

And then they lifted off and were gone. Tears ran down my face. Ylva nodded, eyes moist.

"What do we say to Thrizzle?" I asked.

"That's our next job. We're ahead of schedule but I thought we should be, in case anything went wrong."

"Like Shagfen not wanting to leave?"

"Like that."

"Do you think they'll avoid detection by the temple leaders?" I asked, squinting in the direction they'd gone.

"Amgath has been testing and exploring. She'll enter Sartren in a remote area. She'll stay in touch and I'll let you know." Ylva put a hand on my arm and we were in the forest near the fort. She dug in her pocket. "I've been wanting to give you this." She handed me a palm-sized heron, carved from stone. "You should keep this one with you."

I caressed the smooth cold shape, delicate yet sturdy, and felt I might easily take the heron form. As I held it, it grew warm to the touch. "I want a special pouch for it, to rest here." I indicated my heart area.

We hovered over Thorgisl's tower and the Jutland fort. He might have seen it all by scrying. I felt terrified.

Ylva touched my arm. "Ready?"

"No."

She stopped.

"How are we going in?" I asked, realizing she'd told me nothing of her plans. "Should we call to the Thirteen in case—"

"*Hegri fljóð*, I've told you not to worry."

Friend of heron, she'd called me.

We stood in the tower room, full sized. Thorgisl looked relaxed, talking with Rousseau as they sat in the hammock chairs examining an instrument made of bone, leather, and metal.

He looked up. "How consummately rude," he said. "Rousseau, would you want to return to your chamber, or walk in the gardens? It hasn't yet begun to rain."

Why is he sending him away? And where's Galfride?

My heart wrenched as my son stood and walked past me, giving me a smile before he descended the stairs.

Thorgisl said," Do you see how well I treat your son?" Then to Ylva, "You have one day left to return the stone to me."

"We need to discuss that," Ylva said, taking a seat facing him, her head still above his.

He stood, as if to gain the upper position. "Will you sit as well?" he offered me, gesturing to a third seat.

I assented, keeping my eyes on him, never trusting.

"Tea? Other refreshment?" He appeared to be holding patience by a fine thread.

When we shook our heads, he again seated himself. "So. What discussion is needed? We had a bargain."

"But did we? It seems that a key negotiator was not a part of our parley." Ylva was calm.

"Oh? And who might that be?"

"The stone," Ylva said.

Thorgisl's smile was a mere gash. "Surely you jest."

"No. I do not. The stone wants to return to its mountain, in its world. We have helped it to do so."

Thorgisl stood, face darkening. "You what?" His voice was low and threatening. "You toy with me? With Kay's son in my custody?"

"No longer," Ylva said. At his response—coloring purple—she held up a hand. "But wait, Thorgisl. I have some other marvelous enticements." She drew from her pocket a tiny dragon. It hunched on her hand. Its swirling, lavender eyes locked onto Thorgisl's; from the side, I could see they were like pools of infinite depth.

Thorgisl stopped mid-fume. He looked as though he'd

never known love until this moment. He barely breathed as he watched the delicate, enchanting creature, its wings folded back along opalescent sides. Gently, he held out his hand, glancing to see if Ylva would object. The sparkling fire-breather raised up and walked onto his palm, its eyes never leaving Thorgisl's. The mage breathed slowly as if a mere breath might disturb, even frighten it. The man seemed to have utterly forgotten us.

We disappeared from the room, and across the North Sea, arriving in front of Ylva's home.

"Do you think the dragon will be safe with him?" I asked. "It's so tiny. And...should he have a dragon?" I wanted to believe this was the consummate solution, but concerns jangled in my mind, only half trusting.

"His mother will keep close track. With Thorgisl's love of the dragon, he will be easier to control. And we can find out his thoughts."

"That's brilliant. But … we didn't get Rouss—"

My son strode toward us. I rushed to him and we hugged.

"How'd you get me away?" Rouss asked. "I thought there was another day. Is everything settled? You gave back the stone?"

"Can I explain?" I asked. "A lot has happened."

Rousseau nodded.

"But is he safe?" I asked Ylva.

"I believe he is."

We walked toward Ylva's ground's level where Duff worked at his high bench. He gave Ylva a kiss, then hugged me. He and Rousseau shook hands.

"Let's check on the others," I said, starting up the stairs. "I promised Marget we'd help with—"

"I know, Ian's memories," Rousseau said.

As we climbed, we heard no music. But no one was on the main floor. The bedroom was empty. So was the top story.

We ran back down to Ylva and Duff in the workshop.

"No one's in the house," I said.

Setting down his tools, Duff said, "Talaith and Boldo took Mora home. She's that much better." He nodded with satisfaction. "Baird, Hamelyn, Gwynedd, and Kyna also left this morning."

Hearing the four names together—a family—my stomach clenched just the slightest bit. *Left together, to go home.* Jealousy toward Kyna—my medieval twin—had not arisen for a long time.

Marget strolled toward us from the hillside. "You've got your son back, safe and sound."

We hugged.

"I'll wait to hear the story. Are things resolved here?" he asked.

"I believe they are." I turned to Ylva.

She nodded. "You three are welcome here at all times. But I imagine you'd like to be home. Let me get your cloth bag.

When she returned down the stairs, she handed me my down jacket in the bag. We wore the same clothes we'd come in. We hugged.

Seconds later, Marget, Rousseau, and I stood by the oak tree, our familiar, shared destination.

Rousseau looked around in wonder, at the abandoned front yard and Marget's derelict housefront. "I can't believe we're here. And it's the same day we left?"

"It should just twenty minutes since we left here." I carried my cloth bag with my down jacket.

"Everything's solved, right?" he asked, as we walked toward the house.

I'd never approached it this way. I glanced at Marget, wondering if we'd walk in the front for once.

"What happened with Thorgisl? You didn't give him the power stone, did you?"

"There's jest th' techy lit'l problem o' Ian's memory," a voice—too familiar, so unexpected—came from behind us.

We spun around to face Galfride.

"Did ye think I'd forgotten about 'im?" he asked Marget. "Did ye think I din't know who ye were?"

The color drained from her face. "Galfride," was all she seemed able to say.

This was what I'd feared from the beginning: that Galfride would learn of our time.

"So, Kyna's cousin." He now turned his sardonic gaze on me. "A verrra distant cousin, wouldn't it be?"

"You knew where Rousseau was from. You must have put it together," I said.

"Well, now, no. No, I didn't know where he came from. I was never the one t' draw him, was I?"

I thought about it. Thorgisl, and Otho. Or perhaps just Otho.

"Where be he?" Galfride turned back to Marget. He seemed to be avoiding my son.

Was this why he'd offered to stay with him, to watch over him? Was he making sure to follow us back? He couldn't, after all, stay close to Marget. What excuse could he make?

"I don't know," Marget said. "He doesn't remember me. Therefore, we have no relationship at this time."

"You think I'd believe that ye wouldn't find out where he lives, wouldn't keep a watch on him?" Galfride hadn't looked this angry in a long time.

My old fear of him returned as my son saw this side of him.

Rousseau watched, disappointed. Galfride had helped him, seemed like a guardian to him.

"Aren't ye gonna invite me in fer tea?" Galfride asked, glancing around at the yard and house, taking them in for the first time. His mouth twisted into a strange grin. "No' much, is it?" He looked at us. "Look at this heap. Be this yer place, witch?"

We turned as one toward the decrepit front of the house, always in shadow among elms' lofty upper story.

"Or are ye disguisin' somethin' nicer?" he asked. His grin was gone. He shook his head. "Ceirwyn, Ceirwyn, so much deception. So many lies." He turned to Rousseau at last. "I don't blame you. Ye never lied. Ye were just there. Comin' an' goin'. Pulled by the winds, ye might say."

My son was clearly at a loss for words.

"Let's go in," Marget said.

"Oh, me, too?" Galfride put a hand on his heart, as if touched.

Marget quirked a ghost of a smile, eyelids lowered.

Then we stood in her kitchen.

"I suppose you'll be a frequent visitor, now ye know where we are?" Marget said, putting on water and stoking the wood-burning stove.

"That all depends," Galfride said, pulling out a chair, turning it backward, and sitting, legs straddled like he was at home.

Rousseau hesitated.

"Sit, man," Galfride said. "We're all goin' t' have some civilized tea and conversation."

Rousseau joined him at the table.

I wished my son would pull back, not follow Galfride's lead, not do what he said so easily.

Galfride leaned forward and spoke quietly to him, something about their time at the fort.

Still standing by the door, I woke my brand. For good measure, I reached into my cape pocket and wrapped my hand around the heron carving. The stone quickly warmed to my touch. I called silently to Ylva.

Marget glanced at me. The men kept talking, hunched forward on their elbows.

"Galfride followed us to my time," I thought to Ylva when she responded to my call. "He's talking about Ian. I wondered if you might—"

A knock came at the back door.

Chapter 35

G alfride gave me a corner-eyed look. Rousseau twisted around, brows raised in question. Marget opened the door and welcomed in the great, red-haired giantess in. Ylva ducked to enter.

Inside, she nodded to the seated men.

Marget said, "Tea?" getting another cup from the shelf.

We all sat around the kitchen table, Ylva taking one end, Marget and I at the other.

"Well, well, how did a Norwegi priestess happen in on us at this time?" Galfride levelled his gaze at me.

I shrugged.

"I missed you all too much to stay away." Ylva's hands dwarfed her hot mug. As Marget finished pouring tea for the rest of us, Ylva added, "Now let's get down to business. What is your purpose here, Galfride of the Many Talents and Gadgets?"

"'Tis yer affair because …?" Galfride retorted, bringing his cup to his nose and smelling deeply.

"I'm not trying to knock you out," Marget defended her brew. Her eyes held ice.

Galfride gave her a wicked smile.

"You still have interest in your old friend, Ian." Ylva felt no need to answer his questions.

Marget turned on the oven and arranged cheese puff pastries on a pan.

"I have offered my services in returning Ian to his memories," Ylva said, gulping tea with a thankful nod to the hostess.

Marget set a plate on the table. "Cornish fairings, anyone?"

Ylva bit into a cookie, brushed crumbs, and said, "We must come to a decision about the best way to proceed."

"Ian's memories were stripped. He were snatched from 'is time wi'out his consent," Galfride enunciated in measured tones. "I ask again. Why is it any affair of yers, Norwigi giantess? *I* can return his memories. I'm quite adept at working with others' minds." He gave me a surly smirk.

My stomach churned. Anger sizzled in me with the memory of him of him controlling my mind. My groin ached with confusion.

"Just tell me where he is." Galfride's tone sounded menacing now.

"Um." Rousseau cleared his throat. "Maybe it's a matter of mental health. Ylva's a good healer as well as adept with mind-work."

Galfride moved his laser stare to my son, and softened. He kept eye contact long enough that I thought Rousseau might drop his gaze but he didn't.

Galfride said, "If I'm a part of every step of the process—I won't have blocks against my contact with him this time—" He looked sharply at Marget, then at Ylva. He did not take my skills seriously enough to include me in the intense eye-gazing. "When are we going to do this?"

"It hasn't been decided." Marget spoke at last. "Aelfwyn has been involved in the discussion."

"What about the Cornish Craft Guild?" He said the title with venom.

"The guild threatened to strip our powers. I found this portal," Marget responded. "I didn't realize he would lose all memory of—" Staring into her cup, she finished— "everything."

Galfride's eyes widened. "He's forgotten *you*, hasn't he? You bungled it, woman." He laughed nastily. "All this time I blamed the witches' council. Saw you as a victim. *You* did this." He shook his head slowly. "You got your punishment, didn't you? Gave it to yerself."

"Enough, young pup." Ylva slammed her hand on the table. "Losing a child is no laughing matter. As you know from your own life, if you'd think a moment. Though you were doing the lad no favors, it would seem. Let's not skim over the details in one place but not another."

Galfride glowered at the Nordic magic-worker, then stood. "I thank you for the tea," to Marget. "I give you twenty-four hours. Then we restore the memories, with none left out. I will be back." He strode toward the door and was gone before reaching it.

Rousseau took a deep breath.

I felt sick. This home had started to be a major haven for my son, a place for irreplacable training. Now it felt wretched, fraught with tension and threat.

"Nothing be ruined," Marget said, lighting a thick wand of tied white sage. "Don't ye love the smell o' this? We have not this species in Cornwall of my time. Jest the broad-leaf sage." She smudged the air around the room.

"I do," I said. "I keep trying to grow it but my soil is too fertile, or maybe I overwater it. I've tried the starkest environment imaginable, according to online instructions," I babbled on, trying to reach normalcy. I put a hand on

Marget's shoulder. "Are you okay?"

She sighed, rested her head on my shoulder. "Lad," she said, holding out the smudge stick to my son. "Finish the house, will ye?"

He took it and we heard his footsteps down the hall, then soon up the stairs.

"It was a bit hard to hear but he said nothing untrue."

"Just harshly." Ylva rose. "I will plan at my home, gather what I need, and return well before the day is up. Do you intend to bring Aelfwyn here? All the Thirteen? I have to say, I believe we can do it well ourselves, without need of them, but whatever you decide, of course."

Marget studied the woman's broad face which hovered above us, nearly touching the ceiling. After a moment's deliberation, she said, "I will be happy to keep it among us."

I felt relieved somehow. This was my time. I was gaining comfort and strength from Marget, and I was building our own force of magic here. Ylva belonged to no time and all times.

She left. I felt some certainty that we were making the right choice. This had become Ian's era as well. I hoped he and Marget would stay after this.

"We need to plan this through carefully. I guess, in a sense, it's fair, even wise, to deal with Galfride now and not be haunted by possibilities. What do you think?" I asked.

Just then, Rousseau re-entered the kitchen.

"Smash it out or it'll burn itself to cinders," Marget said to him, pointing at a bowl of sand on a sideboard.

He did so.

"I agree with ye, Kay. Let's meet in the mornin' and plan. Get lots of sleep if you can." Marget got up, arms wide to give hugs.

"Okay, but if you have any thoughts this evening, don't hesitate to contact me, any time," I said, hugging the other woman, strong and ageless.

"Or me." Rousseau bent and kissed Marget's cheek.

I loved to see the fondness he held for his mentors, Marget and Ylva, who'd healed him from his other-world trauma.

We left, walking out the door and stepping from the porch to appear on the other side of the hedge, in the park.

"I saw Galfride in the front yard, from the upstairs window. I don't think he's left."

"I imagine Marget knows." I slipped my arm into his and gave an affectionate squeeze.

We walked to the street and aimed for the community gardens, glancing toward Marget's home at the corner. I would leave it to her to discern Galfride's presence and decide what to do, sure she was well able to handle him.

Rousseau finally broke our silence as we entered the community gardens. "I can't believe we're back, safe." He huffed a sigh, making me realize how much he needed a good night's sleep.

"I can't either," I said. We made our way to my garden plot. I watered briefly and harvested a few veggies for late dinner.

Walking toward the house, my son said, "I thought everything was solved, all the danger, with Thorgisl. But maybe it's not. And now Galfride, coming here to this time?"

"It seems like there's always something," I said. "But at least we're learning skills for repulsing mental invasions and not being pulled against our will to the past."

"Do you think Otho will no longer try to draw me? It'd be tiring to be ever-vigilant."

"It would." I put an arm around his waist and hugged.

"I do think we'll keep working 'til everything's solved. I have some more share with you. One or two things that are rather amazing and beautiful."

"Really?" He gave me a questioning look.

"Yeah. We can talk over dinner, how 'bout?"

"That works. I still don't know why the stone made Otho draw me, though. Hey, what happened with the stone and Thorgisl, anyway?"

"That's related to the beautiful part. I don't know that all's solved."

Reaching home, we made a quick omelette with toast and sat to eat our meal. I related the astounding scene with the stone in Ylva's caves, the love I'd felt, converted from anger. And about Ylva's gift to Thorgisl, showing him the scenes by laying my hand on his arm.

"That tiny dragon was so friggin' adorable. I want one." He laughed.

"A dragon in this time? Maybe you can ask her if you could visit them in their worlds."

"It sounds like you felt something really special, with that power stone. You'll miss it."

"I do. It started out feeling fierce, a torrent of negative energy. I was scared of it."

"I felt that, too," he said.

"I think it was angry, to be taken from its mountain, its world, the elements it loves."

"Shagfen sounds pretty outrageous."

I put a hand to his head and gave him a mental picture of her as I'd seen her, mostly in darkness—massive, miserable—in her smelly quarters, then on the dragon's back, launching toward her home world.

"Wow." He shook his head, musing. "The things you've seen."

"I want to know everything about your time with Thorgisl," I said as we cleared plates. "But you must be tired. Tomorrow's Friday. Your sister's coming for the weekend—I'll have to find out what time. I have to let Marget know we should start early in the day."

"Why is she coming on the weekend? I mean, she's not working, is she? She could come anytime of the week."

"She's started her graduate project."

"Oh, yeah. She can say more about that when she's here. It sounds fun compared to law school."

"I look forward to hearing about it, too!"

Rousseau showered and headed for bed. I soaked in my beloved bubble bath.

Coming out in my robe to say good-night again, I found my son working on his laptop in the living room, but looking off distantly.

"What are you thinking about?" I asked.

"I haven't seen you weaving," he said.

"I stopped, when I felt Thrizzle. I wasn't sure if it was helping me see him, or him see me. I need to try again and see if I have a better handle on that. Good night, love." I kissed the side of his head.

I lay in bed, exhausted after days with little sleep in medieval time, yet not tumbling immediately into slumber. I thought about Baird not being there when we got back to Ylva's. He'd been so amorous before I left. Was he angry at my not asking him to come with us? This thought-loop was becoming a pattern.

Chapter 36

In the morning, we did our usual, me up first, making coffee, Rousseau wandering in groggily. He sat at the built-in table hunched over a bowl of granola, hand curved on a cup of hot tea. "Are you nervous about what we're doing today?"

I joined him with coffee and cereal. "A little. I just want to do it right, for Ian, for all of us, ultimately. It's tumbled together so differently than we'd planned, or I'd imagined."

"With Galfride following us?"

"Yeah." I nodded, spoonful of Kashi cereal stopped mid-air. "I wanted to do it slowly, carefully. I even discussed it with Shelley—how to bring the memories in a healing way using depth psychology."

"Maybe that could happen after."

I nodded agreement, chewing.

"Do we even know if Ian's up here? Doesn't he have a place in Berkeley?"

"He does. Good point. I don't think I have his number. I suppose Jarl and Joaquin do."

"He doesn't know who Marget is, so I guess it might make more sense for those guys to help out. Do you think they would?"

"It might have been better to have Sophie up here. She's

the natural go-between."

"We could call her, ask her to come up earlier in the day than usual."

"But do we want her mixed up in this part of it?" I pondered.

"She's Ian's friend."

"That's true. I can call her, at the very least, see what her plans are. I don't guess she'd thank us for leaving her out. Maybe we'll find out Ian's whereabouts that way."

"Yeah, call her," Rousseau said, scraping the last of the granola, yogurt and fruit from his bowl.

I picked up my cell phone and pressed Sophie's number. Got her voicemail. Left one of my own, asking her to call, then went to shower.

When I came out, Rousseau yelled, "Sophie called you back."

I dressed quickly in my self-woven clothing and phone her, finally actually speaking to her. "How's it going in your new place, sweetie?"

"Good." She sounded excited.

"Have you been spending a lot of time at the university?"

"Yeah, quite a bit. I'm so loving it. You have to see the building. I get a little office. Well, I share it."

"That's so great, honey. Are you still decorating?"

"I think I've blown all the money I can afford for now. I'll just watch for more things that come along."

"You got all your stuff from Aberystwyth?" I asked.

"I did. The last box came yesterday."

"Have you seen Harper in the Glen play down there?" I tried subtly to lead toward asking Ian's whereabouts.

"No. I think they're playing in Pomo Bluff this weekend. Maybe even tonight."

"Are you still coming up today?"

"I think I'll drive up tomorrow late morning. Are you okay? Rousseau's fine?"

"Oh, yeah. We're great. Can't wait to see you." I felt that plummet in my stomach when I hid parts of our lives from her.

"Okay, well, it's sunny, after a cloudy week. I think I'll go out for a bike ride."

"You bought a bike?"

"Yeah. Craig's List. Good price."

"We should buy you and Rousseau bikes for up here."

"Let's! See you tomorrow."

We hung up. "I'll call Duck 'n Hen. See about the schedule for Harper," I said to Rousseau who was listening closeby.

"Makes sense. Then call Jarl?"

I agreed. "I can also see what Marget wants to do."

"Yeah, that first." He grinned.

I suggested practicing with the scrying bowl, even though we all had cell phones. Rousseau and I climbed to the attic. I pulled the cover off the black obsidian bowl. With our fingertips at the edges, grazing the water, we thought about Marget. Her face appeared.

"Good morning," she said brightly, though her eyes looked shadowed.

"Did you sleep okay?" I asked.

"Fair enough. I invited Galfride in when I realized he was camping in the shed."

"He stayed the night in your home?"

"Yes. He was a cordial guest."

"Did you talk about—"

"No."

"My daughter thought Harper in the Glen might be

playing tonight in this area."

"Can't find yer lad?" Galfride's voice came from out-side the curtains. "I'm surprised ye can't locate 'im usin' that. Can I give a try?" Galfride's narrow face appeared on the water's surface, dark hair tied back, almond eyes stud-ying the scene. "Well, well, well, here we all are. 'Cept fer th' tall redhaired one." He sat cross-legged, making himself comfortable.

Marget studied him. "Can we talk for a moment first?" she said to him.

Ylva appeared on the other side of the bowl and seated herself, her legs engulfing a good portion of the space.

"Should we come there now?" I asked.

"Yes, may as well. We seem to be beginning." Marget seemed flustered.

I knew this was not the way she'd imagined. We'd first thought this would all take place in Kyna's tower. It all felt willy-nilly and unsafe. I covered our bowl with the heavy cloth. Rousseau and I manifested ourselves in Marget's magical room.

Galfride nodded at Rousseau. He seemed to like hav-ing another male there.

Ylva said, "Let's move away from the bowl and discuss a moment," clearly used to taking the leadership role. She pulled pillows from a heap by the wall, tossing them to each of us. We made a circle in the open rug space.

Marget seemed happy to give the reins to her.

"We can search for Ian. But who among us does he know best?"

"He's met Marget at the Duck 'n Hen," I said. "He and I don't have a great relationship."

Marget's brows raised. I had downplayed the tension between her son and me.

"Of all of us, Sophie knows him best—"

"Since his memories were taken," Galfride put in.

I finished my sentence. "But I hesitate to involve her."

"Why?" Ylva said.

"She can't travel to the past. She's already upset that she's being left out."

Galfride raised his brows with interest. "And who might this 'Sophie' be? A daughter perhaps? Be there a love blossoming between her and Ian?" He said *love* as if it was a funny type of common cold that others got, not him.

"Friendship," I said.

Galfride eyed me with doubt and amusement.

I did my best to ignore him. "What's an excuse to get him here?"

Marget suggested, "If Jarl, Joaquin, and Shelley could say, 'remember that woman who joined us when you played in town? She's invited us to lunch'…?"

"But then they're all here. That's not ideal," I said.

"Let's just see where he is and I'll compel him to come," suggested Ylva.

"Or I could, without all this nonsense," Galfride said with growing impatience.

"We want it to be comfortable for him," Rousseau contributed, surprising everyone. "I mean, this has to feel positive. I've been through some mind stuff myself lately. It's going to be awkward with too many people. Especially when his memories return. But I think Ylva can, once he remembers, go in and heal his mind, like she did mine."

"Shouldn't be in there meddlin'," Galfride growled in an undertone.

"That's very reasonable, son," said Marget. "Let's let Ylva take the lead. Galfride, promise that once he's remembered you, you'll work with us. Do you have good intentions? What are you hoping for?"

"Hopin' for." Galfride looked around. "He was my friend." He started irate, but some of the wind dropped from his sails and he spoke quietly. "I lost a lot when I couldn't find him. I was lost. I searched. I looked for you, woman. Gone. After a while, I wandered north, ended up … well, that doesn't matter. He was … we were … okay, some o' th' things we did—"

"You were older. You were leading him," Marget burst out, no longer able to sit back and not express herself. "You took things from my work room that ye di'nt properly know how t' use. And … ye hurt people,"

Galfride shifted away, stood up and paced. "I haven't always … done th' right things."

Ylva interrupted, "Dark energies draw dark to them. I think you pulled some to you. Is that not right?"

"I did. I can't blame it all on others but … I haven't always acted as myself, no."

"What now, though?" I asked. "You've been helping us. I don't always know why, if you're working with others, if you have aims we don't know of." This might be a bigger question than he'd answer at the moment.

"I just don't want Ian to return to… malice," Marget said.

Galfride clearly hated being outnumbered by three older women, with great power among at least two of them. He weighed his words, glancing frequently at Rousseau, who kept silent. He'd eased himself to lean against the wall, legs outstretched. I longed to do the same but wasn't close to anything.

Ylva said, "We can keep watch, monitor what happens after."

"Ylva, you're getting stretched with all you need to watch," I said, privately, from my mind to hers.

"I get help when I need it. Not to worry, *Frendi*," she said to me alone. "So," to the rest, "we find Ian, draw him here, and restore his memories, carefully, working with Marget to start from the beginning and lead up to the present. We have agreement that Galfride will act in accordance with decency, doing no harm. Are all agreed?"

We nodded and watched Galfride. He spread his hands, a chilling play of emotions moving across his face until he said, with smarmy sincerity, "A-greeed," then did a *tah-dah*, as if performing to an audience.

Ylva, Marget, and I glanced at each other to see if we felt it was genuine. Rousseau just looked pained by the discomfort he felt for Galfride, perhaps along with wariness.

Ylva seemed confident she'd bring about what needed to happen and moved to the scrying bowl.

Chapter 37

The rest of us gathered again around the bowl, Galfride easing in beside Rousseau. Ylva folded her great legs, one bumping against mine. Marget tucked in between me and Rousseau. That left a gap between Galfride and Ylva. She settled herself more comfortably, filling the gap. Galfride eyed her warily.

Fingers touching the bowl's rim, we combined our energies.

Soon we saw Ian driving up the highway. Ylva sent a spell. We watched as he reached town and turned in the direction of Marget's house, pulling up in front of the old oak. Looking around, he stepped onto the dry lawn. Brow puckered with a confused look, he crossed the yard and entered the seldom-used front door. We heard his footsteps as he climbed to the attic room.

Opening the door, he came to the curtains and put in his head. His lank blondish hair fell forward. He wore an earring in the shape of a harp. He gazed around at us. Seeing me, then Rousseau, he grinned his overlap-teethed smile.

"What the hell, Kay? Why are you… Why am I…"

Ylva stood. His eyes widened as she reached her full height. Spreading her hands, a further spell compelled him to lie down on the rug. Obediently, he closed his eyes as if in an exhausted daze. She knelt beside him and touched his head.

Marget came over and put her palm on his chest. The rest of us circled him, drawing close to support the process, whatever was needed. Our thoughts were enmeshed, traveling into Ian's mind. We saw memories going back to his teens, arriving at the oak, wandering, confused, taken in by a foster family.

This I hadn't known. Neither did Marget. It hadn't lasted. Marget took him back to their earliest memories, his birth, his childhood in the house in Cornwall, flowers growing in the thatch, birds nesting there. She told briefly of the time when Galfride arrived in her area and came to live with them, until he drew the attention of the Cornish Witch Guild which ran them all out.

Ian's eyes flew open. He struggled to sitting. Now he saw Galfride, and recognized him. He whirled to his mother, flew into her arms. Then pulled away, mouth open. "You ... made me forget?"

"I didn't mean for you to forget *me*," she said, tears streaming down her face. "Then I didn't know how to bring you back to me without ..." She glanced at Galfride.

Ian stared a long moment at Galfride.

Memories seemed to tumble into his mind, with accompanying pangs of guilt, remorse, longing.

Galfride had aged; he was no longer the teen Ian had idolized.

Galfride held back, watching him, emotion carefully schooled, held at bay.

Slowly, Ian got to his feet and approached the other man. "Galfride?"

We watched as the men embraced, carefully.

It seemed to me the younger man had misgivings. He turned to his mother. "This is catastrophic. All the time lost. The years of confusion, feeling 'not right'."

"You remember the incidents that led to our banishment, the danger we were in?" She glanced at Galfride. "They threatened to strip us of all our powers." Her hands were so clenched, they were mottle red and white.

"Powers? I've lived without powers these years." His voice strained around a knot.

Galfride had leaned against the wall. "Perhaps he and I can have a quiet talk," he suggested, teeth clenched with the effort of staying civil.

"I'd like to have some time with my son," Marget said firmly. She pushed to her feet. Rousseau gave her a hand up.

"I won't be far." Galfride's jaw worked.

Perhaps I should invite him to stay with us, but was extremely uncomfortable about doing so. I looked at Rousseau, wondering if he would offer.

Galfride said, "I take my leave." He looked one last time at Ian, seeing if he would stop him, run after him, but the young man only nodded a farewell.

The rest of us made to leave, Ylva first, kissing us.

"Thank you for your help," Marget said. "I am indebted to you. I could not have done it…"

"The work is not entirely done," the shamaness said, putting her great hands on Marget's shoulders. Before she could disappear back to her mountain, I said, "Can I walk with you?"

"Of course." She waited as I kissed Marget.

Ian eyed me strangely. With the new clarity came anger over the deceptions, I was sure.

"You knew?" he asked.

"Only recently."

"Sophie?"

"She knows what I know." I put a hand on his arm.

"It's only been a short time," Marget said, interceding. "We've been planning how to bring your memories back in a way that wouldn't harm you."

I looked from Marget to Ian to Galfride, then back to Marget, brows raised in question. Dare I leave her?

"We'll be fine. You go on." She bowed her head to Ylva.

Rousseau and I followed Ylva downstairs. In the back garden, I asked quietly, "Should we stay? I'm not sure about leaving Marget alone with Galfide now that Ian remembers him."

"I'll keep an eye out. If Galfride is threatening, I'll bring him to me."

"Thank you, Ylva. Hopefully soon we'll solve everything and you'll be able to get back to your own life."

She stroked my hair. "You worry too much."

Rousseau grinned.

I asked, "Have you been in contact with Amgath? Did the stone reach its mountain?"

"I watched, *Hegri fljóð*." Heron woman. "Build your protective shield around us and I'll show you." I created the sphere as directed, including Rousseau. Resting her hands on my head, she gave me the images of Amgath soaring through mountain tunnels, wiggling through the tight bits, arriving in a vast subterranean cave with a misty blue sulfur lake that sent ripples of light around the walls. The dragon hunch-walked into the water.

Shagfen clung on. As the luminous lake waters took her weight, her eyes—long twists on a strange, stretched face—opened wide. She broke into a blissful smile, watching the opalescent dragon swim away, dive deep, and come up under her playfully.

"That's fantastic," I said. "And the stone?"

Amgath crawled from the water. Shagfen unfastened the leather case and let it down into the dragon's hands. In a crevice full of ferns and flowering vines, she set the stone gently into a natural basin, as if made for it. Perhaps it was. I felt the stone then, a radiant pulse, as it settled.

Butterflies flitted in an out of the crevice and over the lake. Bright salamanders curled by the amber stone, draped over. Frogs and crickets sang. The stone hummed.

Rousseau watched it all with me, leaning against my shoulder.

"Thank you, Ylva, for all you've done for everyone." I hugged her, head at her diaphragm. She hugged back, then left us.

Rousseau and I left the yard, invisible in case anyone was there when we appeared on the far side of the fence. Since the park was deserted, I made us visible. We walked through the neighborhood, I felt aware of the stone aware of me.

Was there too much allure in the stone's compelling love? Might I be drawn as my son was to that other world? I took Rousseau's hand to feel his warmth.

"Are you worried about Galfride and Ian?" he asked. "Not to mention Marget. Is she safe?"

"I am concerned. We just can't know what direction this might take. Will Ian go to the past, or is he more attached to this time? What if Galfride is partnering up with Thorgisl? They certainly looked cozy in that tower room. He might want to bring Ian in, for a power team."

"What about Sophie?" Rousseau asked. "Maybe she'll tie Ian to this century."

"There's that. Certainly, old Cornwall would be different, returning as an adult."

STRANGE ALLIANCES

As we walked around the corner toward home, Marget gave a cry that broadcast to me involuntarily. I saw, through her eyes, Galfride grabbing Ian. "Come home. Ye don't belong here."

THE END

Marie Judson is a Northern California native, with Masters degrees in depth psychology and education. She's been a fantasy reader since her teens and loves complex tales of symbols with buried meanings that hold wisdom for our modern time. She also adores tales that involve forbidden romance, which you will find in her books. She's been a coffee roaster, a high school teacher and a college professor. She loves singing harmony and tries to grow vegetables.

Follow her at **www.mariejudson.com**